The Beggar's Garden

The Beggar's Garden

STORIES

Michael Christie

HARPER
PERENNIAL

Published by Harper Perennial, an imprint of HarperCollins Publishers Ltd.

First published by HarperCollins Publishers Ltd in a hardcover edition: 2011
This Harper Perennial paperback edition: 2011

The following stories have been previously published in slightly different form:
"Goodbye Porkpie Hat," in *subTerrain Magazine* and *The Journey Prize Stories*
(vol. 20); "The Quiet," in *Taddle Creek*; and "The Extra," in *Vancouver Review*.

HarperCollins books may be purchased for educational, business, or sales
promotional use through our Special Markets Department.

HarperCollins Publishers Ltd
2 Bloor Street East, 20th Floor
Toronto, Ontario, Canada
M4W 1A8

www.harpercollins.ca

Library and Archives Canada Cataloguing in Publication information
is available upon request

ISBN 978-1-55468-830-2

Printed and bound in the United States
RRD 9 8 7 6 5 4 3 2 1

For Cedar

Contents

Emergency Contact

They sent the wrong paramedic, one I'd never met before. He had sideburns sculpted into hockey sticks and stunk of canola oil. He was in my doorway with the gulping eyes of a rodent and the shocker thing in a red nylon duffle over his shoulder. His partner was old and wheezed beside him from the three flights of stairs. It had taken me a while to answer the door because I was on the toilet, unable to pee for nervousness. When I stood, my hamstrings went pins and needles and I steadied myself on the towel bar while taking a minute to arrange my hair.

Is the patient inside? Sideburns said, looking primed, as though he'd been about to force the door.

No, I said.

Oh, sorry, he said, deflating. Then he sent a confused glance down the hallway in hopes of spotting the actual emergency.

This is 308, is it not? the old one said.

I'm the patient, I said.

Sideburns took a rapid, teaspoon-sized breath and strode in. They guided me to the floor right there, the old one cradling my neck so my head didn't snap back, setting it on the bristles of my welcome mat. Then they rolled me to my side and a foamy pillow appeared beneath my ear. A light whipped my eyes. Breathing? someone said, and someone said, Good. I prided myself on my good breathing as I felt the sleeve of my housecoat roll up. Something squeezed my arm like a tiny, forceful hug and then it whooshed. A hand leapt inside my nightgown. Cold metal went on my chest. With someone listening to it, my breath sounded louder to me in my head. I felt like an instrument valuable enough to be measured and checked. There are rules for what they are doing, I thought as they rolled me to my back and I stared into the pagoda-shaped light fixture on the ceiling until it blew out my vision. The old one was still wheezing, like little stones trapped in his chest, and I worried about him then figured if he keeled over then me and Sideburns would just shock him with the shocker thing and he'd be ready for more stairs.

To be honest, I was surprised the fire department hadn't come. Usually they're first, especially for something like a heart attack. My stairs pose no problem for them, their lungs like great immaculate bellows after carting miles of hose up twenty-five flights of those training stairs I've seen near the highway. Beside the training stairs is a cinder-block building they burn for practice, which they must look forward to, X-ing days off on charity calendars that depict themselves shirtlessly soaping their engine. I picture them bunking down together in a big room, a slide pole in the middle, them bidding each other gruff goodnights, dreaming collectively of their most secret desire, the great inferno worthy of their courage. When they came before, they all had the same moustache and seemed disappointed that I wasn't on fire or at least dead. To be honest, I prefer the paramedics.

And the paramedic who had come last week I prefer most of all. He'd spoken tenderly and stayed for nearly an hour. After he checked me out, I made him green kool-aid in the plastic jug, stirring it with my wooden spoon that's stained green from all the times I've used it. He sipped, his elbow on my counter, pursing his lips until they disappeared, and said it was a slow night.

I asked him what days he worked.

Four on four off, he said, and I have tomorrow off.

Next came the exciting moment when he said my nightgown was an interesting colour, which meant he liked it very much, because people love to be interested, especially by the slumber-wear of the opposite sex.

I know this because I've always had guyfriends. It's just how I am, I'm a social person. I don't say *boyfriend* because I'm not a pedophile. I like grown guys. Men. I once had a guyfriend, a life-guard at a public pool, who said he loved me for me. If someone tells you they love you for you, it means they will love you as long as you act like who they love—that is who they want to love. So that's what I did. He said he liked cheerful, so I danced around his house to the radio and made cheerful kinds of food like pies or triple-decker sandwiches. In the end, he told me I loved too hard and that he didn't love me anymore. This confirmed my suspicion that he was lying the whole time, so I guess I won.

Since the night the paramedic came, I'd passed five days of yearning and rehearsal, the bathroom mirror foggy with the lip grease of practice kiss marks. I'd rearranged the furniture twice, discovering a lively configuration I knew he'd enjoy. Tonight after dinner, I'd put on the same interesting nightgown before dialling 91 at least thirty times, snatching and replacing the phone for over an hour. There should be someone who picks up when you just dial 91, someone reassuring and pleasant, a service for people in almost-emergencies, because that's what this was, not really in the life-threatening category. I just needed to see someone specific, but it was the sort of longing that could corrode something essential inside me if it stretched out for years. I reminded myself that emergencies are things that *emerge*, out of nowhere, and that there's nothing more out of nowhere than love, before raising the phone a final time.

Nine-one-one, police, fire or ambulance? the operator had said, and I heard keys clicking while I envisioned a sportscaster microphone curving from her ear into her wiggling lips.

Definitely ambulance, I said.

Hold please, she said.

Ambulance, a nonchalant-sounding man said.

Hello, I said.

Ambulance, he said again right away, exactly the same.

I'd planned on requesting the paramedic directly, but I didn't know his name and something in the operator's demeanour suggested an unreceptiveness to such requests, so I decided to take my chances. The important thing was that they'd send one. Fate would handle the rest.

I need an ambulance, I said.

Can you tell me who is in distress, ma'am?

Well . . . I am.

All right, what kind of symptoms are you experiencing?

My mind starved for something perfect to say, something that wasn't really a lie, because I'd read in a women's magazine that lies are toxic to budding relationships.

I'm having a tightness in my chest, I said, which felt as true as anything else at that moment.

You right now yourself, ma'am? How long has this tightness been going on?

Oh, a while now, I said, and my chest ratcheted tighter when he confirmed its tightness by naming it.

Are you experiencing shortness of breath?

Yes, I said, then noticing the rustling in the receiver that was from me.

Are you seated currently?

No I am not.

I'm going to need you to sit down, and please stay on the phone. Then I heard more clicking and he said paramedics were on their way.

Him telling me what to do had me feeling essential, like he couldn't do this without me, like he needed me, which was true—he couldn't send an ambulance somewhere if there wasn't someone there who was waiting for it. I'd always secretly wished for a friend who'd call and give instructions: Bake a cake, he would say, or, Dance to the radio. And he'd speak with such gravity and conviction, I'd comply without any internal complaining or laziness, attaining beautiful, undreamt-of summits of personal fulfillment.

Is your skin pale, cool or moist? the voice said.

I don't know, I can't see myself, I'll go to the bathroom—

No, ma'am, don't get up, just stay where you are. Is there any pain? he said.

I listened to my body with my mind like an ear to a railroad track. The rumbling of something began faintly, almost the hush of a seashell, intensifying gradually as it approached, a train en route from a distant city I once knew as my home. My veins began a glacial ache, each of the thousands of bones in my feet felt cracked and prickly, and my organs suddenly seemed misshapen and crammed together all wrong. These discomforts fortified one another until they swarmed me like sickened wasps.

It hurts everywhere, I said, then hung up because I was bored of talking and needed to prepare for my paramedic without some voice I didn't even know ordering me around.

———————

Vitals are fine, the old guy said. Blood pressure one-twenty-two over eighty.

All this staring into the light on the ceiling made me feel like I was talking to god even though I've never been able to believe in him.

Are you new? I said to Sideburns.

What do you mean?

To the job—I don't know you.

I know what I'm doing, ma'am.

No, I don't mean—just why haven't I seen you before?

Oh, I'm new to this district.

I thought so. What's your name?

He glanced to the old one, who shrugged while ripping velcro.

What's more important right now, ma'am, is how you're feeling. Is there any pain or tightness here? he said, planting his palm dead centre on my chest, not on my breasts, because I was on my back and they hung at my sides because I am no spring chicken. Like a satellite bouncing important signals back to earth, his hand made it so I could feel the beats. My heart was good and dependable and I felt negligent for not offering it thanks or considering it more often. I desperately hoped it didn't feel like the rowing slave in the galleon of my body, but I knew I'd forget it again soon, so I told it I was sorry in advance.

I think I feel better, I said.

Have you had difficulties with your heart before?

Oh yes, I said, many.

When?

In the past, but it's gone away now, thanks, I said, hoping they'd just leave so I could commence the project of storing up enough courage to call another ambulance.

Well, the old one said, we're still going to take you to hospital to check you out, do a cardiogram, keep you in for observation.

I don't want to go anymore, I'm better, I said, then rose, retying my housecoat.

Your call, said Sideburns.

You are not my paramedic, I said, but only to myself. Sideburns' cool, uncaring nature only proved how special and one-of-a-kind my paramedic really was. He would have taken as long as he needed to convince me of the importance of precaution, of regular checkups and expensive tests just to be sure. He'd have maybe even given me a hug while, of course, being careful it didn't sail uncontrollably from the shores of compassionate to those of passionate in the way we all know hugs often do.

But if Sideburns left and I called again, they might not send another. They'd smell something fishy because it would be my fourth this month and I knew someone somewhere must keep track. I was already surprised this one had come.

Sideburns reached into his bag and produced a metal clipboard that flipped back. He handed me a pen.

Sign here to deny service, he said, putting his rubber-gloved finger to an X.

My paramedic was working tonight, of this I was sure. I'd counted the days more times than my own toes and had even bought him a greeting card at the dollar store. The prospect of waiting a minute longer was insufferable. All ambulances must eventually go to the hospital—it was the only place I could be sure he'd end up. And how suspicious it would seem if I went there on my own and just waited around.

I looked out the window. A red-bearded man was picking through the dumpster behind my building, a rack of grey cloud over everything. For that moment, I felt a hundred feet tall. Then I shrunk back to my normal size, which is maybe a little heavy but not too shabby.

I think I might want to kill myself, I said.

The other paramedic stopped writing with rubber gloves on in his clipboard and shot his eyes my way. Suddenly the thought of writing anything rubber-gloved depressed me unfathomably. I shut my eyes to appear as depressed as possible and found myself emitting a long, defeated breath like a punctured tire. I decided to keep eyeing the window, approximating a moody philosopher contemplating existence.

Sideburns came closer, plucked the clipboard from my hands.

Let me get this right, he said. You've just had a heart attack which you miraculously survived without any apparent complications, not any you're worried about at least, but now that you are fine you've decided you want to kill yourself?

I felt real tears come but not quite enough to make whole drops. They teetered on the edges of my lids as cars do on cliffs in movies. I whipped myself with the thought of never seeing my paramedic again while blinking furiously in order to show Sideburns I meant business, but the drops disappeared like my eyes just drank them.

Yes, that's right, I said.

Well, do you have a plan?

I paused because pausing means deep consideration.

No, I said.

He turned and shot his hands in the air then slapped his thighs. The old guy grabbed the bridge of his nose and wrestled it.

No . . . actually, yes. I do.

He turned back. Okay. May I ask what it is?

I stuck my hand to my chin like that thinking statue and searched my mind while focusing on my paramedic, realizing I wasn't even completely lying, I *could* want to die if I never saw him again and was unable to give him his card. Sideburns was still waiting so I indexed all the suicides I knew of—falling from a bridge, bleeding, eating pills, hanging, rat poison, gun in the mouth—and they each seemed equally terrifying and brave.

I'm going to make myself stop breathing? I said.

And how are you going to do that?

With my mind?

O-kay, he said, and approached his partner for a bit of whispering.

I knew what they were saying, not the words but the general

idea. There are laws for this, for what I said. They were serious words, ones they couldn't ignore. Whether Sideburns liked it or not this was a blood pact we'd made: my saying it, his hearing it. And when he strolled back to me, I knew that he knew that I knew that he knew, going to infinity. He flipped to a fresh sheet in his clipboard and started writing.

How long have you felt like harming yourself, he said, as if reading from a book he detested. Oh sorry, I know the answer to that one—let's just do this on the way, shall we?

I need to clean up first, I said, and went carting some crumby plates to the sink. Nothing is more depressing—here I mean actually depressing—than returning from hospital to a messy place, but I didn't say this because I figured from that point the less I spoke, the better for everyone. I rushed to my room to pack. I whipped my interesting nightgown off over my head and wadded it with two others, stuffing the wad with three underwear, a magazine, a hairbrush and medications into a bag. I only needed enough time to find my paramedic, but I liked to be prepared because I spent some time in a hospital as a kid and know the comfort of having your own stuff. People say *in hospital* the same way they say *in love*, because you really are different when you're there, that is, if they keep you, which means they think you need help, which is nice of them to care about you that much.

I put on the fancy purple jogging suit I never have reason to wear, then removed it to change my underwear and put it back on. I brushed my hair twenty times on each side. I pulled his greeting card from under my pillow, closed it in a book then placed it in my bag.

Greeting cards have messages that say what you really want

to say but don't want to write yourself because that would mean you had to really mean it. If someone hates what a card says, or doesn't feel the same way, then you can just say: Sorry! I picked the card at random! Or if they really did like it, and you can tell, then you say: I spent hours reading cards until I found the perfect one just for you! And they know how you really feel about them. Really, they're a win-win situation.

After hours of reading at the dollar store, I picked one that said *Love is in the air!* inside, with a picture of two teddy bears on the front riding in a biplane with hearts painted on its wings. But I wanted to really express myself this time, so inside I wrote more:

> *Dear Paramedic,*
> *You saved my life! (Just kidding) But I just wanted to say*
> *you are the best and most caring paramedic on the force (are*
> *you a force?) and I appreciate everything you did for me.*
> *I'm very interested in getting to know you better. Coffee?*
> *Airplane ride? (more kidding)*
> *Maya*

I didn't write my phone number because I didn't want to be pushy. We'd probably write them down on a piece ripped from the envelope—this way we would be more spontaneous.

Got everything? Sideburns asked when I came out.

All packed, I said.

Can you make it to the ambulance?

I think so, I said.

On the way out through the lobby, I saw Marvin, an elderly man who lives in my building, sitting in his chair. His eyelids droop so much that wet crescents of pink are visible always. I'll be back in a few days, I said, feeling like a movie star with my entourage, an imaginary animal fur twining around my neck, but Martin didn't once look up from his racetrack papers because he is a certified compulsive gambler as well as the nastiest person on two legs.

The sun made me woozy and I asked the ambulance driver to take my arm.

Up you get, he said, and boosted me into the rear of the vehicle.

I lay down on the stretcher. He threw a white cotton blanket over me, which at first I wanted to kick off then realized I needed when the doors shut and the air conditioning kicked in. It felt dangerous to be wearing my shoes in bed even if it wasn't a real bed. The old guy was driving and I prayed he wasn't one of those old people who'd rather maim someone or kill himself than admit he couldn't recall the rules of the road anymore.

Are you going to strap me down?

Didn't plan on it, Sideburns said.

What if we were in an accident? Aren't these straps like seatbelts for the patient?

You're the boss, he said, and leaned over to buckle me tightly across my thighs and chest, which reminded me of my chest pains that had by then mercifully subsided. With my heart attack ancient history, the straps had me feeling all gathered in, a scattered thing at long last collected.

Yes, this suicide business was technically a lie. I did not crave death, not immediately anyway, but I'd always trusted myself to reject immortality if it were offered to me so this lent what I'd said a partial truth. I lay conjuring the unbearable climate of an actually suicidal mind and stayed focused on that, pitying this person who loathed life for reasons unexplainable to others. I decided that while locating my paramedic and giving him his card, I would help the paramedics and doctors out by providing free training for dealing with suicidal people, and the performance of this good deed would detoxify any and all of the lies necessary to unite us.

Oxygen bottles clinked and plastic bags of life-giving juices swung with the potholes and turns and I crossed my arms contentedly over the straps.

———————

Friday night, said Sideburns, offering this as explanation for the packed waiting area.

I sat in one of the only empty seats and watched him chat with the intake nurses. Then he and the old paramedic went outside to hack down halves of cigarettes, spitting through their teeth and telling each other funny stories, some probably about me, before departing in their ambulance without a goodbye. Just like policemen, there are good paramedics and bad paramedics. If there weren't, the good ones wouldn't be so heaven-sent, and at that moment even for this I was grateful.

There was plenty else to look at while I kept my other eye on the ambulance parking area: people in flip-flops and shorts, others in pyjamas, still others swathed in elegant black for nights on the town cut short. People get hurt on weekends because they let their guard down when they try to be carefree. They forget their guard is often what keeps things from going awfully wrong. I wondered whether my guard was up or down right then and decided it was both.

An ambulance pulled in but it wasn't him. Some paramedics I loosely recognized pushed through the crowd of people with a stretcher, on it a muttering old woman who looked to be sculpted of ash. They disappeared through some doors marked No Entry.

On the televisions hanging from the ceiling, people's pets were getting makeovers from a man wearing a kimono and a golden top hat. The owners put their hands to their cheeks and couldn't believe their pets were their pets.

Do I look sick? a man beside me asked.

That depends, I said.

On what?

On what you're supposed to look like normally.

At this he raked at the reddened turf of his scalp with his fingers. He had a deep, fat-man voice and a kind, puddingy face that I felt the unbearable urge to jostle in some way.

They tell me I got nothing wrong with me but I got this pain in my guts. Won't stop. He patted where his shirt strained to envelop a large, hard belly that seemed to me deeply powerful like a sizzling cartoon bomb. I saw the crater-like dent in his shirt demarking his belly button.

You don't look sick, you look good to me, I said, squinching my eyes, resisting the urge to pat his belly while giving him an appraising once over. He smacked his lips, about to disagree.

Maya? said a large woman in a cream cardigan and a ton of silver jewellery.

That's me, I said, standing, then remembered my suicidalness and bent my smile back into a hyphen of despair.

She asked for my health number, which I recited from memory. The nurse shrugged like number-taking was the most loathsome chore in the world. Some hate the efficient memories of others because their own are shot to hell. She probably found herself at least two nights of the week in the middle of her living room wearing only one slipper, carrying an egg beater, without the faintest idea what she was supposed to be doing. I decided to pity her.

She asked about my medical history, which I won't tell you because it's mostly boring. The paramedics had already explained my current situation and I was pleased I didn't have to talk about harming myself again because since I'd been there around all these caring and interesting people, I was feeling much better.

 Emergency contact? she said.

What? I said.

Someone who we can notify in case something, you know, transpires.

I sat, pausing, but actually thinking this time. She had a picture atop her computer monitor of a kid in a judo uniform who shared her brassy hair and fatigued expression. The truth was I had nobody—who would give a hoot if I died, I mean. Sure, like everyone I had parents, and even a sibling or two, but they were petty, disinterested people in a faraway town, people to whom I hadn't spoken since the advent of caller ID.

No, there was only my paramedic, who, when he learned of my untimely death, would scuttle himself on a series of all-night drunks, spending hours transfixed by the digits of his alarm clock, guessing when the numbers would turn—saying, Now, no . . . okay, now—all in an effort to flee the searing fact that he'd, just one week ago, overlooked the unmistakable warning signs of my fatal sadness.

Can mine be 911? I said.

Funny, she said, as if what I said was the negative of funny. What we mean is family, next of kin, close friends, relatives—

Can I pass? I said.

She nodded knowingly, kept typing.

———————

Back in the waiting area I found the same chair and watched for ambulances, hoping I hadn't been gone long enough to miss him. I lifted my feet for a turbaned janitor making spirals with a mop. I've never smelled the janitorial products of a hospital anywhere else, and I figure the company that supplies them must be a good investment because the smells have never changed, not since I was a kid. The gut guy was gone and I read my new ID wristband a few times, just my name and DOB written there beneath soft vinyl. The date wasn't so long ago but at that moment seemed ancient. I've always liked how they make the ID bands impossible to remove without destroying them, how for this reason you could never wear the bracelet of another, how they, and the belonging they bestow, must be earned. I felt unique and proud to have one, even though my mission there at the hospital was ultimately a selfish one.

When I was ten I broke both arms falling from the roof of my house while helping my dad clean the gutters. I got two casts that ran from my wrists deep into my armpits. Not able to reach my face, I had to be spoon-fed every meal by nurses. I was instantly entranced by the trays of gorgeously compartmentalized food, by the fluffing of pillows and by the lovely regularity with which the nurses asked each morning how I'd slept, as if there were so many different ways it could have gone. Dutifully, I sought to describe these sleeps as best I could.

Effervescent, I said one morning, something I'd learned from a dictionary in the lounge the previous day, and the nurse's hyena laugh brought another nurse to see if we were okay.

During this time, I refused to wash my hands, smearing them on railings and doorknobs before hiding under the covers to lick each finger meticulously. I would locate the sickest kids, corner them and inhale deeply at their collars. I was polite with the nurses and never watched television, suspecting they looked down on it. I even considered re-breaking my arms by falling off my bed, but I feared the nurses would know I'd done it myself. Also, I feared the crash would wake my roommate, a kid who'd buckled his face on a spruce while riding an ATV. He groaned intermittently and breathed as if through a straw filled with pudding. Sometimes I even swore the room smelled like spruce. His parents came every second day in matching leather jackets, and his father's girlish sobbing was pitiful to hear. As she drew the curtain closed around them, the mother would regard me with contempt for my breathing clarity and uncollapsed face.

Happily, I managed to stay long enough for other things to go wrong. Before my casts came off, I had my tonsils out, and then, not long after I was spooning up my own solid food, I got pneumonia. I wept in the arms of a nurse when I was finally sent home.

Now here I was, back at the hospital, and even though I'd packed a bag, I had to remind myself I wasn't here to stay this time.

Hours passed and the ambulances grew more frequent. The injuries migrated steadily from those self-inflicted to those inflicted by others. The television programs, in turn, became more violent and I wondered if there was a connection.

A drunk man in a tank top that said Ask Me If I Care held a diaper to his caved cheekbone and sought for nearly an hour to convince his girlfriend to call his mother because it was her birthday.

Here, I'm dialling, he said, waving his phone with his free hand as she cupped her ears and shook her head, while saying over and over that this was his shit.

A worn-looking woman with a shelf of sparkly cleavage stared unflinchingly up at the television. She clicked her furry heeled boots on the waxed floor and shifted uncomfortably in her seat. She didn't flinch when the nurse finally called her, once out loud, then over the intercom. She jumped when the nurse's silver-bangled hand met her shoulder.

I investigated each person called before me to the examination rooms for signs of illness. Most of them didn't seem that bad off, but of course neither did I. It's hard to see that someone wants to end their life just by looking at them, so I trusted in their greater need for medical attention and didn't get frustrated.

Finally, the nurse called me and I gave one last look to the empty ambulance area and followed the blue line as instructed, walking it like a tightrope.

There was no tissue paper on the green vinyl bed so I spooled some out and sat down. I studied the tools for looking into people's different holes. They were attached to a little box with curly headphone cords, all hung up like a celebrity kitchen. People like hanging tools on the walls because it helps them remember they can handle any kind of situation.

Put this on, a cheery nurse with a lip problem said, handing me a gown. Then she zipped shut the curtain with a grating metal-on-metal sound.

I set the gown on the paper, took out a tongue depressor and depressed my tongue, but it almost made me puke so I stuck it back in the jar. I didn't put the gown on because my problem was in my mind not my body so there would be no need for an examination. I waited, listening for the sound of the paramedic's voice from outside the curtain.

The curtain zipped again. Hi Maya, I'm Doctor Gerwer, said a white-coated man. He had hair that seemed too blond for his face and steel, efficient-looking glasses.

I understand you are having some trouble, he said, that you've been experiencing some troubling thoughts.

Oh, they aren't too bad, I said. I have nice ones too so they balance out.

Well, it says here you've been feeling like you may harm yourself?

Everyone wants to impress their doctor and I'm no different. I pronounce clearly and try to present him with symptoms he'll find remarkable. I want to thrill him with the story of the greatest disease in the history of diseases, a disease that has chosen me only because it knows I and I alone am worthy enough to endure it. I want to lead him to a diagnosis that's so clear-cut, all he has to do is sign off on it, then we can go for drinks and chat about how brilliant I am for diagnosing myself with no formal training, and about how hopelessly out of touch most people are with their own bodies. But unfortunately, I didn't want to kill myself at all anymore, and being away from the ambulances made me antsy, so I stamped out my storytelling urges.

Yeah, but I'm fine now.

He took a slow breath and seemed like he was thinking. I scribbled a mental note that the pausing-equals-thinking trick really did work.

Do you think it's possible to force yourself to stop breathing?

Oh, no, I said.

But this is what you told the paramedics? Correct?

I made a remembering face. I guess so, I said, then shrugged as breezily as I could manage.

He made some notes.

Well, Maya, I think it would be best for us to have you as our guest here a few days to see if we can get you all sorted out.

I really don't want to stay, I said. I'm feeling better.

I'm afraid it's something that we strongly suggest.

I couldn't believe I was turning down a free visit to the hospital, even if I'd be in the psych ward where the nurses weren't as nice and definitely didn't fluff pillows, but that's the kind of sacrifice you have to be willing to make for love. I knew I needed to distract the doctor and the best way was to give him something he could feel good about.

What I *have* been having is a pain in my guts.

He scrunched his face. Let's see, he said, putting his hand to my belly, testing me like a steak.

Is the pain here? he said, pressing deep with the two fingers you use to take a pulse.

My guts didn't really hurt but his pressing could have hurt if he had done it even just a little harder so I said yes.

Hmmm, he said. Have you felt this kind of pain before?

No, I said, I don't think—Oh! You know what? I did eat some chicken today that had been in my fridge for a while.

Oh sure, he said, chicken can grow all kinds of nasty bacteria. What I do is label food I put in the fridge with a date, so I know how long it's been there.

That must be it, I said. I'll be sure to do that smart labelling thing, thanks, Doc, this pain is already feeling better, thanks so much for your help. I stood, clapped my hands and started gathering up my things. I was sure my plan had worked, but he just looked at me, puzzled.

Why don't you wait here and I'll have someone walk you over to the psychiatric unit, where you'll be more comfortable, he said, and left the room.

It felt like something had rolled down a steep hill inside me and struck something valuable. Convinced I would never find my paramedic, my body became heavy with real, actual despair, not the kind that makes you kill yourself, but the kind that makes you give up on something you desperately want and just go home.

When I was in the hospital with my broken arms there was a lady in the gift shop who gave me penny-candy fish or bookmarks with funny sayings. She didn't have to be nice to me, but was anyway. When I was older I returned to the hospital and a different lady was behind the counter. She said the other lady had died. I asked her for some free penny candy and she scowled.

Nobody does something kind for someone else if they don't love them, even a little. I'm not stupid, though, I knew my paramedic was supposed to come to my apartment to help me, that it was his job, and people do jobs for money not because they want to. But people choose careers in health care because they love caring for people. The problem was my paramedic and I wouldn't be given the chances other couples were, happening into each other on the street, or joining the same life-drawing class. He'd chosen to find my nightgown interesting, which means he must have loved at least some little part in me, and I couldn't let that slip away.

I passed the nurses' station and none of them looked up from their computers or cups of microwavable soup. I came across a pair of orderlies striding the blue line in the direction I'd come from and ducked my head.

Then came the thrilling moment in the lobby when I saw him, wheeling a guy on a stretcher through automatically parting doors. I called to him but my words were outstripped by what he and the other paramedics and nurses were yelling to one another about colours and codes.

I'd prepared for complications like this by accustoming myself to the thought of him caring for other patients, so I wasn't anywhere near jealous. His job was important to him, he was career oriented, that's why I liked him, and trust is something that must be unconditional.

They were moving quickly toward the No Entry doors so I had to trot to catch him, even though at that moment I was finding it difficult to breathe.

Hi, I said, tapping him on the shoulder.

He turned and I saw that our time apart had infused his face with an even greater surplus of beauty. He began to speak but I accidentally interrupted him by blurting, Your card! horrified that I must have left my bag in the examination room.

Wait here! I said, and thanked the god that I don't believe in for the blue line that I was able to trace back, because otherwise I would have got lost because people do silly things in the throes of passion with their guards down.

I whipped open a few wrong curtains, saying sorry to the different sick people, some of whom I recognized from the lobby, until I found my old examination room, where there was now an old man laying on his stomach, his withered butt peeking through his gown. I found my bag tucked under a little stool and the old man didn't stir. So even though it wasn't nighttime, I changed into my interesting nightgown because I was worried my paramedic hadn't remembered me without it to trigger his memory. It crossed my mind that the next person to undo each of its five neck buttons that were shaped like mini-seashells might not be me, and my heart felt like four different hearts who were all best friends, pumping away in unison for a good and noble cause.

When I got back my paramedic was gone. I pushed through the No Entry doors and spotted him and some others down a hallway. They had stopped beside an elevator, waiting for something or someone.

Hi, I said when I caught up to him. He was holding some bags of fluid up in the air and his armpits were sweaty, but not too sweaty, a good, healthy amount.

Hi? he said, glancing down at my nightgown and I could tell he still found it profoundly interesting.

You can't be in here, said a bearded security guard, his hand on my back.

It's okay, the paramedic said to him, which he didn't have to do, and this warmed my heart and proved that I and I alone remained his favourite patient. His eyes were so blue that I bet on a clear day, looking up at him from underneath with his hands planted in the grass on each side of your face, they would look like holes bored all the way through his head.

Can I help you? he said.

Here, I said, holding out his card, this is for you.

He didn't reach for it and I prayed I'd spelled *Paramedic* right because he was regarding the envelope with a funny expression.

He laughed. Sorry, we don't really accept gifts, he said.

He was trying to be professional, but I couldn't help but take this personally, especially because my card was nothing if not personal. If only I could tell him what was inside the envelope, then he would know why he actually wanted to accept it as a gift, but that would ruin the whole surprise effect that is so great about card-giving.

You should open it. You'll like it, I said, winking, with a feeling that I was already giving too much of the card away.

He said he couldn't right now because he was in the middle of an emergency. I looked down at the unconscious man on the stretcher whose legs were both wrapped with large pads of bloody gauze, and he seemed pretty content to me.

The elevator chimed and the medical people started pushing the man through the doors.

Do you want to grab a coffee after work? I asked, with no other choice than to ruin the most exciting part of the card completely.

He mustered a strange expression, the bewildered kind people give when they've just heard something that is so absolutely impossible that they can't even consider it. Did he think he was too good for me? For my card?

Sorry, he said, and walked into the elevator and I saw now that he was just as heartless as Sideburns or any other guyfriend I'd ever loved—perhaps more so—and that he was probably just accidentally horny the day he came over and found me so interesting. I yearned now to prove him wrong, to wound him and show him how much he did in fact care for me, deep inside him, on frequencies that his heart couldn't detect, with a tenderness and compassion crafted only for me, and during this contemplation I found myself warming again to the whole killing-myself business. I wondered how many people had actually killed themselves because of the callousness of others, or even just so they didn't have to feel like a liar anymore, and I figured it was probably all of them.

I took the deepest breath I could and locked it away in my chest. I felt my eyes bulge and my lungs began to chip away at the air. Miniature crystal bells tolled in my ears and it was as if I was pressing my stomach to a brick wall, peering through a window, and then I knew I was envisioning our future, his and mine. I watched the paramedic and I on a queen-sized bed, spending entire days entwined, our arms going to sleep from constant embracing, breaking only for one of us to make toast while wearing the rumpled clothes of the other, settling for the lightest toast setting because the longer toasting time seemed like a painful eternity to be apart.

How much do you love me right now? I would say, returning with fresh toast slices on our last clean dish.

I love you this much, he'd say, stretching his arms past the edges of the bed, as wide as was physically possible for him.

Only that much? I'd say.

Then I love you as far from here to Neptune.

Do you love me more than you did yesterday?

He'd think a minute, and here I mean really think.

Yes, I do, he'd say.

Then you didn't really love me yesterday, I'd say, not really.

But I didn't know yesterday that I could've loved you more today.

What if you love me more tomorrow?

Oh stop this, he'd say, kissing me in rapid fire. And then he would say that he didn't care, he just loved me today and tomorrow and forever and I would believe him and we would have sex with each other's bodies as well as our minds because the mind is the largest erogenous zone and we would live with no need for greeting cards because we would speak in our own voices without fear and each day would be the day before the day he would leave me.

Then my imagining stalled because by this point my lungs were crawling, like two lobsters having a death match in my chest, and I was on the floor. My paramedic was feeling my neck and talking at the others saying the word *seizure*. It was a beautiful word, as pure as lightning. Maybe I *was* having a seizure, I thought, grand mal, probably, which is French for really bad, and that seemed apt for the way my paramedic was abandoning me with such cruelty.

But then I saw it: in his panic, in his furrowed brow, his sudden sweaty gleam, in his desperate wish for me to continue my life, which was plain to all those present in that hallway. I saw the brilliant, steadfast jewel of his love, and I wondered if someone could tell you they loved you over and over, so rapidly that the sound of the words would blend into a constant tone—kind of like a dial tone—but infinitely more beautiful. Wouldn't that sound be the most comforting sound in the world? Wouldn't it be the greatest painkiller ever invented? Better than morphine, or phone calls, or cooking shows? As he tenderly sought my pulse and gently pried open my mouth to clamp something plastic-tasting between my teeth, as he cradled my head in his hands like a man holding a newborn child that he was sure was his own, this was the sound ringing in me, burrowing into my joints and tendons and bones, into my heart and into my guts. I bit down on the plastic and offered myself to the sound, wholly and without reserve, and it was then I felt the sound penetrate to the very doorstep of the dead part of me, the part that had been strangled long ago by someone or something I could not name, and there the sound wavered, diminished and was turned away.

Discard

Earl drives from his motel into the fray of the city. He stops at a downtown supermarket where he selects two pre-roasted chickens from a warming cabinet and places them in his carry basket.

"Sunday supper?" says the clerk, a man of his age.

Earl is surprised such a person would be working as a grocery cashier. "With my grandson," Earl says, feeling suddenly disloyal for the admission. He pays and, to spare the man the trouble, bags the chickens himself.

He drives the short distance to English Bay, parks, and pops open the domed-plastic container. Steam bursts from the joint as he tears a leg loose. Half-listening to the radio, he eats nearly the whole bird, digging morsels out from between the bones with his fingers. It is winter, and night in this place comes much too early for Earl—a vacuuming kind of dark that settles in by four-thirty. He sits watching the lights of the countless freighters tremble in the void of the inlet. They resemble distant cities, so numerous it's impossible to tell where one ends and another begins. He glances at the green digits of his dashboard clock: 8:30. He's not late but should be going.

Earl recalls the day not long ago when he bought this car—a small, efficient thing, well suited for a city—and how he laboured that night for hours to set its clock and finally was forced to return the next day to the dealership for a kid in a blue jumpsuit to set it for him. He'd always rather do a job himself, even if it took three times as long, and when his wife was still alive there were many nights where his dinner sat cold on the table while he fiddled, red-faced, with something in his workroom.

Earl steps into the sea-rich air and tosses the picked carcass into the trash. As he backs the car away, his headlights catch a primer-grey sea bird descending greedily upon the barrel.

Soon he's trolling the narrow streets of the West End, hunting for a nook he can shoehorn his silver hatchback into. He nuzzles up behind a carpet-cleaning van only a few blocks from where he is going. He reaches for his aluminum cane on the rear seat, and is pleased to find the second chicken container still warm as he tucks it under his arm. Lately, Earl has been feeling increasingly brittle, and his knees wobble and click as he enters an alley lorded over by two dizzying concrete apartment buildings. His new doctor has fitted him with a pair of tight nylon stockings because blood has been pooling in his legs, not making the return trip. This began two months ago on the airplane when his feet blew up like violet bear paws. The stockings haven't helped much. Earl suspects the dampness of this place doesn't sit right with his circulatory constitution, if there is such a thing.

He reaches the dumpster where his grandson will be. Beside it is some scrap vinyl siding and an oak desk, the heavy kind schoolteachers once preferred. The lid of the dumpster is shut, but not locked. He's noticed that more of the bins are being chained and padlocked, and there have been arguments about this on the radio. He's heard interviews with city planners who want the dumpsters gone, and with security guards who pour bleach on bins full of perfectly good food to thwart scavengers. The logic of this escapes Earl. Who cares if a person gets some use out of what nobody wanted anyway?

He hoists the dumpster's lid and peers inside. Six nearly identical tightly cinched grocery bags of kitchen waste, a large browning houseplant, and a box with a plastic window through which Earl can see an untouched birthday cake that reads: *Happy 28th Charlie! Love, The 'Fam.* The only explanation Earl can imagine for the uneaten cake is that in the frenzy of preparation, Charlie's overzealous family accidentally ordered two.

The dumpster is against a cinderblock wall and the lid won't stay flipped back. Earl sets it on his head and stretches an arm deep inside, his heels lifting shakily from the ground, so as to lower the chicken in its plastic coffin as close to the bottom as he can before releasing it. The metal lip bites into his sternum and his eyes fill with blood. Just as he lets go, there is sudden tension then a cold snapping in his left knee and it throws his weight funny and the container tumbles wrongly from his fingers. Earl watches the domed plastic pop away from the black base when it lands, springing the contents loose. The chicken comes to rest half on the plastic, half on the slimy bottom of the dumpster.

"Damn."

Earl pulls himself from the foul pocket of air, tingles of bad circulation in his ears and fingertips. He tests his knee and it appears to be fine. That the rotten thing has a mind of its own enrages him more than any pain could.

Earl checks his watch. He'll be here soon, the same time every night, much too soon for Earl to drive back and get another one.

———————

A few months previous, when Earl still lived back east in the brick bungalow on Miles Avenue, his grandson appeared to him in a kind of vision. It was a time when Earl was adrift in the wake of his wife Tuuli's sudden death at sixty-four of an aneurism that occurred while she was curling at the club where they were both members. Since the funeral, after the casseroles that appeared on his doorstep were long consumed, Earl had been subsisting on cans of condensed milk and loaves of white bread bought from the corner confectionery and eaten in a single day. He'd retreated to the basement he had finished himself, with its chestnut panelling and dense industrial-pile carpet that Tuuli had claimed hurt her feet. He preferred this room to the others—it was the least shot through with her memory—and there in the basement he watched hour after hour of television with little regard for what his eyes fell upon.

Many weeks quietly unspooled in this way, until one night Earl came across a news special about homeless people in Vancouver. The reporter spoke in the overemphasized way of reporters, like she was instructing a fool, but also as if she herself was exhausted by the overwhelming nature of the homelessness situation. With one hand gripping an umbrella, the other an almost comically large microphone, she strolled past a soup kitchen, along a lineup of downtrodden men, with their beards and shopping carts, all of them tinged with misery and grime. He'd never before seen someone known to him personally on television, but there in the line Earl saw his grandson, like an apparition, inhabiting the body of one of the men. The boy's red hair had made its way into a stringy red beard, and the same defiance and glazed recklessness dwelled in his good eye. But it was the other eye that convinced Earl, spun halfway into his upper lid, what people nowadays would call lazy.

It had been nearly fifteen years since Earl had seen Kyle. Not since the slushy day he'd fetched him from out front of the holding cells where the boy had spent the night for public drunkenness, aggravated assault, and God knows what else. Earl drove him straight to the bus station, put six 20s in his hand, and turned his back on him. He was sixteen years old.

Earl realized, there in his basement, that a rarely visited part of himself had long ago decided the boy was dead. His first thought was to call his daughter, Sarah. But that wouldn't do. She was a fragile creature, the kind of girl who'd be bent all out of sorts by something like that, one who was born sure that every miserable thing on this earth was her own damn fault. And what would she do, anyway? Go and get him? Bring him home? She lived in Cold Lake, Alberta—a cruel, wind-beaten place—with her four-year-old daughter and the girl's father, a flight sergeant named Reginald, a man Earl had never met, who for two weeks of every three flew thousands of kilometres over empty tundra. Since she'd left home, Sarah had called Earl at all hours, when she heard noises at night in her basement, or after eating some food she suspected had expired. She'd been a disorganized but well-behaved girl, and it had been a great surprise when she'd become pregnant at seventeen by a boy named Dennis who lived a few blocks north over on Whalen Street. If the two had been dating, Earl and Tuuli had never known. Dennis had worked with Earl at Hydro one summer, digging and backfilling kilometres of trench for underground cable, only to be laid off when the ground froze, but eventually secured a better-paying job in a diamond mine five hours north. Earl had found him to be a good worker and had no unkind words for anyone who took pride in holding down a job.

Sarah decided to keep the baby, and when Kyle was born she merely continued living at home without ever asking their permission. But neither Earl nor Tuuli minded. Sarah was the sort of girl you heard about on the radio who'd do something like put a baby in the oven to dry it after a bath, so they slept better with her close by.

Dennis sent money with good regularity and came for visits on his longer stretches of off days. He had most of his things at their house, in boxes, which Earl had locked in the tool shed because Kyle would get into them. Earl had once caught seven-year-old Kyle brandishing a dull Mexican switchblade, and another time found a skin magazine hidden in his room; Earl threw both the knife and the magazine in the trash, because there are things you don't bring into another man's house. When Dennis would visit, he'd come on a foreign motorcycle that held his body at an absurd angle, and pass hours wrestling with the boy in the backyard while Kyle roared and his ears turned crimson. With Dennis around, Kyle was transformed. He went from a quiet and for the most part respectful child to a frantic performer, an attention seeker. He'd tear about the house with one of Tuuli's old dresses fluttering from his shoulders like a cape, talking nonsense, singing and carrying on, all the while shooting expectant glances at his father. "I want to show you another thing," he'd say, leading his father by the finger, and when they got where they were going, he'd have forgotten what he meant to show but by that time was on to something else. Showing off was the only way to describe it. Earl had never cared for spectacle of any kind. In his experience, any person who craved the attention of others usually wasn't much worth paying attention to, and this was something the boy would have to learn. In the throes of Kyle's nagging, Dennis found little peace, and Earl pitied him. He had to lock the boy in his room and mow both the front and back lawns so Dennis and Sarah could take some time alone.

Over the years, Kyle was left increasingly riled up and difficult after Dennis's visits, and Sarah took little interest in righting him. Soon, the boy's sole pleasure when his father was away was to send him letters, and this had been pretty much the only way they could convince him to learn how to write. But Dennis never replied. And by the time Kyle was eleven, the visits had dwindled to nothing. Tuuli had tracked them on a calendar she hid from her daughter in the glove compartment of her car, marking days with circled D's. Kyle grew sullen and neglected chores he'd once done happily. Sarah was called to the school principal's office a number of times for his disruptive behaviour in class, but each time she was to go, she got a stomach ache or migraine and stayed home. As much as this pained him, Earl felt it wasn't his place to intervene.

"We can't just do nothing," Tuuli had said on their way back from bowling. It was a dry summer evening, the windows down, the sky full of minced, pink clouds, the kind of night Earl would later turn over in his mind for hours.

"He's a good kid most of the time—there's something off with him is what," he said, "and with a mother who can hardly do up her own shoes, who can blame him?"

"Oh, Earl, he hasn't a single friend, the neighbourhood kids treat him like the plague."

"Well, if he acts like the plague, he'd better get used to kids covering their mouths," Earl said, and Tuuli frowned. Earl shifted his grip on the wheel. "He just needs to take responsibility for himself. He'll settle down when he's working age. There's no use beating ourselves up over it."

Shortly after, one of Sarah's friends from high school found a job as a banquet waitress on a Norwegian cruise boat, and she told Sarah there was a spot for her.

"I think I'd regret it if I didn't do it," Sarah said to her parents over oatmeal one morning. Kyle was at the end of the table, fiddling with the brown sugar container.

"That's enough sugar, Kyle," Earl said.

"We've always wanted to go on a cruise, haven't we, Earl?" Tuuli said.

"That's plenty," Earl said, feeling his throat close as the boy continued heaping it on.

"It will be good experience," Sarah said, and Tuuli took her hand while Earl nodded then stood in an effort to disperse the rage building in him as he eyed the wasteful peaks melting in Kyle's bowl like dirty glaciers.

It was clear what Sarah meant by this, even to Kyle. She was fragile, too young for a child, everyone knew it, always had, and now with Dennis gone there was nothing for her in this place, and no opportunity to better herself. The work would be just the thing for her. What good was there in asking the boy what he wanted? They'd always picked up after their daughter and this wasn't much different. And so it was that when Sarah set off on a bright Friday afternoon for the airport to meet a great white ship anchored off the coast of Florida, while her son played lawn darts against himself in the backyard, Earl and Tuuli became the boy's guardians.

Though they'd done their best raising him, it had come as no great shock to Earl that the boy had ended up where he had, rooting around in the garbage, eating at soup kitchens, and probably living off the dole.

The night Kyle appeared on his television, Earl lay sleepless on the left side of the mattress, the side he still found himself migrating to even though his bed was no longer shared, mulling over the existence of this boy—who was really now a man—he'd for so long pushed from his mind.

The next morning Earl changed into his work clothes and pulled on socks for the first time in weeks. Outside, he shook his head at the sorry condition of the yard and set about carefully weeding then mowing his lawn, finally edging it with a tool he also used in winter to chop ice from the driveway. In the afternoon he turned the vegetable bed and planted two rows of potatoes. The following day he rose at six and repainted the small bungalow exactly the same washer-fluid blue it had been for as many years as he could accurately recall. The repetitious quality of the work eased his thinking. And at the end of it, Earl was left with a curious feeling of obligation to his grandson. Not that he'd done him wrong, but perhaps Earl could now, after all these years, talk some sense into him, have him give his head a shake. He saw this as plainly now as he did anything else in his yard: he needed something to do, a project. Work kept a person from wither, from rot, and he was wasting away in this place. Tuuli would have thrown open the curtains, stuck a to-do list in his hand, and roused him from the basement long ago, but he didn't have her anymore, so he had to take the initiative himself, and this also scared him.

Though the housing market was poor, the small city's industries having all folded in on themselves like stoned Goliaths and its young people, or the ones with any ambition in them, all packed off to seek work elsewhere, Earl had managed to sell his house to a Finnish couple distantly related to his wife for what he felt was a fair price. He phoned his daughter and told her he was going on a trip around the world. "Good for you," she'd said. "Treat yourself, you deserve it." Earl said he'd send postcards.

When he arrived at the airport in Vancouver, he took a taxi and sat up front, making a point of shaking the driver's hand before paying him, leaving no tip. He rented a room in an outlying motel with weekly rates and purchased the silver hatchback with a portion of the money he'd received for the house. The city was not new to him. As a young man, he'd hitchhiked out west and worked loading grain ships for a summer. He'd passed most of that time in the murk of beer parlours and the arms of deceitful women. It was a period of his life he cared not to revisit, part of a span of lost years he couldn't fully conjure in his head if he tried. Tuuli had never pressed him about it, another of her many kindnesses, and for this he was grateful.

He drove downtown, found the soup kitchen from the news report with no trouble, and parked across the street each day for a week, long enough for the prostitutes and drug dealers to give up on approaching his car. Earl had never seen people so wretched. It was as if the country had been tipped up at one end and all of its sorry bastards had slid west, stopping only when they reached the sea, perhaps because the sea didn't want them either. Why a man would choose to live in this desperate, brutal way rather than in a house with a family surrounding him Earl would never know. Was it so hard? There'd been plenty of jobs when he'd come in his youth, you could have your pick. But even then there were those who'd rather take what another had built than build it themselves. So perhaps the place hadn't really changed, only managed to attract more of them.

One drizzly Thursday evening, a red-bearded man took his place in line. His hockey jersey bore the number of a player the Canucks had traded south well over ten years ago; the sleeves, once home-team white, were now mottled brown and grey.

It was Kyle. There was no doubt. He waited his turn and went inside, soon emerging with a paper bowl of something steaming he blew on as he set off down the street. Earl put the car in gear. He followed the boy for some time with no purpose in his mind that he could have honestly described if he were stopped and asked. He'd never actually considered what he'd do once he found him, and now that it had proven so easy, he was beginning to suspect he'd made a terrible mistake. Stopping a man he didn't know from Adam to offer advice on how to live his life seemed futile, silly even, as well as potentially dangerous.

Earl gassed for a block or so, then pulled over to allow Kyle to walk ahead. He knew his grandson could pick out detail only up to a distance of about ten feet, that's what the doctors had said anyway, so he trailed closer than he would have anyone else. Kyle walked briskly, his free arm swinging. He looked more robust than he had in the news special. A man tracking his own grandson like an elk, Earl thought, shaking his head at what he'd been reduced to. After about ten blocks, Kyle stopped at the edge of a small, vacant parking lot and disappeared into a row of large bushes beneath a billboard that flipped back and forth between two pictures like a set of vertical blinds. Earl pulled over.

He waited, tapping at the wheel with his thumbs. He failed to imagine what would make his grandson want to live in all this filth and confusion. Vancouver had always seemed more like an encampment than a city to Earl, about as permanent as a card table set up for a Friday-night game. Perhaps it was drugs. But the boy looked all right, physically, that is, healthy even. What Earl knew of drugs were the snivelling junkies of television forensics shows.

A sudden honking made Earl jump and he saw his rearview full with a hulking shape up tight to his bumper. He stuck his arm out and waved the bus around. It only honked again and lurched closer. As Earl pulled away, he saw his grandson emerge from the bushes with a loaded shopping cart he must have had stashed there. Earl made a right and had to go a few blocks south because of one-ways. When he returned to the lot, his grandson was gone. He applied sudden force to the small wheel, ceasing only when he feared it would break off. He spent the next three hours crisscrossing the neighbourhood and swearing under his breath until he finally spotted him, now without his shopping cart, outside a dingy building called the Grandview Hotel. The tired neon of the hotel's sign was familiar to Earl, and he had a feeling he'd spent some time drunk in a room there, perhaps a long time, but he pushed it from his mind. He watched Kyle pull a key from his trousers, unlock a side door, and step in.

The next morning, Earl parked out front of the Grandview Hotel for the whole day, plugging the meter, cluttering his dashboard with the wrappers of hotdogs bought from a street vendor. There was no sign of Kyle. He returned to his motel that night and got drunk on the wine coolers he'd bought because he'd not been in a liquor store in twenty years, not even when Tuuli died, and had thought the festive bottles were a new kind of beer. Something about the distance from home, or the fact that he no longer had one, or that he no longer had someone to explain himself to, made drunkenness more reasonable to him than it had been in years.

The next day he was parked in the same spot even earlier than the previous day, watching the weak sun climb into the mountains to the east like the first leg of a roller coaster. He'd bought a road map and a mechanical pencil at a drugstore, and now he unfolded the map, located the Grandview Hotel, and made a star with his pencil. At exactly seven Kyle appeared, and Earl followed him, quickly sketching his route on the map when he stopped to let Kyle walk ahead. Earl followed him all day, and the next. After a week of this, he had learned that his grandson made exactly the same journey at the same time each day, seven days a week, taking on average eight hours to push his roaring cart up alleys and over bridges, through a circuit of dumpsters—mostly for condos and apartment buildings—that traversed a good part of the city and ended at a series of second-hand stores and street vendors, where he attempted to sell what he'd found. By the end, Earl had produced a meticulous map, and it delighted him that he was able to pinpoint the boy at any time of day.

But even after Earl completed the map he continued to follow his grandson, for no reason other than he liked to watch Kyle work, because work was the only way to describe what he was doing, whether he was getting paid for it or not. After much frustrated flipping through the manual, Earl had mastered his car's trip odometer and he clocked Kyle in at about twenty kilometres a day, which impressed him. At times Earl felt like the support car for one of those disabled people who wheelchaired across the country for charity. He watched his grandson tether impossibly large objects to the rickety cart and push them great distances to the places they could be sold or stashed for later. The boy's labour seemed to belong to another time. Earl thought of pharaohs, forced marches, treks across deadened earth in search of new beginnings. He found himself strangely proud of his grandson, proud of the steady way he carted the things he found and of the resourcefulness the task required. Earl knew that he himself had never worked so hard in his life.

The first thing Earl left was a rain poncho. It had kept him dry for years atop hydro poles, but he had no use for it now, clocking most of his time in his car. He left it poking from a grocery bag beside one of the dumpsters, and the next rainy day he was pleased to see Kyle wrapped in it. He remembered Easter egg hunts, hiding foiled eggs in the garden and tool shed for Kyle to find, ruddy joy in the kid's face as he tore around the yard like a crazed detective.

Now Earl leaves cheap sneakers and chickens, cases of sports drinks, tarps, and packages of size medium underwear, and it pleases him to think Kyle values these items that appear magically each evening in his dumpsters. He likes to think that his grandson feels he is, in some small way, lucky. And it is for this reason that Earl decides he has to at least right the chicken resting half on the bottom of the dumpster. Kyle might not eat it if he thinks it's contaminated. In truth, Kyle has taken everything set out for him so far, but the thought of him going hungry tonight is more than Earl can bear.

He attempts to pull the oak desk over but can't get it to budge. Then he scans the alley and spots a floral-upholstered armchair next to a scraggly bush and a motorcycle that likely hasn't kicked over in years. He drags the armchair toward the dumpster, walking it on its legs, halting intermittently to lean on his cane. He resists sitting in the chair because it smells of vomit and cat litter. Finally, he butts it up to the dumpster, then sets a foot on the cushion. Earl lets his cane fall to the ground and with a grunt he unsteadily mounts the chair, wobbling and sinking into its springs. He feels ridiculous, and for a moment smiles at the idea of someone passing by the alley and taking him for another old dumpster-diver about to take a plunge for sunken treasure. Earl kicks his leg up to the edge of the bin and feels his stockings cinch tight on his calves. He draws a bracing breath and attempts to hoist himself over the lip of the dumpster, wary to not land on the chicken. He is just about over when he hears a sick silence as if someone has placed two drinking glasses over his ears and the sky swings over him and the side of the dumpster heaves up, striking him mercilessly in his ribs, and it is difficult to unravel the sound of the lid slamming from the faraway sound of his head against the bottom and all this is followed by a bleached, dizzy rushing in his ears.

———————

In near perfect dark, Earl pulls himself into the fetal position. The rushing has subsided slightly and he begins to make out fibres of light where the lid of the dumpster is bent a little. His hip is blowing pain and at the side of his head there is wetness. His elbow is pressing into something. He feels the urge to stand but needs a minute more for his body to stop shaking. He fears for a second he is trapped. He can't remember the last time he was trapped somewhere, perhaps only in a childhood game. But he's not trapped, he just needs to collect himself. Then he realizes it's the birthday cake box that his elbow is sinking into. With his other hand he reaches and touches the dead houseplant. After the birthday cake is gone, I'll eat this, he thinks, crushing a brittle leaf in his fingers, chuckling to himself, until the pain in his hip forces his teeth together.

With the lid shut, the smell is sickening. Years of leaking garbage bags have left a gummy film on the dumpster's bottom. He attempts to pull his head away from the stench but there is more pain so he stops. While he waits for strength, the smell brings to Earl's mind with a staggering vividness the day of Kyle's accident, a few months after Sarah left for the cruise ship.

He and Kyle were at the dump in Earl's truck, stopped waiting for the junk truck ahead of them to be weighed, its sides built up with scrap wood and brimming with bald tires. "They do it so they know how much we got rid of when we leave," he told Kyle, who hadn't asked, but Earl thought the boy might find it interesting. The boy's eyes were fixed forward. "You don't have to talk if you don't want, doesn't bother me," Earl said. "Anyhow, we have a job to do." Earl briefly considered how much it would cost if he were to leave the boy there, or for himself for that matter. He calculated it wouldn't be much for either.

On a dusty road further in, they passed a bulldozer spattered with what looked like soiled toilet paper. Kyle rolled down his window and the truck was deluged with hot, putrid air, a smell so bad it graduated to taste. The little muscles of Kyle's jaw wiggled and Earl felt the dust starting to make paste in his eyes and he wiped at them with his cuff.

They entered what was like a coliseum of garbage, great slopes that loomed and shifted in the rippling heat. Outside their truck swarms of gulls, so far from the sea, shrieked pure treble and men were yelling at each other over the noise. A man in coveralls rapped at their window. He asked if they had any batteries, or paint, or wood, or metal. Earl turned to the boy; their cargo seemed somehow more his than anyone else's.

"No," Kyle said.

The man raised a stick to the end of which he'd attached a mannequin's hand, making his arm appear grotesquely long, and pointed to where they should unload.

Earl clunked the truck into reverse.

"Why does it matter where we put it—it's all just garbage, isn't it?" Kyle said.

"They need to keep things orderly, even at the dump," Earl said.

The boy was bouncing his knee. Seagulls twisted overhead and the punishing smell found Earl again as he stepped from the truck. He felt the bulldozers in his chest as they churned the waste upon itself. For a moment he questioned whether it was wise to have brought the boy along. Earl didn't really need his help but had woken that morning with the notion that it would be good for Kyle, a sort of medicine.

"You going to help?" Earl said, and the boy got out and crossed his arms.

Earl dropped the tailgate with a bang, stepped up, and the pickup sank further under him. He couldn't think of any words that would make this easy for the boy—it was like ripping off a bandage, or jumping into a lake—so he grabbed one of the boxes that Kyle's father had left behind and hurled it to the foot of the mountain of garbage.

He turned to Kyle and saw that he was weeping, two fat streams down his reddening cheeks, and Earl's chest fisted with pity. He felt an overwhelming compulsion to lower his eyes, to focus on doing the job they'd come to do, let the rest take care of itself. He threw another box, turning before it landed with a crash made tiny by the roar of the bulldozers.

The boy still didn't move. Earl figured he was only making it worse for himself.

"You can work, or you can walk," Earl said, and the boy glanced to the road. Earl wondered if he really was considering the fifty-kilometre hike home. Kyle made two shaking fists at his sides, exhaled, then released them. He turned his slick face away and leapt to the tailgate. He snatched up two shoeboxes and threw them. Then he grabbed a larger box, slid it over, and kicked it from the truck.

"That's it," Earl said. "Who needs this junk anyway."

Earl started on the heavy garbage bags of Dennis's fancy clothes that swished when he launched them. As they worked, Earl could see the tears had dried and Kyle was maybe even enjoying himself a little. After a while, they made a kind of game of it, aiming for fragile things like old lamps and panes of glass, and this made the time go quickly.

With their cargo gone, Earl drove his grandson home, where they sat in the backyard, waiting for Tuuli to thrust open the squeaky storm door and set a plate of egg sandwiches on the picnic table. The midday sun was hot. The boy seemed all right now, as far as Earl could tell anyway. Perhaps the work had done him good. Kyle said he was starving, so Earl walked over to the small vegetable garden he'd been tending with increasing care since he had retired and pulled two carrots. He rinsed them under the outdoor tap and they sat, crunching.

Later, after eating their sandwiches in silence, they played lawn darts, both shirtless in the heat. As always, the boy used the yellow darts and his grandfather the red. Kyle claimed that he was going to win this time and Earl replied, "We'll see."

From the start, the boy played poorly, sending his darts in great lofting arcs and cursing them as they thudded into the grass, feet from the ring. Earl nearly offered him advice on technique but figured this was not the best time. But letting the boy win wouldn't do him any good either, so Earl threw his own darts as best he could.

The boy's next throw hit the door of the tool shed, leaving a mark, and Earl spoke softly—"A little too much"—as he licked his finger and rubbed the paint while Kyle kicked at the dirt at the edge of the vegetable garden.

"Not everything turns out like we think it should, chum," Earl said.

Kyle considered this, twisting the dart in his hand. "I'm going to work with Dennis when I save up some money," he said.

"You wouldn't last two days in that mine, not with your attitude."

"He's going to be mad at you when he gets back, when he sees all his good stuff went into the garbage, and that my mother is too retarded to take care of me."

Earl threw his last dart of the round, and it landed nearly dead-centre in the hoop across the yard. He turned and took Kyle by the shoulders, shaking him a little so this time he'd actually listen. He was sick of having to spell everything out for a kid who took pleasure in acting like a fool, a kid who refused outright to make the best of his situation, and he told him in no uncertain terms what he thought the chances were of Dennis ever coming back.

Earl would later admit to Tuuli he knew what Kyle was going to do before he did it. Their eyes had met before the boy slithered from his grip. Kyle took a step back and bent low and swung his arm upward with as much force as his small body could muster. He'd thrown the dart straight up, like a space launch, and they followed the yellow plastic fins until they were lost in the sun. Earl searched the sky for it, acutely aware of what was happening, of what was coming. He found only blurs of cloud behind the grid of telephone and power lines that criss-crossed the small yard. It's going to hit where it's going to hit and there's nothing we can do about it, he remembers thinking. He was still hunting for it in the sun when he heard that awful, hollow popping, like opening a new jar of pickles, followed by the hush of his grandson collapsing into the soft grass.

"Nice and easy," Earl said as he held it still while Tuuli, who'd never had a licence, drove. There was frighteningly little blood, and he remembers thinking he would have felt better if there were just a little more. It had lanced the corner of Kyle's left eye, squeezing in snug to the tear duct, the thing sticking up proudly like an antenna, its yellow fins bright above the boy's clenching face. Halfway there, Kyle started to panic and Earl had to grip his arms to keep him from pulling it loose.

———————

Earl opens his eyes without remembering closing them and knows he must have passed out. He manages to sit by pushing his back against the wall of the dumpster. His calves throb in his nylon stockings. He decides his hip is not broken, and his next thought is that the chicken has gone cold. He can't see his watch, but Kyle is certainly late and Earl keeps himself from speculating on the many ways a street-dwelling man could be harmed. Minutes pass. Earl's breathing slows, and his mind becomes more collected. The terrible smell has weakened. Or perhaps it is him. Even the nose gets tired, Earl thinks, then he wonders how this odour strikes his grandson when he lifts the lids of the dumpsters he frequents each week, if he smells it at all.

He hears a rumbling that is not a car, then footsteps. The lid comes open and the streetlights bathe Earl in a yellowness that hurts his eyes. A hand grips his arm, and though he does not quite feel ready, he is hoisted to his feet.

"Up you get," says a voice from a man standing on the floral armchair from which Earl fell what seems like ages ago. He feels hands in his armpits and he is dragged up over the lip by a measured strength and dropped on his feet in the alley. His knee quakes, then holds.

"Sleeping one off in there?" Kyle says. "I wouldn't. That's a good way to get squished."

Earl looks down to examine himself in the light. On his shoulder there is a darkening ellipse of blood, his shirt is untucked, and the front of his pants and coat are splattered with grease, soil, and a yellow gravy-like liquid. He puts his hand to his head and feels a small gash beneath a clotted mat of his thin hair, and doing this, brushes his face with his forearm and realizes he hasn't shaved in weeks.

"This yours?" Kyle says, holding out an aluminum cane. Earl realizes he's been standing without his cane for some time. Adrenalin, he figures.

"Yes, that's mine," he says. "Thank you."

"Good find," Kyle says, handing it to him, and Earl is relieved to have it back.

"A real bump you took there," Kyle says and grabs Earl's head, turning it roughly. Then he makes the sound one uses to call a chipmunk. "I think I got somethin' for that," he says, and goes rooting in one of the many bags that hang from his cart.

Kyle returns with a tube in his hand and squeezes a pea of opaque gel onto his dirty finger. He leans in, turns his good eye to the task, and begins to apply it to Earl's wound. It is a gesture of such tenderness that Earl feels all at once entirely unworthy of it. In his weeks of watching Kyle, tracking him, mapping his route, he had never been this close to him, and this proximity warms him now, something similar to the softness in his chest that came when Tuuli used to cut his hair in the kitchen, or when he watched Sarah float boats built from milk cartons down McVicar Creek. Kyle pulls back to assess his work, and for a moment Earl thinks there's a catch of recognition in Kyle's good eye, but the moment passes and Kyle walks back to the dumpster.

"This is one of my bins, don't you know that?" he says and lifts the lid and peers inside. "But you're half in the grave anyways so I'll let you slide. Just don't make a habit of coming round here too much—it's not like you can't find your own, there's plenty of 'em around." Then he reaches in and pulls out the chicken in its container.

"I'm guessing this is yours too, right?" he says, admiring the bird.

"No," Earl says, then clears his throat. "It's yours."

"You know I keep finding these things," Kyle says, "all over the place, people just buy 'em and throw 'em out. Don't make any sense. Sometimes I think they just come from nowhere, that things come out of these bins that nobody ever put in." Kyle attempts to brush some grime from the skin with his dirty hand. "You hungry? You look like hell anyways, you drunks don't know when to take a pit stop. Here, we'll go halfers on this, how's that?"

"That'd be fine," Earl says, suddenly wobbly. He sits in the armchair.

Kyle sits cross-legged on the pavement and tears the bird in half with a cracking sound. He sets Earl's portion in the lid of the container.

Earl isn't hungry, but he accepts his ration, pinching a bit of meat and placing it in his mouth. Though it has gone cold it doesn't

taste half bad, nothing like the dumpster smells. Kyle stops talking for a spell while they eat, and Earl gets his first good look at
him. His shoulder-length red hair is drawn into a ponytail and he
is wearing the polar fleece Earl left for him a few weeks back. Earl
can see now that it is a bit small and decides to next time buy him a
size up. He sees that the eye is aimed outward and it looks cloudy,
as though filled with yoghurt. Earl could not remember it looking
that way when they'd removed the bandage. It had been crooked,
but clear. The doctor had fit Kyle with a patch for his good eye in
hopes of forcing the bad one to aim straight, but Kyle refused to
wear it. When the swelling diminished, Earl insisted Kyle return to
school. Only two days into the week he was suspended for breaking two fingers of a boy who Earl had thought was the closest thing
Kyle had to a friend. After that, Kyle was caught by floorwalkers
at Zellers stealing odd things like women's perfume and clothes
that weren't even close to his size. He lit fires and tore up Earl's
garden. No longer just a show-off, he was a wild animal, and Earl
couldn't help but think the dart had injected some manner of evil
deep in his head. The boy seemed to have set out to break their
wills. And though she wouldn't say it, Tuuli feared him too. Earl
responded with a severity and rigidity he'd never known himself
capable of, tactics he'd never employed when raising Sarah. He
decreed curfews and ratcheted down bedtimes. He called in favours
with folks he knew around town and got Kyle jobs—stock boy, gas
jockey, even farmhand at a U-pick strawberry place—but he was
fired from them all. "Can't take instructions," "Pumped diesel into
a Honda Civic," or as one of Earl's old buddies from Hydro had
put it, "Got too much angry in him." With each disappointment, he
found himself punishing the boy more and more severely, and now,

as he watches his grandson devour the chicken, Earl knows that he behaved in ways that would repulse him today. Only recently, drinking alone in his motel while listening to men argue about money in an adjacent room, Earl remembered striking the boy, though the years had washed out the details, whether it was closed fist or open. He doesn't remember taking any joy in doing it, but this offers little comfort. In his darker moments he fears he did worse.

Earl realizes he has lost his appetite and stands to toss the chicken back into the dumpster. Light-headedness forces him to sit for fear of falling. "You want some cake? There's a whole cake in there," Kyle says with a full mouth.

"No," Earl says, "I'm stuffed."

Kyle rises shouting, "Lookat this thing!" He rushes over to the schoolteacher's desk. "What a beauty." He runs his hand over the wood and opens the drawers.

"This thing is worth money, I can smell it, look at this wood, this is solid wood—oak, you know, that's why it's heavy, particle board ain't heavy—it's probably an antique, that's what it is, definitely an antique, somebody didn't know what they had, just threw out a good thing that they had, you believe that? I bet we could get at least forty for this thing if we can get it to Harold before he shuts down."

"It's too heavy for the two of us," Earl says.

Kyle scans the alley and walks to a moving truck that's parked in the adjacent lot. He pulls a large pin that's attached to a chain and unlatches the side door. He disappears inside and returns with a rolling carpeted dolly.

"Look, buddy, if you can just help me get this thing up this hill, I'll be able to get it to Harold myself."

Though the alley rises in only a modest slope, with the heavy desk it will be gruelling, and after his stint in the dumpster Earl doubts he is up to the task. But when Kyle begins to flip the desk over and the cupboard doors swing open and the drawers all come sliding out, Earl can't stand to watch him do it alone. When they finally get it over, Earl's breath comes in tense, shallow gasps. Then Kyle lifts one end of it and has Earl slide the dolly underneath. "Wait," Kyle says, and goes to stash his cart behind a parked car. Clouds are sweeping overhead and it must be later than Earl thought because the windows of the office towers have darkened except for a few. If he hadn't fallen into the dumpster, he would have been asleep hours ago. It is turning into a fine evening, warm and fresh-smelling. They find that the desk rolls easily enough, but when they reach the hill, the going slows, and Earl's knees grind and his calves throb with stagnant blood. Earl stops again to chase his breath.

"Come on, push, you bag of bones," Kyle says, and Earl lowers his head and puts his shoulder to the desk, offering up all of the little strength he has left.

Goodbye Porkpie Hat

Purpose

I'm lying on a sheetless mattress in my room, watching a moth bludgeon itself on my naked light bulb. Over near the window sits a small television I never watch, beside it a hot plate I never use. I spend most of my time here, thinking about rock cocaine, not thinking about rock cocaine, performing rudimentary experiments, smoking rolled tobacco rescued from public ashtrays, trying to remember what my mind used to feel like, and, of course, studying my science book. I dumpstered it two years ago and ever since it has been beside my mattress like a friend at a slumber party, pretending to sleep, dying for consultation. I read it for at least two hours every day; I know this because I time myself. It's a grade-ten textbook, a newer edition, complete with glossy diagrams and photos of famous scientists who all look so regal and determined, it's as though the flashbulb had caught them at the very moment their thoughts were shifting the scientific paradigm forever. I like to think that when they gazed pensively up at the stars and pondered the fate of future generations, they were actually thinking of me.

I excavated the book in June. The kid who threw it out thought he would never have to see science again, that September would never come. What an idiot—I used to believe that.

My room is about the size of a jail cell. One time, two guys came through my open window and beat me with a pipe until I could no longer flinch and stole my former TV and a can of butts, so I hired a professional security company called Apex to install bars on my window. I spent my entire welfare cheque on them, just sat and safely starved for a whole month. I had to pay the guy cash up front because he didn't believe I could possibly have that kind of money. It felt good to pay him that kind of money, he did a good job.

Someone is yelling at someone outside, so I go to the window and look out into Oppenheimer Park, which is across the street from my rooming house. There I see only a man calmly sitting on a bench, smoking. Everyone says this park was named after the scientist who invented the nuclear bomb. It has playground equipment, but it's always empty because no parent would ever bring their kid there, on account of it being normally frequented by people who are like me or Steve or worse. The park is infamous, an open-air drug market, they say. From my window, I've seen people get stabbed there, but not all the time, good things happen in the park too. Some people lie in the grass all day and read. The people who are reading don't get stabbed. I'm not sure why that is.

I'm finished studying, so I go out and cut across the northeast corner of the park, walking west up Powell. I approach a group of about six Vietnamese men. You can always tell the drug dealers because they are the ones with bikes. I purchase a ten rock with a ten-dollar bill, all of my money until Wednesday. Eye contact somehow seems to make things more illegal, so I stare at the ground while one of them barks at me. He is cartoonish, his teeth brown and haphazard like tusks. He shifts side to side on his toes like a warmed-up boxer and aims nervous glances to the street. "Pipe?" he barks. "No," I say, "I have one, thanks."

Crack melts at a tepid eighty, and if you heat it too fast, it just burns off with minimal smoke. Smoking it is one thing I'm good at. I don't really feel the crack craving people talk about; I would describe it more as a healthy interest than anything else, like I'm fine-tuning a hypothesis, or conducting a sort of protracted experiment. I know it sounds strange, but I feel if I could get high enough one time I would quit, content with the knowledge of the actual crack high, the genuine article. Unfortunately, a paltry approximation is the only high I have been able to afford so far.

In an alley, my brain has a family reunion with some long-lost neurochemicals, and I crouch beneath the party, not wanting to disturb it, shivering and euphoric. A seemingly infinite and profound series of connections and theories swamp my mind. It is a better-than-expected stone and it makes me long for my room and my book.

A man and woman are suddenly five feet away, arguing; I am unsure how long they've been there. I have an urge to explain something complex and scientific to them, to light their eyes with wonder. The man is talking.

"Hey bro."

"Hi, are you guys doing okay?" I sputter, feeling sweat rim my eyelids.

"Oh yeah, she's just being a harsh bitch." The last word he turns and yells in her face, actually puffing her bangs back with it. After an emphatic pause, he turns back. "Hey bro, how about you give us a toke and make us feel better?" he says to my clutching hands with a smile and an assumed entitlement. I'm briefly embarrassed for being so absurdly high and unable to share it with them or anyone else.

I tell him, "It's all gone. Sorry," with what I feel is a genuine sincerity, my high already beginning its diminuendo.

"How about giving me my pipe back then?" he says, steps closer.

I've been on the receiving end of this type of tactic before. I tell him sorry, there is only one, careful not to combine the words *my* and *pipe*, a pairing that would no doubt signal the commencement of my probably already inevitable beating.

The woman tells him to leave me alone. Her cropped shirt reveals an abdomen stretch-marked and harbouring unearthly wrinkles in the texture of a scrotum or an elderly elephant. The man is yelling now. Blurry and ill-advised jail tattoos populate his arms, and I watch them wave above my head. I wonder if any woman who has told her boyfriend to leave somebody alone has ever meant it. If ever, I conclude, it is a statistically insignificant proportion. Amidst his racket, the urge to smoke another rock comes over me in a bland revelation, like I need to do the dishes. I hear rats scrabbling inside the wall and I try to think if I have ever seen a rat look up, into the sky I mean, and wonder if it is possible for them to see that far. As I'm trying to stand, the man kicks me in the chest with his fungal shoe and I feel a crunch inside my shoulder and it begins to buzz, and I bring my other arm up to shield my face.

I hear my pipe hit the ground, but it doesn't break because crack pipes are made of Pyrex, the same glass as test tubes. People dumpster them from medical supply laboratories. They are test tubes with no bottom, no end, all that smoke and mania just funnels through them unhindered. My lungs have tested the tubes and their acrid samples, but unfortunately there has been no control group, so the results of these experiments are often difficult to observe.

I am crumpling to the ground, hearing him pick up my pipe and smelling the tang of fermented piss. When urine evaporates it leaves a sticky yellow film, and I am thinking about how urine is a solution, not a mixture, of this I am absolutely sure and the beating continues from there.

Materials

In the room beside me lives an old junkie named Steve, who at some indeterminate point took to fixing between his toes, the rest of his veins being too thickened and prone to abscesses. He blows his welfare cheques in about three days, pupils whittled down, head pitched on the stormy sea of his neck like an Alzheimer's patient. He warns me by banging on the wall when he suspects he may be about to shoot too much dope. I've rescued him twice by calling in the Narcan injection, plucking the needle from his foot before they arrive with their strange antidote. I guess you could say he is my only friend.

Steve knows nothing of science. Doomed to forever repeat the same experiment, he arrives on his sticky floor at the same vomit-soaked conclusion over and over. I'm well aware that experimental replication is a cornerstone of the scientific method, but not to the extent Steve takes it.

In his nasal junkie voice, he calls me a tweaker or a coconut because I smoke crack, but it doesn't bother me. He doesn't mean anything bad by it. One time he sold me a kernel of soap, saying it was a rock he found on the street and he would let go for cheap. At first I didn't believe him, but it was the way he held it, with reverence, two hands together, a child holding a cricket. I didn't speak to him for weeks until he almost overdosed, and when he woke up, he'd completely forgotten ripping me off, so I forgave him, plus I stole the money back anyway. And I guess I was lonely.

Steve has been bringing me food. He says he might as well, because the guy on the other side of his room doesn't do shit when he bangs on the wall. Tins of grey meat you open with a key, and day-old hamburger buns from the gospel mission. My left collarbone is broken and my face raw and taut with swelling. Bones float and snarl in my shoulder like an aluminum boat continually running aground, and I have had dizzy spells. Last week, I stumbled to the welfare office, picked up my cheque, saw my worker, Linda #103, told her everything was okay while she made her empathy face and told me I should go to the clinic. "I should," I said, and staggered to the cheque-cashing place, returning home with a small fortune in Tylenol 3's and a tin of tobacco. The T-3's came from a guy I know who long ago convinced a doctor of his unbearable chronic pain, resulting in a bond I suspect is not dissimilar to love. I gave Steve some 3's for taking care of me and he took them all right away, hand to his open mouth, in a yawn.

———————

It's a month later, I've been up for days trying to memorize the periodic table, and I'm so high my stomach is boiling. I sold the T-3's and bought some crack because I've found that it's what best alleviates the pain and the dizziness, but now the crack is all gone and the reckless similarities between magnesium and manganese are beginning to make me want to dig my teeth out of my head like weeds. I'm watching my light bulb grow brighter and grinding my molars and wishing I had someone to apologize to. I guess it's ironic that only when I'm really stoned do I feel optimistic and strong enough to never want to do it again. I'm telling myself that when I get my next cheque I'm going to get a big bag of weed and some groceries and just get healthy again.

It's morning, my room is a haze, I still haven't slept, and I'm lying face down in bed listening to the inside-my-head sound of my eyelashes crunching into the pillow that reminds me of distant steps in snow. I'm fluttering them faster and faster, imagining someone running toward me, their breath steaming into the air, and suddenly I hear my fire escape rattle.

I snap into a sitting position on the bed and there is a man at my window. He wears an old-style porkpie hat and a three-piece tweed suit, and is smoking a tailor-made cigarette that smells American. He grips the bars of my window as if he has been momentarily locked up for a petty misunderstanding and smiles warmly.

"Hello, Henry, my name is J. Robert Oppenheimer."

The man's speech is soft and melodic. His eyes are soothing and blue, lit by an inquisitive intensity. I recognize him from my science book.

"I recognize you from my science book," I say, my teeth chalky and soft from grinding.

"Of course, Henry, and dare I say I recognize you as a fellow of the pursuit? Would you agree? And by 'pursuit' I refer to the intrepid and arduous quest for knowledge. Care for a cigarette?" His eyes linger on my science book as I tentatively snatch a smoke through the bars, unsure which of us I would describe as being inside.

I find my hands are shaking as I light the smoke. I'm not used to tailor-mades and get panicked by the restriction of the filter as I wait for the drag in asthmatic anticipation. I exhale and begin to calm. His eyes flash as he speaks.

"I feel it's the best way for a man to buckle into some erudition—just a meagre room, a book, and some tobacco . . ." He is taking strangely long drags from his cigarette, and as he exhales, his eyes scan the room and land on the vials that once held my crack supply.

"I'm sorry, Mr. Oppenheimer, but—"

"Call me J. Robert, what my students call me."

"I'm sorry, J. Robert, I mean thank you . . . but I'm pretty sure there are two dates under your picture in my textbook, or rather what I mean to say is that—"

"I'm deceased? Throat cancer, unequivocally abhorrent, avoid it at all costs. Only truly evil things expand infinitely, my friend." He grabs the bars and gingerly sticks his long, spindly legs through, then his arms, assuming the position I imagine would be most comfortable were one trapped in a giant birdcage. I can see his socks and they don't match.

"What're you doing here, J. Robert, if you don't mind me asking?" I mumble as he grips my eyes with his, brandishing the smile of a forgiving and benevolent parent. There is silence, he is still smiling and staring, I'm not sure if he heard me. He seems to be thinking.

He smacks his lips and lifts his palms upward and out in a gesture of peace and his long arms sweep farther into the room than I would have imagined they could. "Look, I'm not concerned with the past; I can see by the shape of your face and shoulder you are not particularly interested in revisiting it either. I'm here to elucidate, provide guidance, this sort of thing. Do you have any questions so far?"

My mind accelerates with a myriad of science-related questions, questions I've never had the chance to say out loud, and all of them seem too elementary for his finely tuned understanding. "Did you know the park out there is named after you?" I sputter, my clamping jaw carving jagged chunks out of my syllables.

"Ha. Of course it's not, Henry, it's named after Vancouver's ghastly and colitic imp of a second mayor, David Oppenheimer— no relation. Why would they name it after me?" He lights up his third cigarette in one mechanical motion and blows more smoke into my room.

"Everybody around here thinks it is," I say.

"Regardless, your question is churlish and time is precious, so moving on, I will cut to it . . ."

He clears his throat.

"In my humble opinion it is not possible to be a scientist unless you think it is of the highest value to share your knowledge. Would you agree?"

"Yes," I say, still wondering if churlish is bad.

J. Robert's eyes again find my empty crack vials. "And accepting this axiom you must agree as a scientist that it is invariably good to learn, that knowledge is good. Yes?"

I nod.

"Do you truly believe that?"

"Of course," I say, sounding decisive and intelligent.

"Excellent. So now we arrive at the crux of my proposal, Henry, and that crux being . . . In the spirit of scholarly inquiry, I hereby formally request your assistance in the procurement and consumption of the drug commonly referred to as crack cocaine."

"I have no money." It is the first thing I can think of; next is wishing to have denied ever smoking it.

"Aha! A pragmatist! Of course I have more than adequate funds to suffice for our purposes; think of it as our research grant, and when I say 'our,' Henry, I am illuminating the fact that you will be an equal participant in the inhalation of the psychoactive substance in question."

I say nothing. His eyes are so kind and forgiving, they make me want to turn around and see if they are actually meant for someone behind me.

Method

Although he is too foreign-seeming and well dressed to be a cop, J. Robert's eagerness and complex questions put the dealers off. However, even when turning him down, they treat him with more respect than they ever did me, calling him sir, and one of them going so far as to ask why such a fine gentleman would want to get high with a goof like me. Finally, after promising to report all details of the experience, I convince J. Robert to stay back while I complete a transaction. The man is impressed by my large request and American money and says he is from Seattle and is just selling to get home. He stuffs J. Robert's money into his jeans before telling me he has to go pick up more vials because he doesn't have that much on him. I follow him nervously with J. Robert trailing a block behind. He leads us to a rooming house and I wait for a minute while he runs upstairs. I don't have to find out what J. Robert would do to me if I got burned for his money because the man returns with a plastic bag rattling with vials, and I act like the whole thing was no big deal.

The sun is out and fluffy clouds bump together in the sky above the park. Clouds are glorified smoke. My days are defined and determined by the comings and goings of various types of smoke. We are walking briskly now, J. Robert slightly ahead of me. We come upon an old drunk woman lying at the edge of the park, passed out before she could reach its boundary, pickled in the sour jar of her body. I get a whiff of mouthwash vapour, strangely sweet and ironically fresh. Her mouth is loose and open, jaw pushed slightly forward, like she is concentrating on something fragile and complicated. "Alcohol evaporates faster than water," I say, but J. Robert is too far ahead to hear me. It's as if this woman is sublimating, I think, solid straight to gas, her life's horrid memories fuming from her rubbery ears. I tighten my grip on the bag of vials and quicken my pace.

———————

He tosses his suit jacket over my TV, unbuttons his sleeves, and shoves them up his arms. "Your apartment is significantly smaller from the inside, Henry." This is the longest I have ever gone between buying rock and smoking it. He rubs his hands together, sits cross-legged on my mattress. "Teach me everything," he says, "everything you know."

As I'm laying out our supplies—pipes, steel wool, lighters, mouthpieces—it starts to rain. It feels as if the room's air is being sucked through the bars out the window and up into the churning clouds, and I feel cold. I explain the entire process to J. Robert, savouring the details, making it sound as complicated as possible. He studies my face, sometimes moving his lips along with me as I talk.

He raises the pipe and his hands are shaking.

"Like I said now, don't scorch it."

I can't believe I'm telling a genius to be careful. He does a good job melting it and starts to get a toke, but he lowers the pipe trying to watch the rock burn and the liquefied crack dribbles out the end into his lap.

"Goddamn it!" he says with an intense and boyish concentration.

I start coaching, "Don't stop! Keep smoking it, tip it up, that's it, now inhale—go go go go . . ."

He brings it back to his lips, musters a pretty good one, but blows it out too early.

"I don't feel anything, Henry. Goddamn it, show me properly, you buffoon!"

"Here," I say, blowing on the scorched pipe to cool it down. I load another rock, cook it, take a big hoot, then hold it to his lips and he fills his lungs. He holds it, blows it out, and shivers. His porkpie hat is tipped back like a newspaperman and his forehead is varnished with sweat.

"That was the one, Henry . . . Oh yes . . . I'm getting the picture." He closes his eyes and leans back on my bed. "I'm experiencing the prologue of an extremely pleasurable sensation now—differing vastly from what I imagined, however, but quite promising."

I help him smoke more rocks. Then he starts chain-smoking cigarettes, pacing the limited circumference of my room.

"It's no secret I'm a vastly superior theoretician than experimentalist; this is a reality I have always accepted." I can't imagine how deeply he is thinking.

"Oh, Henry, without your steady hand, your know-how, I would be a stranger to these marvellous sensations. I feel such a marked increase in self-control, vigorous and capable of productive work."

"I'm glad I could help," I say.

He kneels beside me. "Henceforth, I shall refer to you as 'Hank,' because, Hank, I propose you just keep on doing what you do best, hitting those little delectable balls out of the park for me just like Hank Aaron smacking his home runs. Hey, old man? We can be partners. What do you say?"

"Okay," I say, "partners."

Either he or I wants to smoke another. So we smoke another. Then he begins a series of brisk jumping jacks in the centre of my room.

"Christ, a man with your kind of prowess, Hank, we could've really used you at Los Alamos. Just imagine it: the world's greatest intellects, working together in seclusion, a truly cooperative effort to stop the greatest evil mankind has ever known, nature's deepest secrets unfurling before us like the desert mesas."

J. Robert is grunting with exertion and the rain is making the trees outside tell him to *sssshshhhhh*.

He finishes, which serves as a good reason to smoke another.

"We could've had a building erected specifically for inges- tion; this substance would have tripled both creativity and pro- ductivity. A sizable supply could have been requisitioned, and of course rationed and distributed equally. Oh, we would have had a functional device years earlier, we could have vaporized Berlin as soon as Hitler jumped a border, for Christ's sake. Hank, I once tired of your platitudes; now I see you for who you are: a great probing and unflinching mind, steadfast and brilliant, but yet modestly so; not a pompous blowhard of pseudo-academic tripe, but a scientist, in the most unmitigated sense of the word."

I can't believe what he is saying; my throat burns and I feel like I'm going to cry. I stand up and start telling him about some experiments I've been performing and start moving my hands dra- matically like he does as I talk, and I'm explaining about how I have always felt I was born in the wrong time in history and about if I just maybe had a chance to meet some peers or like he said some fellow scientists with similar interests, and now that he is here . . . Suddenly there is a bang on the wall. It's Steve.

J. Robert comes with me. We are companions. Steve's door is open and we find him nodding out on his bed with his legs splayed in front of his frail body, semi-conscious, his head drifting downward toward his feet. I shake him and he comes around.

Steve whines something about his high being ruined. J. Robert introduces himself and immediately offers Steve some crack, offending him deeply.

"I don't smoke that shit, Bob, it don't do nothing for me. And as far as I can tell the sorry people who really like it, I mean the people who really get it in their blood, are the ones who already hate themselves the most."

His eyes are rolling back in his head, and he is speaking completely through his nose as if it were a kazoo. "That's why I shoot dope, because I'm selfish, because I treasure myself. And I just don't mind that self feeling like it's floating in a warm sea of warm tongues every single minute for the rest of its life, that's all. Is it so awful, Bob? My advice is you leave my crackerjack friend here out of your—"

J. Robert's voice booms theatrically. "Sir, I must ask you to hold your tongue! Treasure yourself? How asinine! It's philistines like you who cloud the great minds of our nations with your rhetoric of self-worship. This crack cocaine unleashes the truest and noblest potentials in our society! And furthermore . . . ," but he leaves it because Steve has nodded off again, and this time I don't wake him up. I'm just glad he knows so little of science; if he doesn't recognize J. Robert he can't rat him out. Rat him out to whom I'm not sure.

Back in my room, J. Robert's fuming anger is transforming into a sort of agitated sadness. I think it is probably also due to the fact that he is starting to come down, but I don't tell him.

He comments on the naked futility of existence, on the merciless-ness of my light bulb, and then says something in what I think is Dutch. The rain has stopped. Luckily, he wants to smoke more rock, which is good because I do too.

"What made you want to smoke crack in the first place?" I say.

"Excellent question. Because, Hank, to have a sound and crystallized view on something, I feel one must experience it first-hand—to know what one is talking about, that is—and this crack just seems like an area I should form an opinion on."

I notice sweat stains forming in the armpits of his crisp white Oxford shirt. I want desperately to pick up where we left off, before we were interrupted, eager for him to listen to some more of my theories.

"You know, J. Robert, these pipes are made of Pyrex, the same glass as test tubes."

"Simple physics," he says. "Ordinary glass would shatter if subjected to this type of treatment, just like us, huh, Hank? Steeled by the girders of inquiry and knowledge!" He shakes my shoulder and it stabs me with pain, but I don't tell him to stop.

The scientific conversation doesn't last. J. Robert has loos-ened his tie and is pacing and anxious; he wants to go outside, see the sights, meet the locals, get some air, and of course buy more crack. I fear J. Robert will forget about me if we leave, or that he will disappear and never come back. I tell him we have more than enough to last us the night, and that this neighbourhood is ugly and dangerous and unscientific and we should just stay here and just smoke and talk. He snatches his jacket, begins stuffing his pockets with vials. "Hank, my colleagues call me Oppie. And Oppie is not going to tell you what to do, but Oppie and his narcotics are going outside, into this night—this night whose force shall break, blow, burn, and make us new!"

Results

I was twenty-six when I first smoked crack. *Crack*. It sounds so ridiculous even when I say it now, so pornographic. I started late in relation to most. I'd just moved to Vancouver, like everybody else. I was at a party I'd overheard some people talking about that afternoon at a coffee shop. Right when I got there, a girl I didn't know asked me if she could borrow some money. I asked her what for but she wouldn't say. I told her whatever it was I would like to be in on it. I was drunk. I didn't think I would have sex with her but I guess I hoped.

After the first glorious toke, I calmly asked how much of it was hers and how much of it was mine, took my share, and left. I fumbled through the dim rooms of the party and out the door, deciding to smoke rock forever.

It's still forever and we are wandering the streets at the mercy of Oppie's arbitrary fancies. He is oblivious to traffic or fatigue and often breaks spontaneously into a run. I give chase and am barely successful in my effort to stay with him. When I do catch up, he puts his arm on my shoulder, breathing heavily. He seems surprised to see me and tells me he's glad I'm here.

The pavement is wet and reptilian, the air thick with evaporation. People are out tonight, like every night, hustling, smoking, chatting, shaking hands, screaming. Everybody is buying, selling, or collecting things of certain or possible value. Oppie is smiling and saying hello to random people, handing out cigarettes and American change to any and all who ask.

Faces swing into our orbit and out again like comets, trajectories forever altered by Oppie's generous crack policies and philosophical musings. He is electric and alive. His interest is insatiable. Lecturing as he walks, he relates mind-bending scientific concepts with ease and grace. We are a team. Although nobody recognizes him, I feel proud to be partying with such a distinguished man of science. Prostitutes approach him and he respectfully tells them he has no interest in "erotic labour" but gives them rocks and kind words. He is a gentleman.

Sitting on a bench in Pigeon Park, we form an accidental alliance with a Native kid whose face, crusted with glue, is making sad and sluggish approximations at consciousness. Oppie is offering him the pipe, but I don't think he even sees it. Oppie blows out a hoot and continues with a conversation I wasn't sure we were having.

"Take this young man, for example, Hank. Here is a fellow theoretician, a physicist; he studies zero as we infinity. He's asking the same question we are, but he's approaching it from the bottom up, beginning with base assumptions, attempting to divide everything by zero. And as you well know, it is at these extremes, these margins, these points which a curve will avoid like poison gas that things really get interesting!"

"You can call it whatever you want, I guess, Oppie, I think he's just trying to kill himself."

"Oh no, not kill." He is scratching under his shirt collar. "Destroy, Hank—he seeks to destroy himself."

When we leave, I turn and see that the kid has managed to stagger after us for a few blocks. But he can't keep up.

Oppie ducks into a corner store to buy more cigarettes. I'm

straining to remember what it was Oppie actually did as a scientist. I know he made the bomb, but I'm not sure why or when. I can only remember his picture.

I decide to ask him when he returns. "Oppie, when you were working at the place in the desert with all the other scientists, all working together like you talked about, did you imagine making a better life for people in the future? I mean, did you wonder about how things would be for them?"

He spins and grabs me by the neck of my T-shirt. His hands are weak and the cherry of his cigarette dances millimetres from my face. "I want you to listen to me very intently, you smug son of a bitch. In our minds, the Krauts could have dropped one on us at any time, understand? We never had any idea what was going to be done with it, is that clear?"

I lie and say it is.

———————

Later, we are on the bus because Oppie wanted to "experience the authentic transport of the proletariat." The bus seems to have cheered him up, so I ask him where he lives and he says he's been sleeping between the stacks at the university library. I ask him how a genius can die of smoking-related throat cancer and whether he knew it was bad for him, and he tells me to stop tormenting him. I want to ask him what it's like to be dead, but I don't want to push it.

"Hank, I feel crack cocaine may affect you in a profoundly more negative fashion than it does me," he says a little snidely. "I believe it has permanently altered your judgment."

Sometimes I do worry about lasting damage, tracks laid down that can never be picked up, that sort of thing. I often try to remember what it was like to not know what the crack high feels like, and I can't. In this way, crack rewrote my history. I remember my mother, who quit smoking cigarettes when she had me and said she dreamed of them almost every night until the day she died. Even when we ate chocolate-chip cookies in bed while watching TV, she would tap the cookie with her index finger after each bite, ashing the crumbs carefully into a little pile on her plate.

"Don't worry about me. Just hope it doesn't run out," I say to Oppie, hoping it won't run out.

A woman with a baby is sitting across from us and I wonder why the baby is up this late. Oppie plays peek-a-boo with it for a few blocks by hiding his face behind his hat. Then Oppie lights a smoke, takes a big drag, and blows it right in the baby's face, chuckling as the woman freaks and we get kicked off the bus.

Back on the sidewalk, I notice Oppie's smile has become strained and his face bleached. He insists on carrying all the vials himself, and he has begun to mutter. His walk has warped into an exaggerated parody of someone trying to walk with confidence. I wonder if he is a ghost and whether ghosts get the same high. I try to imagine the goings-on inside his brain. What an instrument to be flooded with so much cocaine! His mind is like a Ferrari entered in a demolition derby. He mutters something about the "allure of alkaloids" and then something about someone named Prometheus and a vulture and a rock. "You want more rock?" I say, and he nods like a little boy. I need to keep him away from people for a while.

We run out of rock shortly thereafter, and I try to convince him we should slow down. Oppie pulls out a roll of bills like the cavalry and hands the whole thing over to a man whose face I will never remember.

"Hank, I think this new batch of stones may be cut with something vile," he says later, glancing at me suspiciously.

When I shut my eyes there is a dioramic theatre of brilliant neon, and I have resolved to keep them open so as not to lose Oppie if he starts to run. We've ducked into a doorway shielded from the street by a tiled staircase, and in a further effort to slow him down, I suggest maybe he should try to cook up a rock on his own for once.

"Well, that certainly contravenes the terms of our agreement, Hank, now doesn't it? I supply the goddamn rock, you the steady hand and experimental know-how! Isn't that it?"

He is starting to yell again, so I don't press the issue. We smoke more and I hold the pipe. I'm saving the better hoots for myself because he doesn't really need them, and because he is starting to annoy me. He begins kicking the bus shelter in front of us with his leather boat shoe, over and over, trying to break the glass and laughing insanely. When I tell him they are made of shatterproof glass now, he says he knows that, although he doesn't stop.

We find ourselves back in the park that isn't named after him and I'm beginning to think Oppie is losing his mind. Occasional forays into madness are, from what I understand, pretty standard for a genius, but this seems to be of an assortment darker and more potentially irreversible. He is mumbling in a heinous amalgamation of the many languages he seems to know. His teeth are yellowing and his fingers are blackened from gripping the charred pipe.

Aside from the playground there are a few trees and a brick structure on the perimeter of the park, but mostly it's just a field.

Oppie is rocking back and forth, staring into the park's dark centre. I'm thinking about whether this is the highest I've ever been and conclude statistically it must be, but somehow I feel clear and alert. Could there be an upper limit? A cap, like terminal velocity or supersaturated solutions? I figure we need more data. I can see my room from here, and although I want to go home and read my book, and although I know there is probably already enough resin in my pipe to keep me high at least until tomorrow, I resolve to stand by him, to ride it out; that is, if it can be ridden. He needs me.

He hasn't said anything for about an hour when my scientific thoughts are dispersed by his voice, raw from smoking and disuse. "By the mere existence of this city, would it be safe for me to assume the Cold War went all right, Hank?"

"Yeah, it went okay, Oppie."

"Oh good," he says, clearing his throat. "That's good."

Discussion

At the country-and-western karaoke bar, it's me, Oppie, and the woman who told her boyfriend not to break my collarbone, our beer glasses hydroplaning around a small, slick table. She is wearing Oppie's porkpie hat in the flirtatious way some women grab and wear men's hats, perched on top of her hair like she is balancing it there, her neck stiffened, hoping the novelty of it will provoke a new appreciation of what's beneath.

She is smoking too many of Oppie's cigarettes, and I want to tell him she broke my collarbone and watch him rise to my defence, reducing her to tears with a bombardment of scathing quips. I decide against it. She and the beer seem to be providing Oppie with some kind of ballast, amnesty from the psychotic twister in his mind.

Earlier, after we'd left the park, Oppie scampered into a dense patch of traffic and disappeared. When I found him he was a few blocks over with this woman on his arm. This place was her idea. Oppie introduced me as Professor Hank. I scoffed when he said it, annoyed by how proud he could still make me feel.

The karaoke microphones have been monopolized by an old drunken couple who have feuded, proclaimed, wept, reconciled, and so far barely made it through a single song without one of them regressing to a bout of screaming "I fucken love you!" into the other's face. Somebody said the guy who runs the karaoke got bottled a few hours ago and went home.

I'm in the bathroom now, hoping Oppie will be there at the table when I get back. Everything, even the ceiling, is wet. The urinal is ancient, a stainless-steel trough. I'm pissing and it sounds like a sink. This is the kind of place where the line between beer and piss is blurry and rusted out, where one seemingly unifying golden liquid soaks everything, spewing and slopping from spouts and cups.

I look at my steaming face in the dirty mirror and I come to the grim conclusion that I have to smoke more rock or go home. I consider stealing the stash and making off, but this seems too fiendish, and plus I think he could find me anywhere.

I return to the table, where his arm is around her and she is talking. "They named that piece-of-shit park after you, huh? If you ask me, sweetie, there shouldn't be a public square inch in this neighbourhood."

Oppie is smiling and vacant. He carefully finishes his beer and rises weakly from his chair. She turns to me and asks if she has seen me before and I tell her to shut up. Oppie mounts the stage and the old couple unexpectedly surrender the microphones to him. He brings them both to his mouth at the same time and begins.

"Good evening, ladies and gentlemen, my name is J. Robert Oppenheimer and I'd like to thank you for this opportunity to speak before you this evening. I want to commence by buying everyone in the house a beverage as a sign of my esteem and gratitude."

No one cheers because no one is listening. A synthesized slide guitar strikes up the next song.

"No takers? Good, because I'm all out of money, which means there are only a few ivory nuggets left between me and something dark and unknowable."

Oppie clears his throat. Someone yells something in the crowd, but it's not directed at him.

"Crack cocaine, ladies and gentlemen. Some believe only the truly unhappy enjoy it, or rather need it. However, this hypothesis seems flawed. I have found its benefits extremely promising, but sadly not without cost. Like most things, it is a good servant but a bad master. Thus I believe control to be paramount, wisdom and knowledge trumping blind fear and temperance. To speak of regret is to ignore realities and inevitabilities. Humanity, my friends, must experiment—that is its nature. Want versus need, nature versus nurture: these questions seem redundant, boorish. Knowledge cannot be outlawed. It must be doggedly pursued! Alas, eggs are broken, unfortunate experiences are experienced, but, however, in my opinion, humanity is stronger for it."

No one is listening. Oppie sways feebly in the awful stage light. His hair is grey and sparse, his cheeks hollow and triangular. He looks so different now from my science-book photo. He is pacing the stage, compulsively touching and scratching his face as he speaks. He looks like one of this neighbourhood's regular discarded men, who in a dirty tweed suit is taking an unscheduled narcotic vacation from the drudgery of his blister-packed medication.

"And so I stand before you, yet I am dead of throat cancer, as my colleague pointed out so perceptively earlier this evening. How is this possible? Who can say. What is possible is that if I go to sleep I will never wake up."

I wish he had a lectern, something to put his hands on.

"Therefore, I must conclude, further study is merited. And I must forge on—like Currie, with radioactivity humming in her oblivious cells—with courage, conviction, and a deep, unshatterable hope and faith in the value of this experiment. And for this greatly undeserved opportunity, I humbly thank you."

The woman, still wearing his hat, stands, clapping proudly. When he gets back to the table I ask him if he wants to leave, to go back to my room and just talk science and smoke cigarettes. He says I haven't heard a word he's said all night.

Conclusion

We are in the parking lot next to the bar.

On the street, the car is waiting for Oppie. It billows grey smoke as it idles. A sheet of paper taped to the back window indicates it is insured only for today. I know her boyfriend is behind the wheel, but I don't look in because it doesn't matter. Oppie is leaving.

"We are going to go and appropriate a few computers from the university library and sell them in an effort to procure some powder cocaine that Brenda here is going to cook and formulate into some real pure samples, genuine freebase, no more vials and uncontrolled specimens," Oppie says as I load our last rock. I want to tell him to stay, but I am too tired and confused and plus I don't really want him to.

He does not ask me to come with him and I do not want to go. I'm worried I will regret it. I've never smoked real freebase. Someone else will be helping him now and they will probably do a better job than me.

I hold the pipe to Oppie's lips a final time. He exhales and his voice is a scoured whisper. "Well, that's the last of it, Hank. You truly are one of the finest minds of your generation. How I'm going to miss your steady hands and gentle flame."

He is really tweaking now, his eyes drifting inquisitively to pebbles on the pavement, his shoulders and arms whipping restlessly like he is trying to get rid of something disgusting taped to his back. As if he is trying to shed his body entirely.

The car is honking in the street and I'm going to cry.

"These people are not scientists, Oppie."

"No, but they can help me—they know things, my boy."

"Were you serious about worrying you'd never wake up?"

"I guess so, Hank. I'm not sure. Crack may not be the panacea, but I enjoy it like nothing I've ever experienced. I refuse to stop. Not now, not when I feel I'm so close to a breakthrough."

"I'm sorry I didn't take better care of you."

"Nonsense, I planned for all this to happen."

He touches my shoulder and it twinges painfully. He says, "To be frank, I think the world in which I shall live, from now on, will be a pretty restless and tormented place; I do not think that there will be much of a compromise possible for me, between being of it and being not of it."

I watch him get into the car and he is gone again.

The Queen of Cans and Jars

Her younger sister, Wanda, called that morning to ask if she wanted to move into her coach house.

"What's a coach house?" said Bernice.

"It's like a smaller version of our house, but on our property," Wanda said.

Many years ago, when Bernice was still in the shoe department at Woodward's, Wanda was hired as a medical secretary by a brutish orthopaedic surgeon, owner of two of the hairiest arms Bernice had ever seen. They wed after six months of secretive courtship—naturally, there was already a wife—after which he treated Wanda to a smorgasbord of plastic surgery and whisked her off to Kelowna. Now they spent half of the year in Dubai while he, in the twilight of his career, girdered together the bones of the inconceivably rich and she chased golf balls about an island of irrigated turf in the centre of the desert. Wanda called weekly when back in Kelowna, speaking mostly of wine tours and the chore of locating good-quality home furnishings for their expansive lakeside palace, which Bernice had seen only in photos.

Sitting at her kitchen table, Bernice imagined a series of houses cracking open like Russian dolls, smaller and smaller until the last revealed itself as a tiny pink stucco matchbox.

"What would I do there?" she said.

"Relax?"

"What about the store?"

"Oh, haven't you been doing that long enough?"

"And where would I put my things . . . in this . . . coach house?"

"Well, of course you'd have to downsize," Wanda said.

This new word chafed Bernice like ill-fitting slacks. *Downsize* seemed so smug and perniciously simple, as if the physical evidence of one's life, and the space it occupied, could be erased just like that.

"I couldn't. Why would I leave? I'm comfortable here, and there's so much to do," Bernice glanced about her apartment, eyes landing on just a few of her beloved things. Wanda called her stubborn and Bernice said she'd think about it, immediately steering the conversation to the custom walnut deck for which Wanda was suing a contractor for poor workmanship, a saga her sister would never resist retelling.

———————

On May 14, 1978, while sorting laundry in the basement of their building, Bernice had found a dry-cleaning ticket in the pocket of her husband's trousers. She stopped into the cleaners on her way to work the next day and exchanged the ticket for a green evening dress with a mink collar, almost twice her size. She laid the dress over the kitchen table that evening and waited in the living room doing a crossword. Gus came home from work and entered the kitchen. She heard his keys on the counter. She heard the icebox open and close. Then, without a word, he left their small apartment. She waited up, but he did not return, that night or any other.

Some weeks later she quit Woodward's after twenty years there and set up a thrift shop just three blocks away in the basement of New Westminster United. She began by handing out the sweaters and slacks Gus had left swinging in their closet to some old down-on-their-luck drunks and went from there. Shortly after she left Woodward's, the department store slid into decline, and she liked to imagine it was due to her absence, though it was probably the malls and ever-bigger stores she'd heard were going up all over. Woodward's finally declared bankruptcy in 1993, and with it died the last reason for decent people to come down to this neighbourhood, once the teeming commercial hub of the city, now staggering deeper and deeper into the woods of poverty, neglect and despair. All the old businesses on Bernice's block had long vanished, swapped for cheque-cashing places, pawn shops and convenience stores. Over the years, through her thrift-store window, she'd watched the crippled loggers, hobos and drunks—battered leftovers of the city's industrial heritage—joined by the heroin junkies, who were joined by the crack addicts and then by those suffering every other variant of destitution. It became a neighbourhood at which people in their downtown-bound cars gawked like they were on safari. She'd seen social services come and go like occupying armies, stuffing her mailbox with their optimistic, densely acronymed brochures. Most of them seemed out to get the poor wretched people more money, which to Bernice was much like heaving a thirsty man overboard, but she tried not to judge the social workers either. They were all trying their best.

The decline had only deepened the need for her services, and Bernice had to find volunteers like Tuan just to keep clothes on the racks. Busy as it was, the store only narrowly broke even. "As long as you need it," Bernice would say to her pitiful customers, punching *No Sale,* a button more worn than any other on the register.

That afternoon she and Tuan were organizing the shoe racks, combing them for singles—what she called shoes without a mate.

"I'm leaving the store. For good," she said, trying the words out, listening to how they sounded amidst the shelves of used cookbooks and the mannequins in the display window.

"Thank you," he said, relacing a pair of brittle, yellowed boat shoes. Tuan was volunteering at the store while the pastor and his wife helped him with his immigration application. Bernice never tried to correct his English because she didn't want to offend him. The pastor once said Tuan had a master's degree in philosophy, so she figured he'd pick it up soon enough. Anyway, she liked small talk kept to a minimum.

"This ones is stink," Tuan said, pinching his nose, dangling a pair of steel-toed boots like roadkill before venturing out back to toss them in the dumpster.

Alone, she surveyed the store. There was, as always, much to do: organizing, pricing, sorting, displaying. This was no junk shop. When second-hand things were presented well, with care— techniques for which she'd learned at Woodward's—clothes folded or carefully hung, books categorized and alphabetized, knick-knacks arranged attractively, they became items folks could picture in their homes, welcome into their lives.

"Donation!" she heard Tuan yelp from out back.

Lately, more donations were arriving than she knew what to do with, the two storerooms nearly to the roof with them. The rear doors of the church opened to a squalid alley where they pulled up in all sorts of vehicles to pop their trunks, lift their hatchbacks, say *this can go, and this, and this,* handing Tuan and Bernice their garbage bags and boxes. The donors were always pleasant but seemed uneasy, uttering few words. Perhaps they were ashamed of their surplus, Bernice had often thought, the sheer weight of it.

Today it was a tall, stately woman, definitely a women's ten in shoes, with sunglasses nested in her hair and cheekbones that rose neatly on her porcelain face. From her silver vehicle climbed down an unsteady, moon-faced girl in a princess dress. Flakes of sun leapt from her plastic tiara.

"Give the bag to the nice lady like we talked about," the woman said to the girl, who took careful steps toward Bernice as though approaching a windy cliff. Bernice had been witness to these lessons in charity before, parents sandbagging Christian values nice and early in hopes they wouldn't be washed out in the tsunami of adolescence. In the girl's eyes, Bernice knew, she probably seemed something closer to witch than saint.

"These are my clothes," the princess said.

"They don't fit you anymore, Cricket," her mother said.

"What if I shrink?" the girl bleated, pressing the bag to her bulbous, sequined belly.

"Now that's enough of this," her mother said, checking a thin gold watch riding the underside of her wrist. "Let's get moving." She reached into the back seat and set the last of their unwanted stuff at Tuan's feet. "Now," she ordered, and Bernice caught a whiff of the woman's minty gum.

"Will you promise to take care of my clothes?" the princess asked Bernice.

"Oh, certainly," Bernice said, keeping to herself the fact that other kids would likely soon be wearing her clothes, possibly muck-seeking children who might not take care of them at all. The girl knotted her glassy lips and handed over the bag.

As she watched them drive off, Bernice envied the rush of benevolence and general lightness these donors must feel returning to their homes, suddenly unburdened, free from what they no longer wanted or needed. She and Tuan dragged the donations into the storage room, where they could be gone through, appraised. Few of Bernice's customers had kids, so the princess's clothes would go to a shelter for battered women and their children a few blocks over.

Opening the boxes and bags was always thrilling, like the unsealing of mummies' tombs or the vaults of gangsters. As a girl, she'd dreamed of becoming an archaeologist until she discovered how many years of schooling were required and turned her ambitions toward more modest, attainable goals.

The most startling treasures she unearthed were the brand new or the valuable: clothing still tagged or wrapped in tissue paper; unopened specialty appliances like rice cookers or fruit dehydrators; futuristic basketball shoes, their jumping springs never tested; designer labels she vaguely recognized from billboards. Once there were sixteen mason jars full of change, mostly silver, that she'd dumped into the church collection bucket upstairs; and always plenty of new dishes and kitchenware still stickered with prices of magnitudes that never failed to astonish her. Could they all be unwanted gifts? If not, how could someone pay so much for things they didn't need? And if they had once needed them, what had happened in between?

Equally baffling were the odd and used-up things the donors somehow imagined the poor could actually use: cracked helmets, expired urine-smelling vitamins, tiny musical instruments, perfumed negligees, mute synthesizers, their keys greyed with skin cells, couches shot through with black mould, long-expired canned goods, sacks of wormy flour, bloodstained sheets, broken crutches, ten-year-old phonebooks. She'd once got a silk parachutist's jumpsuit decorated with fluorescent polygons, and Bernice and Tuan roared at the thought of one of her customers sporting it to collect bottles then falling asleep in a park like an off-duty superhero. But it disturbed her, the way people failed to distinguish what was useful from what wasn't. The ability to do so seemed to her an inseparable part of getting by in this world.

She tore into the princess's mother's boxes, and under some musty, purple fitted sheets, inside a faux-rosewood case, she found a velvet pouch of collector's souvenir spoons. Shuffling them, she picked out the only one she didn't already have, its handle grazed upon by a gilded buffalo. She fogged it with a breath, polished it on her slacks, then held it up.

"Manitoba," she read, feeling how the word made her mouth go as hollow as a birdhouse, then set the spoon aside. Later, she dropped it into the pocket of her camel pea coat before turning off the lights, locking up and walking for the bus.

Her apartment was half dwelling, half museum. She'd assembled her collection over the years, piece by piece, each object assigned its own special place within the whole. Something rested on every available surface—wide-eyed dolls, ceramic candy dishes, commemorative platters, a wooden Indian, plants both real and fake, three Bakelite radios, a stuffed squirrel, bottles and containers from products long discontinued. There were exactly ten decorative lamps in her bedroom alone, and every square inch of the apartment's floor not obscured by furniture was layered with a thick icing of ornamental rugs. On her walls, paintings and hangings shouldered for space—velvet landscapes, nets of macramé, portraits of winsome children. This collection was not random; there were some themes: near the living room window lived a sanctuary of owl-related items—owl ashtrays, tiny china owl figurines, a hooting clock—and in the bathroom a nautical motif—a tugboat soap dish, anchor-embroidered towels, a miniature ship's wheel for the toilet flusher.

It wasn't that these things were valuable. Most were just plain strange—tacky memorabilia and dead concepts of beauty to which Bernice had taken an unexplainable liking. Perhaps it was their very oddity she found so reassuring. Here in her apartment, she gave room to the rescued, the unlikely. They were evidence that not everything was used up and wasted, pitched away and ruined, a reminder that people made things and those things could be, if properly cared for, kept, possibly forever. She was, however, running out of space.

She clicked on some lamps in the living room and laid her coat over the arm of a chair. Then she set about hanging the

Manitoba spoon above her kitchen table in the decorative display rack. Donated years ago, perhaps her favourite artifact of all, the display rack was solid wood, probably maple, shaped like a shield, housing nearly one hundred spoons in total, all dangling from their hilts in fine array. She had spoons from countries the world over, others commemorating great events like the Queen's visits to Canada or Expo '86. At first she'd felt selfish bringing the spoons home from the thrift store, or any of the other donations she fancied, as if she were stealing from or somehow depriving the poor. But little good some sterling spoons or knick-knacks would do them; most of those poor folks didn't have homes, and certainly not spoon racks. It was the sad truth that the nice things would simply be wasted on them, and besides, there would always be more donations.

She sat at the table with a mug of tea and admired how the new spoon greatly altered the overall appearance of the rack, how the whole room sung with newness. She'd never been to Manitoba, but Gus had ended up in Winnipeg for a few years when he first immigrated from Lisbon, before the extreme weather and dearth of good work drove him west. She'd noticed him at Woodward's in the food floor's noisy cafeteria: a short, rigid man with a fanning black moustache that put Bernice in mind of a cartoon walrus or a Russian spy. The makeup girls said he drove one of the taxis that queued for blocks out front of the store. Each day, over the sandwich her mother insisted on tucking into her coat pocket, Bernice watched him devour a whole fish—one he brought each morning and somehow convinced the guys at the lunch counter to cook for him specially—with a green cloth napkin sprouting from his collar. In him she'd glimpsed the same stormy assemblage of charm, absurdity and selfishness she'd loved in her father. Their few instances of eye contact eventually drew Gus up the escalator, into the women's shoe department.

He came every day for a month.

"One time, you don't even have to say nothing," he said, fists over his chest like he was staunching a fatal wound.

"You are much too short," she said with the playful abrasion she'd picked up from Carol, her supervisor, not intended to discourage.

"Okay, okay, I'm going . . . ," he said.

Left to herself, Bernice despaired she'd pushed too far, and continued to arrange a display of powder-blue baby shoes that were already quite orderly.

Ten minutes later he was back. "I'm ready now for you, yes?" he said, clip-clopping in a pair of size-thirteen Italian pumps that nearly brought him to her eye level.

He took her to a Portuguese place on Commercial Drive, where he swatted everyone on the back and belted every tongue-rolling syllable of every tune the discordant band managed. He stained his teeth lilac with a vast quantity of red wine then took her in his taxi on a tour of the city, relating stories mostly about different buildings, pointing with crooked fingers as he drove.

"You know more about this city than I do, and I grew up here," she said, watching a man furiously wave his briefcase at them as they pulled away from a stoplight.

"I must," he said, patting the dash like a stallion's flank. "It's this job to."

She loved the way he attributed personalities to neighbour-hoods: this one was cruel, that one depressed, this one tipped better, that one was vain. Even her own—across the inlet, where her father's house stood, the same house she'd slept in each night of her life so far—he called "ungrateful," and at this she smirked. The very next thing he said was he wanted sons or daughters, it didn't matter which, and though she loathed her large gums, she showed them. Sitting at her delaminating kitchen table, Bernice hated to think what word he'd use to describe her neighbourhood if they were to drive through it in his taxi today.

"Goddamnit!" barked a voice outside and Bernice jumped, banging her knee on the table, rattling her spoons. She went to the window to see a soiled orange velour chesterfield balanced atop a shopping cart pushed by a wiry, emaciated man, grinding down the alley. The scene reminded her of ants she'd once seen on a nature program. She turned to find the awfully vigorous teenaged faces of her nieces and grandnieces magnetized to her fridge. To them, Bernice was famous for the Christmas presents she mailed each year, though the girls didn't know their gifts were always second-hand. Could she really move to this coach house? Leave her shop and her apartment behind like the donors did the boxes of their unwanted things? She had no friends to speak of. Most of the shopgirls she knew from Woodward's were either long dead or had cashed in on skyrocketing house prices and moved to more affordable cities like Kelowna to spend their money on their grandchildren and strict regimens of all-inclusive cruises.

Why *have* you stayed so long? she thought while commencing to dust her collection, more for something to do than anything. She began to suspect that a great part of her life had been expended waiting for something to happen, though she couldn't say what that something was. She'd given up fantasies of Gus's return years ago, thinking of him only when hanging clothes he would have worn, or happening upon his initials embroidered in the cuffs of a donated Oxford shirt. Neither did she have illusions of how much actual good her thrift shop did for the neighbourhood. Sure, it had achieved some modest benefits. A few people, with her help, had got on their feet and left, leaving being the only way to survive a slum, because there were no jobs, and to be offered drugs every ten paces or beaten near dead for your groceries was no existence for anyone. Duster in hand, she arrived at the spoon rack and saw only two empty slots remained.

Later, as she got ready for bed, she half-heartedly imagined melting all her spoons down and buying a plane ticket to Portugal, or maybe just Winnipeg, not to find Gus, but a man like him, a better one. Tucking herself in, she wondered if they had slums in Portugal and decided to keep her eye out for donated books on the subject, and also on the price of silver.

———————

Karla, a dedicated thrift-store volunteer, had died a week ago and today was the funeral. It was held outside the city, so Bernice took the bus. After three transfers she stepped from the vehicle's hissing doors and asked a boy in a pristine white tracksuit lazing on a bicycle with gold-plated rims where the church was. He flicked his chin grimly at what looked to Bernice like a mall at the centre of a monstrous parking lot, so vast it reminded her of the sweeping landscape paintings often donated to the store, the ones that never sold because, she figured, they amplified people's loneliness.

"That's a church?" she said.

"No doubt," he said. She now saw how the gold was just paint and had bled from the rims to the tire. He also had a skid of grease on his calf where it had met the chain.

Bernice thanked him and set out across the lot.

She'd always wondered if Karla was a prostitute. There was a hardness to her, a kind of cheerful vacancy, but she'd never taken for herself any of the more tartish clothes that Bernice made sure to throw away rather than give to the prostitutes who came in flocks and bought anything scanty and headlight-catching. Karla began as an occasional weekend volunteer until Bernice had offered her a regular position after she'd been impressed with her hard work. In fact, Bernice had to order her to take smoke breaks or she'd work right through them, get antsy and start dropping breakables. But what Karla did set aside for herself were children's toys, anything that was handmade or unique. The room she lived in must have been brimming with toys. Karla had said once that she'd had a son taken from her by family services. He lived in foster care in a town called Merritt, and when Bernice asked if she'd ever thought of visiting, Karla shook her head and went for a smoke in the alley. She'd died of ovarian cancer and Bernice couldn't help but picture the disease, in a kind of science filmstrip, X-ray view, as the accumulate of all those nasty men taking root in her, setting up shop, and Bernice shuddered as she traversed the empty spaces of the lot.

There were a handful of new cars huddled around the church. Conifers wrapped in burlap for winter stood around its brown, rectangular lawn.

"Karla made some bad decisions," her father began in his eulogy. "We all have choices in our lives, free will and the like, but I can feel she's happier now, at peace."

To say someone was more content in death made Bernice's scalp prickle. She drove her knees together until they shook. She doubted Karla was sprawled on a chaise-lounge-shaped cloud having a chuckle at how things had shaken out for her, prostitute or no.

In their tearful speeches mostly about themselves, the family mentioned little of her life but their own respective roles in her courageous battle with addiction, as if she'd sprung from her mother's womb already decided on the perfect way to wreck her life.

"Karla was in my employ," she said after the ceremony to the mother, whose nose hooked in the same not unattractive way Karla's had.

"She had a job?"

"A volunteer job."

"Umhmm."

Bernice raked her mind for something more to tell her, this parent who should already know everything, but in truth they'd discussed their lives as much as she and Tuan had.

Bernice watched her hug the other mourners—lightly, so as not to disturb each other's hairdo, her black shawl gently shimmering—and pictured this mother feeding baby Karla, rocking her. She marvelled at the money spent on things like piano lessons and figure skates, the time teachers spent after class unpaid to detangle in her mind the multiplication of fractions. And with all that went into the girl, that this sad display would stand as the summation of her time here crushed Bernice's heart like a baby bird.

Bernice went to the pencil-lead-coloured coffin and pulled from her purse a wooden caterpillar that wobbled when pulled by its string. She set the toy beside her in the white satin interior. Karla had a ponytail—a style she'd never worn—and her face was puffy and spatulaed with makeup.

On her way out, Bernice turned and saw her father pick the caterpillar from her coffin and place it on a table. Then he and one of the funeral staff electric-screwdrivered the box shut, the tiny motor mewling painfully.

———————

She couldn't find the bus stop, and she wondered if it might have been relocated during the funeral. The sun crinkled her eyes as she walked to another parking lot—this time, she gathered from the nearly full lot, that of a real mall. She went inside to seek directions.

She entered through a store where everything was supposed to cost a dollar. Walking the cluttered aisles with not a salesperson in evidence, she recalled the scoldings Carol would dole out if a customer went thirty seconds in the shoe department without a warm greeting. The dollar store was organized with no apparent logic and the items were all tawdry bits of plastic, a fact the signage and overall design of the store seemed to celebrate. Woodward's had had dollar-forty-nine days each Tuesday. They drew lineups down the block, but people still got good value for their money, and the products were made to last. She stopped in an aisle of towering stacks of plastic containers.

She wondered if Gus shopped in stores like these now. He and the owner of the green dress, or the owner of some other dress. She decided he probably did. The smell of plastic was making her light-headed. Finally, she was approached by an employee, who Bernice asked to escort her into the mall itself, where she sat on a bench. After a short rest, she located a pay phone in a dingy hall-way that led to the janitorial area. She had to ask a custodian where she was before phoning for a taxi that would cost more than the thrift store made in a week.

The next morning, a pumpkin-faced man wandered in the door, pants soaked with urine—his own, Bernice hoped.

"Oh, Charlie," she said, pulling her lips taut, guiding him to the washroom beside the overflowing storeroom. "Nothing I haven't seen before," she said, as she peeled away his shirt, its tails soaked and sour, and saw the man's pink blotchy flesh hung in pouches as if melting from him. Yanking off his pants, she dis-covered on his shins numerous weeping sores that someone had bandaged long ago, possibly months. She tutted at the red streaks that leapt toward his groin.

"You see these?" she said, tracing one with her fingernail.

Charlie looked down at his lower half incredulously as though for the first time in a year.

"You want to lose your legs, you old goat?"

Charlie shrugged and placed his hand on her back. A pleas-ant sensation unrolled from where his hand pressed, akin to tick-ling, but warmer. She let it mix into her blood a moment, recalling how comfortably Gus fit beneath her chin when they hugged—a disparity she'd first found embarrassing but grew to adore—how they'd waited to be together until their honeymoon in Tofino, where he rented from a fishmonger he knew a smelly cedar cabin smack dab in the middle of all that water and air, and how they sat on the gravelly beach drinking wine. "Here," he said, sweeping his arm, exhaling as if at the end of a journey, "this sea faces the right way."

Bernice stood abruptly and Charlie's hand swung limp to his lap. She snipped some gauze, re-dressed his shins and found him a new shirt and pair of pants, better brands and materials than she should have.

"Now you go straight to the hospital and get those legs looked at," she said and Charlie grinned lavishly, opening his arms wide, teetering like a chopped-at tree. "Off you go," she said and ushered him out.

His rancid pants and shirt she flung into the dumpster. She took the squat brown bottle of rice wine he'd forgotten and poured it down the drain, calling it payment for the new clothes. Her opinion, one she would never have spoken aloud, was that these people behaved mostly like little children—careless, impulsive, selfish. Perhaps no one had ever taught them to care for themselves, she had no idea. It was just that possessions didn't seem to matter to people anymore, not how they once did. She gave them nice warm coats, good-quality jeans and blouses and skirts, she gave them toasters and dishes, sometimes even furniture—all of which they lost, or ruined, or sold, or even just threw away. And they treated themselves no better than the things she gave them.

She'd always liked to think if she found something perfect enough for them they'd have to keep it, care for it and in doing so acquire a taste for caring for themselves. But when dealing with people like Charlie she feared there was something missing, something essential they lacked, something that her thrift store could never provide.

On the rumbling bus home from the store that evening, Bernice tried to imagine the coach house, glittery lakeside sun dancing on the floor of her little room. She tried to select just one item in her collection she could part with, just one that wasn't necessary, but this left her feeling cruel. She remembered as a girl the horror of finding even one of her stuffed animals on the floor when she woke and the subsequent guilt at imagining it there the whole night, shivering, crying out, imploring in its silent stuffed-animal language how she, their only caretaker, could be so heartless. No, there was no part of her collection she could be rid of, no part that was less worthy. She decided to put the whole coach house question to rest.

———

She sat on the varnished pew in the teal Orlon skirt she used to wear to sell shoes. "When did you get so dowdy?" she'd said to herself in the mirror that morning before digging deeper into the recesses of her bedroom closet than she had in years.

Never much of a believer, she came to church partly for the singing and mostly for when the pastor referred them to a passage in the Bible. She loved to lick her fingertips, peel the thin pages, discover the numbered verse there waiting for her, right where it should be, charging her with a joy comparable to when she opened the store each morning.

"Blessed is he that considereth the poor: the Lord will deliver him in time of trouble," the pastor began, his voice chalky with feeling. "Fat chance of that," Bernice muttered to herself, and dropped the burgundy King James back into the slot in the pew ahead. It'd been two weeks since her sister's phone call, and Bernice found herself unexpectedly bothered by the lapse. A few nights ago she dreamt that Charlton Heston as Moses from *The Ten Commandments* had pulled up out front of her shop in one of those new truck-style limousines she'd seen lately on the street, the ones the size of a school bus.

"This place is cursed," he'd said, speaking as if he hated his teeth.

In the way one does in dreams, she knew instantly he'd come to drive all the poor, wretched people to another place: a safe, fertile and hospitable land where they could prosper. She saw his tan robe protruding from the vehicle where he'd slammed it in the door.

"It's not so bad," she said, just as hundreds of impoverished souls suddenly emerged from the alleys, teeming from the crack hotels and doorways, running or limping as fast as their rotting bodies could carry them. She watched them open the limo's count-less doors and pile into the vehicle like a clown car in the circus.

Charlton flexed his beautiful face beneath his beard as he electrically raised the window.

"Don't," Bernice said as the limo pulled away, people perched dangerously on the bumper and dog piled on the roof. She kicked off her pumps and chased them for a few blocks, plead-ing for Charlton to stop. It was no good, she would have told him if he'd slowed; these were no Israelites—they packed their mas-ters with them, their horrid childhoods, their illnesses and defor-mities, their plagues, their bedbugs and lice, their rats, roaches and unforgivable sins. And the drugs and drink wouldn't be far behind. Someone would bring those too. Or they'd make new drugs. She watched the car sail through a red light and woke to her cat kneading painfully on her chest.

"Who can make straight what he has made crooked?" the pastor said. Everyone stood to sing a hymn, and Bernice, finding dampness had painted her blouse to her back, sidestepped her way down the pew, past a group of women who each year knit hundreds of mittens for the poor. The same mittens that sat untouched in a box in her shop until finally she had Tuan toss them in the dumpster each April. Who the hell needs mittens anymore? Bernice thought, passing the women, blasted by their high, impassioned voices.

***

The sky cleared, a white midday light landed everywhere and for the first time in she couldn't say how long, Bernice decided to take a walk. She left a "Will Return" sign in the thrift-shop window and passed a few empty storefronts, their signs repainted hundreds of times, now just a soup of faint letters and graphics, the ghosts of failed enterprises emerging from beneath. She passed a window of exhausted pizza slices under a heat lamp; beyond them just a few packages of discount cigarettes were displayed behind a counter. The sign above the store read "Saveway" in red and white, a pathetic imitation of the grocery giant. Surely this would fool no one, she thought, then watched a soiled, twitching teenager disappear inside. She passed a place called Prime Time Chicken with a sandwich board out front that said,

"Leg: 53 cents," and "Wing: 68 cents," the numbers crossed out and written over at least twenty times. Bernice shuddered to think what might cause this price fluctuation.

She found herself approaching the corner of Hastings and Abbott streets, where the Woodward's building stood. She had read in the paper it was to be torn down, finally, to build some new type of apartments for young people. Just as well, she thought; it was of no use to anyone anymore, a whole city block standing empty, an eight-storey palace for pigeons and rats. And maybe that was all the neighbourhood ever really needed, she thought, more young people.

Now the sidewalk was thick with those situated somewhere on the spectrum of ruin. A snarling, agitated woman passed inches from her, pushing an empty wheelchair that Bernice hoped someone wasn't missing. A man with a navel-length beard rode by hunched on a tiny pink child's bicycle. He had a grey propane tank slung over one shoulder, and for a moment Bernice feared he would lose his grip and incinerate them both.

Most of the people on the street knew her and they rarely bothered her for change. Some even said hello. But Bernice was uncomfortable talking to them outside her store, with its known rules of conduct. She had always felt uneasy when speaking not of something tangible, like the fit of a pair of shoes, or the fabric of a garment.

She saw the windows that once housed the famous Woodward's displays, little theatres of possible lives to imagine yourself into, now all stitched up with plywood that was plastered with advertisements as incomprehensible to her as the graffiti painted over them. She strained to see the building as it once was. Most of the streetcars and trolley buses had led right to this corner, where the streets had been alive with restaurants, nightclubs and cinemas. Woodward's itself offered every kind of thing you could imagine and many you couldn't. "Hats direct from Paris, by air," her mother once told her, adding the second part as if it were a punchline. As a child, from her bedroom window, Bernice had studied the great red W glowing across the inlet, perched atop a small replica of the Eiffel Tower built on the roof of the store, staking claim to the city's then modest skyline. She once took a photo of the sign with her father's camera and painted "ANDA" on it, offering it to her sister for her birthday. Wanda, with a mouthful of blue coconut cake, regarded the gift like a dead pet.

It was a friend of her mother's who had arranged the job for Bernice after she graduated high school. That first morning, Bernice had arrived an hour early and walked around and around the block until the store opened. "There are two ways to sell shoes," Carol, her new supervisor, said in the stockroom, a svelte cigarette bucking in her mouth. "Tell 'em the shoes look good, or tell 'em they'll never wear out. Me, myself, I prefer the flattery—it's easier to lie about." Bernice adored her immediately. She was old, which to Bernice meant over thirty, with a residue of tragedy and a fondness for big dark sunglasses and miniskirts that stretched over a high flat butt that seemed to have drifted up on her lower back.

People came from all corners of the world, strolling the store like an amusement park or a museum. There was often music and singing on the first floor, and Bernice couldn't imagine a food that the food floor didn't stock. To her, it was a small version of a city, only a better one: inside, cleaner, more orderly. It seemed to be bursting with goods, an intoxicating promise of endless possibility. It never failed to amaze her what wonders they could make, what unheard-of new things could come.

At first she was timid with customers. She'd never spoken much in school and spent most of her leisure time with her family, rarely with friends. Those nights, she replayed in her head the mistakes and inefficiencies of the day and chastised herself for them. She practised the smooth, pauseless speech of salesmanship on her stuffed animals and memorized the shoe styles by lugging catalogues into the bath. Carol was impressed by her commitment and knowledge of the products, and Bernice found Carol's growing confidence in her to be contagious.

Soon Bernice was scheduled weekends, holidays. She navigated the department as if hovering, helping three or four sets of customers at a time, bursting into the stockroom with styles and sizes balanced precariously in her mind. For the first time Bernice had her own money, all of which, because of her discount, she spent in the store. She met Gus each day at the lunch counter and bought expensive gifts for Wanda and her parents.

Her sister, mouth agape, visited her at Woodward's, and they'd catch a show when Bernice got off. When she neared graduation herself, Wanda begged Bernice to recommend her to the ladies' wear department. Though Bernice knew her sister's presence in the store would lead to comparisons being drawn between them and could threaten the fragile independence she'd established there, she agreed. It was then Carol informed her of the store policy that once one member of a family worked at Woodward's, that person's brother, sister, mother or father couldn't also work there. Management's reasoning was that salespeople doubled as advocates for the store, a kind of advertising network, and by limiting the number of employees who knew each other, the customer base was broadened considerably at no cost to them.

When Wanda learned of this she was mutely devastated. Bernice sensed she somehow blamed her for the store's policy, or thought she'd made it up entirely. Wanda found employment in the concession at a bowling alley on Granville and would no longer eat with the family, even on Sundays. She left home shortly thereafter to begin a series of relationships with men whom Bernice found similar only in their fancy clothes and fondness for finishing Wanda's sentences. Bernice had only seen photos of Brian, the surgeon, the most striking of which was of him skiing in a T-shirt, his hirsute arms planting two neon poles like flags on an arctic moon, with Wanda beside him, flushed beneath her pink headband. Though she'd never met him—Wanda had neglected to invite her to their wedding in Whistler, later saying it wasn't her "kind of thing"—she suspected he was like the others. For the first time Bernice wondered if there was some way she should have assisted her sister, some advice she could have given. But what did she know, anyway? She'd latched herself to Gus with the same recklessness, then spent her whole adult life sorting through the wreckage, with no answers to come of it. A sharp desire to call her sister rose in Bernice.

"Something you want, lady?" rasped a voice from her knees.

"Oh . . . sorry."

She was standing over a man who sat cross-legged on the ground, a small, sad collection of things for sale lying before him on a blanket. She backed up and saw power adapters, thick booklets of compact discs, a cracked computer monitor, a flute missing valves.

Recognition lifted his scowl. "You from the thrift shop?"

"Yes," she said, unsure what to add to inflect the word with more friendliness. He looked familiar.

"I suppose you don't need anything then? Got everything you need, do you?" he said. Though the sun was now muted by cloud, he squinted as if in pain. He had heavy brows, like a cartoon Neanderthal.

"Well, I'm Harold, and you let me know if you got any questions about the items." He stood, allowing Bernice to read his T-shirt—"i still miss my ex, but my aim's improving"—and she smiled.

"Harold, can I ask where you get these things you're selling?" she said.

He blew air loosely through his mouth. "Guys bring 'em to me, they find 'em in alleys, dumpsters, bushes, that kind of thing," he said, twirling his hands as if to imply anything could be found anywhere, even perhaps the air. Bernice then noticed the chapped nub where his thumb once was. She wondered what awful moment had taken it, whether it accidental or intentional, and where this part of him was now, a jar? a lake? a box? Behind him, hanging on a nail in the plywood, she saw a leather jacket she'd once had in her store. It was cherry red, mid-thigh-length, a popular style when she and Gus were dating. It had been in her shop for a few weeks last month and she'd put it on once or twice, wondering if Gus would've liked it, until she'd noticed it missing and asked Tuan, who said he hadn't sold it.

"Is that coat for sale?" she said.

He turned. "Yeah, pretty, ain't it? Real good leather, smells like a ball glove." He rose and took a long whiff of the coat and put it on.

"It suits you," she said, admiring how well it embraced his shoulders and how it hit his wrists perfectly, right where he'd wear a watch, if he had one.

"Ten bucks," he said.

"You should keep it for yourself. It looks . . . handsome," she said.

He smiled and his teeth resembled the wall of a castle. "Got plenty of coats. Ten bucks," he said. He removed it and hung it with finality.

"Well, it suits you, Harold, that's what's important. I wouldn't say it if it weren't true," she said, then feigned interest in a few coverless mystery pocketbooks before slipping away when he was distracted by someone else.

———————

A message from Wanda was waiting on her machine. No mention of the coach house, just one of her sunny updates indexing the things she and her husband had been up to: catered lunches with eminent doctors, notable art purchases, the mounting achievements of grandchildren. Her sister seemed most herself when leaving a phone message, and Bernice suspected she timed her calls for when she was out.

"I'm not going anywhere, Wanda," she said when she called back.

"What, Bernice? Not going where?"

"Into the coach house."

Her sister groaned as if she were reaching high up in a cupboard. "Oh, right, sure that's fine, Bernice. It was Brian's idea really, he mentioned you probably hadn't managed to put much away for retirement and could use a hand, and the girls are all gone now, so—but that's fine, you're happy where you are, to be honest I didn't think you'd go for it."

"Thing is, I'm just not sure what I'd do there."

"But there's so much here," her sister said. "How about golf? Low impact. Easy on the soft tissue."

What she knew of golf was limited to the clubs, nylon pull-overs and spiked shoes donated to the thrift store. The clubs and shoes never made it to the shelves because they held too much potential as weapons, and the pullovers were neither waterproof nor warm. Bernice said she wasn't interested in golf.

"It isn't the only game in town. There are plenty of churches out here you know, good ones, modern architecture, nice and big and brand-new. You could get involved. And besides, we'd be abroad most of the time and you'd have the whole place to yourself."

She saw an image of herself alone, riding a bus to a mall to spend her modest Woodward's pension on little bits of plastic from the dollar store. She could at least bring some of her collection, couldn't she?

"How about storage space," she said. "In your home? I'd have to bring at least some of my more essential things, I just can't be rid of them."

"Oh sure, there's plenty of room, we could conceal a mid-sized army in our closets, but you know, Brian and I have discussed this, and we figured you could get new things, Bernice, here. You could decorate . . . or redecorate, rid yourself of clutter, you know? Simplify."

To her, sitting alone in a room of foreign things was anything but simple.

"I can't."

"You know you're as stubborn as Dad ever was," her sister said, attempting to sound like that was something she found endearing.

Their father had been an insurance adjustor and part-time inventor who often began his frequent dinner-table lessons with "We now know . . . ," as if speaking on behalf of humanity's collective knowledge. The girls competed for his attention, and in pop quizzes or races he pitted sister against sister. Bernice, the eldest, usually won, sending her sister into pillow-screaming rages in her room. "Sore loser," her father would whisper, nudging Bernice's ribs as they cuddled up in front of the TV for a delicious hour past her bedtime. As teenagers, she and Wanda had established an unspoken truce, a pact of mutual aloofness, choosing vastly dissimilar hobbies and pursuits to ensure no comparisons were possible. He'd died in 1993, the same year Woodward's shut its doors, after spending two days with his pelvis snapped in half from a fall on the concrete at the foot of the basement stairs of their childhood home. This just a month after refusing to move into the care facility Wanda had arranged. Her mentioning him now pained Bernice. She'd pushed for him to stay at home, flush with that old feeling of father-daughter collusion.

When they hung up, Bernice lifted her head from her hands and took notice of the spoon rack, the way it already seemed drab, siphoned of newness. She had to go up close to single out the Manitoba spoon, and saw it looked just as sad as any other.

The next day was welfare day and all her customers were off tearing themselves up and throwing themselves in the garbage. As early as tomorrow they'd start trickling in, half-naked and deranged, with blackened fingertips and lacerated faces, their eyes swirling tempests of remorse and paranoia, back for more of what she'd already given them.

Bernice took advantage of the lull to accomplish tasks she'd been putting off. She priced an entire box of kitchen items, arranged them neatly and sensibly on shelves she'd already wiped down, then went on to organize the sprawling women's tops section by colour—all of this before lunch. She couldn't sort clothes by size anymore because labels couldn't be trusted. Today's mediums fit like the extra larges of yesterday. Were people getting bigger? If so, how big would they get? It had to be all the healthy food they ate now, these people who'd never known war, hardship or famine. Worse, their giant garments just weren't made with the care they once were. The seams gave way, the shapes pinched, bagged out and went misshapen. And the materials were of such poor quality, thick and cardboardy, quickly pilled or faded after a handful of washes. She liked old clothes best, they were made to last. Woodward's even had their own clothing line, most of it pretty good quality, for the price, and sometimes these too were donated. Today she found a burnt-orange acrylic cardigan she swore she'd once owned. These discoveries usually brought a good dose of nostalgia, but today it left her feeling old, left behind.

"Bernice?" A woman with short electrified hair carrying a cardboard box was looking at her as if peering through fogged glass. "It's Carol." She set the box down, touching her generously exposed, liverspotted chest as if to prove also to herself she was real. "We sold shoes together."

Bernice smoothed her skirt and took the hand of her old friend, thankful her work that morning had left the store looking its very best.

"I can't believe it!" Carol said, cupping her forehead with her hand, her ring a dazzle of tiny diamonds.

Carol asked what she'd been up to all this time, and Bernice offered a condensed history of her thrift store.

"It must feel so good to give something back," Carol said, and Bernice was tickled by a modest pride.

"Kids?" she said, as Bernice knew she would.

Bernice shook her head. "No time. This place keeps me so busy, anyhow. Just keeping it going takes all the energy I've got. Shame it's in such poor shape today, though, not like the old shoe department, that's for sure."

"Well, I think it looks fantastic." Carol said. "You still with, what's his name, Gustavo?"

She couldn't bear the idea of seeing pity register in her old friend's face, so she shook her head again and smiled in what she felt was a cheerful way, tossing her hand in the air as if she didn't need it either. "Oh, we split years ago!"

Carol hung for a moment speechless, then rescued her. "Got rid of him, did you? Atta girl!"

Bernice found herself in a featureless territory somewhere between laughter and tears and turned to pluck from the floor a dress that had slipped its hanger.

"Well, Pete and I are still together, just barely. No I'm kidding. He's in the car. We're in town because my dad passed and I couldn't bear to just throw his things away, you know, so I thought what better than if people could put them to good use."

"Oh dear, I'm sorry."

Carol said it was okay. Then came a honk from outside. "That's him," she said, embarrassed but still smiling. "I'd better get moving."

Bernice didn't feel up to speaking with Pete, given the possibility of more questions, so she sent Tuan out to help bring the rest of the things inside. They returned with boxes obscuring their vision and Bernice held the door for them. "More where this came from," Carol said. "A real packrat he was."

When the work was done, Carol said, "Well, I'd better run, we've got to get to the crematorium before they burn the wrong old guy. We live in Kelowna now," she added, as if as an afterthought. "Look me up if you're ever out that way." She handed Bernice a square of sharp cardboard.

Later, while rummaging through Carol's boxes—mostly large new Y-fronts and neatly folded men's perma-press slacks—Bernice recalled the shoe-fitting fluoroscope they'd used in the shoe department. It was a contraption the size of a deep freeze, into which the customers, usually children because they liked it best, would stick their feet, snug inside the shoe they were trying on. Protruding upwards from the machine were three viewing stations like the periscopes Bernice had seen in submarine movies, so that the mother, along with Bernice, could "scientifically verify" the fit of her child's shoe. *Don't buy your shoes blindly!* warned a sign hung from the ceiling over the contraption. The kids squealed at their ghostly toes wiggling, the incredible complexity of their own feet something they'd never suspected.

Bernice could guess any shoe size without consulting the machine, but it sold shoes and that was a fact. It wasn't until after Carol had married Pete and quit her job that some men had come and taken it away. Later she heard it had used X-rays, and she shuddered now to think of it. Those nasty rays, or beams or what-ever they were, zapping her and all those mothers and little chil-dren. How she had survived this long she could never say.

While microwaving her vegetable beef soup at lunchtime, she wished she'd stuck a few people's heads inside the fluoroscope to see what was what. She could've saved herself some trouble and put Gus's head in there to check for missing parts, like the bit that made a person appreciate what they had. She drew Carol's business card from her pocket and studied it as she had the shoe styles in the Woodward's catalogue.

"I'm out of sorts," she said to Tuan, who lifted his eyes from a thick book split in half on the glass counter. "I'm going home early."

———

The pastor had met her decision with less surprise than she'd expected. Bernice feared one of the old mitten ladies would be taking over her store, but the pastor had suggested his niece Tabitha, who'd recently had some sort of difficulty with her family up north in Prince George and was looking to make a new begin-ning in the city. She'd be fine, Bernice had thought; the store was nothing a young woman with a bit of tenacity couldn't handle. There really wasn't much to the job, mostly moving things here and there, when you thought about it. That she'd considered herself the only person capable of doing it seemed to her now an incredible vanity.

First she took apart her bed and dragged the pieces to the door. Then she began filling boxes with things and stacking them against the wall over the rectangle of darker wood where her bed had sat for nearly thirty years. She fought the urge to keep her collection organized, tossing it willy-nilly into the boxes, mixing even the owls and nautical items together. Next she moved into the living room, where she teetered on a chair to lift her pictures from the walls. The dishes she wrapped in the weekly fliers that had piled for years in the hall closet. In the end, she'd decided to keep only the spoon rack and her very best items of clothing—many of them Woodward's brand—and these she packed in just two suitcases and set them near the door of her empty apartment. The rest she marked for donation. It astonished her that it had taken only two days to pack her entire apartment.

Tuan and another young fellow with blue hair and metal bits hung in his face came and loaded the boxes and furniture into the van. The few odds and ends that didn't fit, including an old oak desk that Gus used to write his poetry on, she was forced to leave in the alley for the men with shopping carts.

Bernice rode between them to the thrift store, where she was meeting Wanda and Brian later that night for them to take her to Kelowna. As they drove, the blue-haired fellow sang along to the stereo and Bernice swore she heard the word Jesus. Amidst the noisy jangle of the rock and roll it sounded like a swear.

Tuan curved the van into an alley and they approached the rear entrance of the church. Then she watched Tuan carry her boxes inside, struck by the awareness that others would be taking items from her collection home and soon using them as their own. The mitten ladies had organized a going-away party and it would be starting in a few minutes, but Bernice already wanted to leave.

————————

Later that afternoon, Bernice stepped from the chattering heat of the party for some air and was drawn by the low roar of human voices from a few blocks over. As she approached Abbott Street, she thought it was a protest march, but then she saw that no part of the crowd was moving. Hotdog trucks and trucks with satellite dishes strapped to their roofs stood by. The sidewalks around the old department store were barricaded off by high fences and large metal containers that looked like train cars lacking wheels. The surrounding streets were crammed with people who all seemed to be searching the red brickwork of the old department store for clues to a mystery.

She pushed deeper into the swarm. Bodies pressed against her. She could see the plywood had been removed from the windows and that there was nothing left inside, the store entirely gutted. Children were riding their parents' shoulders like lumbering elephants; people carried roughly scrawled signs she couldn't make out without her glasses, and still others aimed tiny movie cameras, lifting them over their heads as if in choreographed salute. It cheered her to see so many people back on this block again, especially people who took care of themselves, people with jobs and children and cameras.

She found a bit of space out front of a soup kitchen, stepping up on the curb for a better view—of what she wasn't yet sure. Beside her stood a young woman, patches crudely pinned and sewn on her clothing as if to suggest a lack of concern for her own appearance, or perhaps appearances in general. The woman turned to her and shrugged as if she too were confused by the spectacle. Her easy, dejected way of holding herself reminded Bernice of her sister at her age. The girl's feet were a size seven and a half.

Then came seven loud blasts from an air horn, silencing the crowd. A distorted voice began counting down from ten. The young woman stuck her fingers in her ears. When the count ended, the voice said "Go," and there were fourteen explosions— she counted—that seemed to chase each other around the structure. She saw flocks of birds, mostly pigeons and crows, launch from the empty windows of the upper levels and she felt great pity for them, knowing there'd be nests and lame birds left behind in the store. Her heart dropped as if her chest were a carnival dunk tank. She felt her hand cover her mouth, and when the explosions ended there came a short pause in which Bernice turned to the young woman, who she saw, also stunned, was timidly pulling her fingers from her ears. For a moment Bernice wondered if there had been some kind of miscalculation, right before a series of greater explosions erupted, triple the power of the ones that still hung webs in her ears, and the structure became liquid and began to fold in on itself, slumping like a set of clothes without a body to keep them standing. In a dense oatmeal cloud, dust and bits of the building rose into the air and enveloped the now cheering and whooping crowd. She brought her silk scarf to her mouth and breathed through it, the dusty odour reminding her of her closet now all emptied out and awaiting the clothes of another. She felt a hand she knew to be the young woman's grip her own, and found herself hoping she was one of the young people who would live in the new apartments they would be building here, and they stood like this, immobile, blinded by dust, in the cacophony of car alarms that seemed to be setting each other off, spreading across the city, block by block.

The Extra

M e and Rick, we rent a basement suite at the bottom of Baldev's house. Actually, we only call it that to Welfare so they'll give us the most amount of money for rent, but really it's just a basement, no suite part. The walls are two-by-fours with cotton candy in between and there's no toilet or sink and it smells bad like your wrist when you leave your watch on too long. We sleep on hunks of foam beside the furnace between an orange lawnmower and used cans of paint that Baldev keeps down there. We take dumps at the gas station down the street and pee in plastic jugs we pour down a drain in the alley. Then at the tap on the side of the house, we rinse them and fill them for drinking and washing our pits and crotches. We used to have different jugs but then we got tired of remembering which was which.

When I say we rent, I really mean I do because my disability worker, Linda, sends a cheque for five hundred dollars a month to Baldev because she can't trust me with my money for the reason of my brain being disabled. But me and Rick and Baldev have this deal where Baldev gives us two hundred of the rent back in cash as long as we don't complain about the basement and how it's just a basement.

Rick needs my help. He can't get welfare because years ago he got kicked off for not telling them he had a job while he was still getting cheques. But Rick says we're lucky because I have a disabled brain and we get more money than the regular welfare pays anyway, so it works out, and we split the disabled money right down the middle. Without Rick I'd be starving with flies buzzing on my face or back in a group home. He says what we're going to do with our money because I'm bad at numbers, and also he cooks me dinners and lunches on his hot plate. He sometimes cooks spaghetti or mostly different stews he gets out of a can. He always makes me wait until the stew is hot before we eat because I eat things cold because I'm bad at waiting. It's just more proper, he says. Then he says it lasts longer in your belly if it's hot. When I ask why, he says because then your belly has to wait for it to get cool before it can soak it up.

Rick could have any job he wanted because he's sharp. He does our laundry and he made a copy of the key to the gas-station bathroom and he gives himself homemade tattoos with a guitar string and gets really mad whenever he thinks somebody is ripping us off. Rick is from Halifax but he never was a fisherman. He never set foot on a boat, he says, and besides there's more fish at your average pet store than in the whole goddamn ocean these days because of those big Japanese fish-vacuums he told me about. But he's not lazy. He's been a roofer, a car parker, a painter, a tree planter, and he once worked at night mopping at a big twenty-four-hour hardware store. But now he just goes to WorkPower with me, which I'll tell you about later. He even used to be married but his wife left him because she was a rotten witch. She got everything, he says. Everything was his house and his kids and all his stuff that he bought with hard-earned money. He even had one of those trucks with four tires on the back. He talks about it sometimes when he's falling asleep after he's had some cans of the beer with lots of X's all over it. Rick says I'm lucky I can't taste the beer. He named it swill, even though I can tell he likes it because it makes him a mix of confused and happy and tired.

Near the end of the month, when the disabled money and the money we get back from Baldev runs out, we get up at six in the morning. Then we put on our steeled-toe boots and bike to a place called WorkPower to stand in line to get jobs. Sometimes it's unloading boxes from trucks, or tearing copper wires out of buildings nobody wants. One time we had to carry blocks of ice from a truck to a freezer in a fish market and the gloves they gave us were thin as the butt of an old pair of underwear. Rick wanted to tell them where to stick it so bad but if one of the bosses complains to WorkPower they won't let us back. I like WorkPower because every time it's different but Rick doesn't like it because he thinks it's shit work. I ask him what shit work means and he says anything that makes you feel or look like shit.

———————

One day after me and Rick got back from a whole day of picking up cigarette butts on a construction site, Baldev came down the stairs from his part of the house, where at the top there is a door that doesn't lock on our side but does on Baldev's side. It's always locked, I've checked.

Rick asked Baldev who the hell he thought he was. He said, You can't just come down here without properly notifying us, it ain't legal.

Baldev nodded like he thought so too and said he had a thing to tell us.

Rick stuck his hands in his armpits and told him to go on and say it.

I am changing, Baldev said. My friends I cannot be able to give you this money-back deal in the future.

Rick got the vein in his forehead that he gets when he thinks he's getting ripped off. It's shaped like one of those sticks that finds water.

So sorry, Baldev said. This is because the property taxes that we have, they are going up.

Well what if the city finds out this here ain't exactly a legal suite? Rick said. But I didn't want Baldev to get in trouble for the basement, he has three or maybe four kids who I hear stomping around upstairs and he has a wife who cooks food that smells good in a way like no food I've ever ate. I told Baldev we wouldn't tell on him.

You must vacate if you are wishing, my friends, Baldev said, ignoring me and what I said. Then he went up the stairs and I heard the door lock.

Rick kicked some of our stuff around for a while but he wasn't that mad because when I told him everything was going to be okay, we'd just work a little harder, he started laughing. Then he said we'd have to go back to WorkPower every day this week if we wanted to eat. I told him I didn't mind shit work as long as my disability worker didn't find out I wasn't as disabled as I was supposed to be, that I could carry boxes and pick up cigarette butts, and then stopped giving me my cheques. Rick said they wouldn't find out as long as I kept my mouth shut for the rest of the night. Then he rode his bike to go buy some beer with lots of X's on it because he can't go to sleep early without at least a few.

———————

The next day, we were in our steeled-toe boots on our way back from cutting weeds as high as our heads at a place that sells motorhomes beside a highway. We had money in our pockets and we went to get some burgers because Rick said he was too damn tired to cook anything on the hot plate.

You eat your hamburgers too fast, Rick said, you can't even taste them. I told him I taste them good enough, but we both know I can't really taste anything too good because on account of my brain being disabled. But sometimes Rick acts like he's too much of the boss so I have to set him straight. If you're wondering why my brain is disabled it's because when I was born it didn't get enough air because there was some problem with my mom or the way I came out. My mom said they knew right after I came out because the doctor poked me on the feet with something sharp but I didn't care. Then he put lights in my eyes but my eyes didn't really care either. The doctor just frowned, she said. Most of the time I forget it's damaged. Maybe it's too damaged to know it's damaged. Or maybe it's not damaged enough for me to notice. Either way it's not very bad.

Rick always leaves his burger wrappers and his tray on the table. He says he doesn't want to take away the people's jobs who clean up, but I throw his out for him because I think they'd still have jobs but just do less if everybody pitched in more. While I was at the garbage, a guy was talking to Rick. He had nice clothes like a disability worker and had one of those pocket telephones in his hand. He talked the same as Rick. Because Rick's from Halifax, he says burr or guiturr when he tries to say bar or guitar, but he can turn it off when he wants. He's really good at being me too, which is funny for a while then makes me mad if he acts too much like a retard because I'm not. Rick told the guy we were working in construction but I could see the guy looking at the long pieces of yellow grass still stuck in my hair. I got bored of their talking so I went to the bathroom and drank out of the tap.

When we rode our bikes home Rick said him and the guy had gone to high school together back in Halifax and the guy had gave Rick a card with his name on it and said he should call him if our construction jobs slow down because now he was working for the movies and they needed some extra people for a movie that they were making. It'd be a lot easier than Work-Power believe me, Rick said, but I didn't believe him because bad things always happened whenever Rick got happy about something.

In our basement he said he always thought he might be in the movies then he asked me to grab him another of the beers that we keep in a bucket of water outside so they're more cold. The rest of the night I had to listen to him practise talking normal, like not saying burr or guiturr. Then he put on the classic rock station, which is music that is older and everybody agrees is pretty good, while he did the kind of push-ups where you do the clap in the middle or just go on your knuckles.

————————

After waiting three days Rick called the guy from the pay phone at the gas station where we take dumps. Rick came back and hugged me and said we were going to have a party because he had just got us both jobs as extras.

I asked him what extras were.

He said they were the people in movies who stood around in the background and made everything seem more real just by being there.

It seemed like something we'd be good at, but I was still worried. I'll do it, I told Rick, as long as I don't have to say anything because I can't talk or remember very good because of my brain being disabled and Rick said no problemo.

That night, during our party, Rick drank lots of beers and threw our steeled-toe boots out on the lawn. Then he went up the stairs and pounded on Baldev's door yelling about room service. I told him to stop because it was three in the morning and he'd wake the kids and they probably had to get up early and go to school. He did what I said and came back downstairs. He looked at his pictures of the rotten witch for a few minutes, then started sleeping.

————————

The next day Rick said we needed some nice clothes because they wouldn't want to film us if we looked like shit.

I don't think we look like shit, I said, and I stuffed my hands into the pockets of my favourite orange hoodie that I was wearing because there was white parts on the sleeves from me wiping my nose on them.

We just have to make sure they don't think we're bums who don't deserve the job, he said, but luckily we saved some money for just this kind of occasion. Close your eyes.

Why, I said.

I'm making a withdrawal from our emergency fund, he said.

I faked shutting my eyes and saw him reach for the pineapple can he'd hid behind an old dartboard, which I already knew was there. He pulled out some money and put some back.

Okay, he said.

We biked to five different second-hand stores to get some clothes for our new job as extra people. Rick got a white shirt that was only a little yellow around the collar, some black pants, some shoes he called loafers, and some shades. I just wanted another hoodie, but he made me get some nice jeans and a T-shirt with a collar on it that had a little picture of a guy on a horse holding a sword in the air like he was going to kill somebody. In the change room, Rick switched the tags on them so they were only two bucks each. But the old lady was nice and didn't make us pay for them anyway.

The day came, which was good because Rick said we were out of money and we had to eat some doughnuts out of a dumpster on our way downtown to the movie place. When we got there, a woman made us wait in a room with a whole lot of other extra people, who were either reading magazines about movie stars or had their ears to their pocket telephones. Some were making appointments to be extra people for other movies and some were talking more quiet to their families and friends.

After a while, they took us into a big room with lots of clothes on racks where we waited some more. Then they brought our costumes. I took mine out of the plastic bag and didn't understand it. One of the clothes ladies had to help me put it on and I was embarrassed because she saw my underwear. I put my golfing shirt on a hanger and she hung it up. The costume was just bits of fur glued to this dirty net made out of canvas that hung off me like a bathrobe made out of a chewed-up dog. I also got these leather boots that were like moccasins, except they had these little blinking lights on them.

What the hell is this? I heard Rick ask the clothes lady when he got his, which was like mine but he had a helmet and these big black plastic horns coming out of the shoulders.

She talked with pins in her mouth and said it was his costume.

What kind of person wears rags and furs and horns and shredded-up leather? Rick said.

She said this is a movie that takes place in the future.

Rick wanted to know how in the hell that explained anything.

I hadn't been working in movies very long but I had already learned that when a movie person doesn't like what someone else is saying they just walk away from them and that is exactly what the costume lady did, which made all shapes of veins bulge under Rick's helmet.

After everybody was dressed up they took us back to the waiting room.

How do you think they know what people are going to look like in the future? I asked Rick who was reading one of the movie-star magazines.

Maybe they're just taking a guess, Rick said.

I always thought the future would look like the Jetsons, I said.

He turned a page and went humph.

Then we waited more in the waiting room.

Do you think we're getting filmed right now? I asked Rick.

No, they'll tell us when that happens.

Okay, good, I said, because I didn't feel like I was from the future yet. Actually I was too bored to feel anything. Plus I guess I was mad we had rode our bikes all day and spent our emergency fund on our party.

I think this is shit work, I told Rick an hour later. I'd rather carry ice blocks.

Then Rick told me to shut up so I kept talking about nothing really just to prove he wasn't the boss.

I felt better when it was time for lunch and we went outside to these big trucks that opened up and had kitchens inside. Us and the other extra people had to line up and wait which was okay because sometimes me and Rick waited for sandwiches at the Gospel Mission so I'm used to it. Rick said all the real actors had food brought to them in their trailers. I told him it was sad they had to live in trailers.

I asked the guy in the truck who had a beard and that knotted rope kind of hair to give me as much food as he could because

I was starving. He laughed and piled my plate with all different colours of food. Can you believe this? I said to Rick when we sat down, but he was watching the star actor who was sitting with a pretty lady wearing sunglasses and an important-looking fat guy who had an old-fashioned hat on his head. Even with my disabled brain and my dead taste buds, I could tell this food had never even seen a can. There was lots of fish and different salads, which I don't like much but ate anyway because I didn't want to get fired. I went back up twice and ate so much my rag-and-fur future costume got tight and started to rip a little which was okay because you couldn't tell because it was already ripped.

After lunch, we went back and waited in the room for a long time. Then they said they were wrapping something up and I thought maybe we'd get a present but they just told us to come back tomorrow.

On the way home I asked Rick if he wanted to get some beers to celebrate.

Rick said this wasn't the kind of job where you get paid at the end of the day, we had to wait for our cheques.

How long will that take? I said. I was worried more about having money to eat than I was about drinking any beers.

Dunno, Rick said, could be a while.

Then I realized my disability worker would find out I wasn't disabled when I cashed my cheque.

Don't worry, Rick said, I gave them a fake name instead of your real one and we just sign it over to me and I'll cash it for you. Until then, we're gonna have to live off the lunch truck.

That's all right with me, I said.

———————————

We went back every day for a week. Then another week. Rick said we shouldn't ask about our cheques because they'd think we were desperate. I said, aren't we? and he said, not yet we aren't.

Our job was to wait in the room for them to call us. We got more used to our future costumes and didn't even bother wearing our nice clothes anymore because nobody really cared, we were all the same anyway once we got dressed up. And some of the other extra people had worse costumes than us like heavy fur robes, fake beards, hats made out of scratchy sticks. It made us feel grateful for ours. I was eating so much at lunch mine barely fit me anymore and I was scared to ask for a bigger one even though they had hundreds more in the other room.

Those nights in our basement Rick didn't talk, which was weird because before he was always putting different complicated plans together like a football coach. He didn't even want to play cards, and usually he hated it when he didn't have any beers to drink but now he didn't seem to care. He did lots of push-ups and went to bed early.

Then one day right after lunch the important fat guy with the hat who I found out was the Assisting Director came into our waiting room and told us finally that they needed us. This was how the movie people talked, they always said they needed something when from as far as I could tell they more just wanted it. He said they were going to need to have this big explosion in the middle of a street that they had closed down. Then he said he was going to need some people to lead our charge and he started looking around the room. Rick made himself taller and put on his helmet. You, the Assisting Director said to Rick, and you and you, to some other people. Come with me, he said, and they went to the other side of the room. I was happy he didn't pick me because I was worried about tripping over my rags and ruining the movie, but then I was scared I would do something even more stupid without Rick there to tell me it was stupid.

Then the Halifax guy came to the rest of us and told us our motivator which is like our reason for living. He said we were these hungry, starving people who were trying to get into where some space stuff was so we could take over the spaceships and get back to our planet where there was lots of food and it was also the place where our families lived. It made no sense to me but I looked over at Rick and now that he was one of the leaders he was taking it really serious. I need you to think starving, Halifax guy said to my group and I saw a lady suck in her cheeks. I'd been hungry lots of times in the past, like the time when Rick lost all our money on the way home from the bar or when we had to send money to Rick's dying sister in Halifax or when we had to buy extra things like our bikes, which Rick got off this guy he knew and were really expensive because they are some of the best racing bikes you can buy. So I just tried to focus on those times but it was hard to believe in my motivator and think starving right after three plates from the lunch truck.

After somebody came to make sure our costumes looked good enough, they took us through some hallways then outside to a street that they'd made to look all burned and wrecked like something really, really bad had happened. There were trucks and movie stuff everywhere. I could see five different cameras and there were tons of people standing around like on the edges of a football field.

They had us wait around more. Then the Director started talking into one of those loud-talking horns. Okay everybody we are only going to do this one time, he said. He was sitting up high on a crane. Someone came and told me to stand in a place. There were lots of us and everybody got their own place. I tried to see Rick but I couldn't see him.

Then all of a sudden I heard Action! and we were all running in a big pack and someone was yelling GoGoGoGo. I was trying not to fall down and my heart was beating like one of those loud things that breaks up the pavement and I started to get a cramp from all of the food that was bouncing around in my belly. A woman ahead of me screamed and tripped over her big stick that had a bird skull at the top and I had to jump over her because if I helped her up I thought I would ruin the movie. Then there was this loud boom behind us and I felt heat go on my ears. I turned and saw the whole front of a building go on fire and there was little bits of stuff flying everywhere and all I could think was that I hoped Rick was okay.

It was the farthest I ever ran and I was almost passing out because my cramp hurt so bad when the Director said cut and they brought us back to the waiting room. Then they got us to take off our costumes and said thanks very much for your time and told us they didn't need us anymore. My legs were still shaking while I went looking for Rick. I walked around for an hour until I saw him still wearing his costume talking with the Halifax guy and the tall pretty lady and the fat Assisting Director over by the trailers.

You can't go in there, a guy with a clipboard said.

In where? I said.

Over there, he said.

So I just biked home.

It had been a few days and I was waiting for the sound of the back gate when Baldev came down the stairs followed by the smell of his country's kind of food that Rick hates but as far as I can tell smells really good, like the lunch truck.

This has come for you, he said, holding out a letter with the government's picture on it.

I opened it but I didn't understand what it said because my disabled brain makes it so that I can't read.

Is this from girlfriend? Baldev said, making his big boobs. Let me tell you Baldev loves big boobs. He puts his hands out in front of his chest to show just how big of boobs he means, which is really, really big. Then he looks down at the boobs and squeezes them. He admires them like he would even settle for having big boobs himself if he ever got the chance. This is maybe the one thing him and Rick agree about.

No, I said, but louder so that he could understand. Baldev, can you read this for me?

Baldev dropped his boobs and took the letter. He saw the government picture at the top and said, no, no, this is not near to my business. Then he went back upstairs.

I sat on a chair trying to make myself read. Once I got a letter from them saying they were going to send somebody to check out whether I was still disabled and see if I could work. After Rick read it out loud, he ripped it up and said there was no

way in hell me or my brain was ever going to get better and that
they were the ones who needed their heads checked. Then he said
something like he always says about how mean the whole world
is. Then we sat down and drank beers and felt better. But nobody
from Welfare ever came, which was good because we didn't want
them to see the beers or that the basement was a basement. Now
I was worried this letter was another one of those and that maybe
this time they really were going to come. I stayed up all night listening to the furnace.

Rick didn't come back the next day or the next. I got hungry
and couldn't stop my brain from thinking about the food truck. I
wondered if it was still there, because if I could dress up in some
old rags and furs again and sneak back, just once, I knew I could
eat enough to last me at least a week. Or how maybe they moved
the trucks to some other movie somewhere else, and I thought
about riding my bike around looking for movie stuff, like cranes
and things blowing up. But I was too tired. I could have got some
emergency money from my worker, Linda, but the letter made me
afraid they'd found out I was working as an extra person and they
would kick me off like Rick or stick me in jail. I didn't even know
where the good dumpster with the doughnuts in it was because I
always just followed Rick.

———————

Then early one morning I woke up to a noise I thought was rats.
I turned the light on and saw Rick going through his boxes of
stuff.

Oh. Hi, he said.

Where you been? I said.

He sat in a chair and leaned his head way back like some-body was washing his hair, and it sounded like he had a cold because he was sniffing lots. I saw he was wearing different shoes and a different coat. They looked new.

Then all of a sudden Rick started talking, not excited like he usually did but still staring up at the boards that I guess were actually holding up Baldev's floor, and even with my bad smell I noticed Rick smelled like lots of beers. He said that after they picked him to be a leader of the future, they gave him a laser rifle that he was supposed to fire at the star. What if you hit him? I asked, and he shut his eyes, blew air out his nose, and said they were going to add the laser beam later. Then Rick said when the Director yelled action and he started running, his helmet slipped over his eyes and he accidentally turned and crashed into the big star right before the huge explosion. He said he was in the only camera angle that they really needed so they had no choice, they had to give him a bigger part in the movie so it didn't seem weird that he was there.

Does that mean our cheques will be bigger? I said.

He said he guessed it did.

Then I asked when we'd get them because I was hungry.

Not yet, he said.

Oh, I said.

It's just like stew, he said. You have to wait. You get impatient.

I asked him if he had any money for us to go get burgers or make something on the hot plate.

No, he said, but there was food and beers at the wrap party. He took a half a sandwich out of his pocket and gave it to me.

Is that where you got those clothes? Were they presents from the wrap party? I asked. I was eating the sandwich as slow as I could, picking fluff from my mouth.

Yeah, he said. Then he got up and said he would go right then and find out where our cheques were.

I asked him if he could read my letter first.

He grabbed it out of my hand and read it really fast.

It's fine, he said, doesn't mean anything.

There's more on the back, I said.

He flipped it and read the back. It's still fine, he said.

Does it mean they know? I said. That I'm not disabled anymore?

No, he said, and started throwing his things into some grocery bags, but none of his important stuff. And you *are* still goddamn disabled, he said. It just means they don't know their ass from a hole in the ground.

Good, I said.

Then he dropped the bags and put his hands on his face.

You don't have to work anymore, it ain't right for you to, he said.

Especially if it's shit work, I said. Like being extra.

He stood there covering his face for a little bit, breathing weird, and I knew he was really angry because when he took his hands away his face was red and there were veins in it like a bunch of blue candy worms. But then he just gave me a long hug that squeezed my breath and left.

———

The good part about living with someone is you can sit there and look at their stuff and know they have to come back sometime to get it. He'd left the hot plate and his steeled-toe boots. Sure, he'd taken the pictures of the rotten witch, but he'd left most of his clothes and his favourite baseball cap. I checked outside and he'd left his racing bike, which made me feel even better.

After cleaning the place up a bit I sat for a while on my hunk of foam. I already forgave Rick for getting mad at me because I called his new extra job shit work. He liked to get mad sometimes for bad reasons, so I decided I'd just have to not talk about it ever again and it would be okay. Then I folded up the disabled letter as small as it would go and tried to throw it in the garbage bucket but I missed. I was thinking about how, after working as an extra person from the future for so long, it was like I was becoming a professional waiter, and how that now I could wait for pretty well anything as long as I knew it was coming. I thought about how long it would take for my belly to eat the sandwich Rick gave me, and about how long it would be before my disabled brain wouldn't be able to stop me from following the smell of Baldev's wife's food up the stairs and knocking on their door. I didn't know how long that would be.

An Ideal Companion

1

Before he did a website for a local organic deli for dogs, Dan had never imagined himself a dog owner. None of his friends had dogs and he'd never wanted one as a child. But at some point while camped at his home-office desk, daylight banished by dusty Venetian blinds, somewhere during all that coding, linking, cropping and resizing, Dan flared with a sudden and insatiable interest in dogs.

He noticed them everywhere. On the street, in his elevator. The breeds were a language he taught himself, a newly discovered planet. He quickly caught on to how much a dog could say about its owner, how people didn't resemble their dogs by accident, and it sure wasn't the dogs who did the choosing. He spent countless bloodshot hours at his computer sifting canine images for the dog that would best represent him, finding all the usual breeds too regal, or showy, or boring, or simple-minded. After weeks of frustration, a felicitous click on a rare-breed site brought to his screen a picture of a dog so instantly familiar to him, a dog of such undeniable beauty and grace, Dan could do nothing but settle back into his computer chair, hands dangling at his sides, and allow a great calm to overtake him.

Originally from southern Spain, the Andalucian wolfhound was a herder, a working dog, not a fashionable furry accessory. During the Spanish Civil War it was used by the Republicans to root out Nationalist ammunition caches as well as keep watch while its masters slept in the woods. An agile dog of medium build with a blunt snout and large ears that rose up like furry candle flames, it had only recently been rescued from extinction. Raredogs.com declared the Andalucian to be making a major comeback, due to its being "confident, reliable, proud, undeniably intelligent, an ideal companion, flush with loyalty and a joyous energy."

Dan could locate only one credible breeder in Canada, a kennel in Saskatchewan stewarded by a couple named Ihor and Sandy Kuziak, whom he emailed before he could weigh the idea any further.

Their reply came within minutes:

One Lucian left. Not a puppy. A good dog. Still interested?
Sandy and Ihor ;o)

His disappointment at the lack of a puppy was quelled by an attached picture of a gorgeous chocolate brown dog with white paws and a blue bandana slung round its neck, its head cocked inquisitively, reclining in a patch of crispy prairie grass.

Who needed a puppy anyway, Dan thought, considering his own age, thirty-six, a number he found hemorrhoidally embarrassing whenever he was required to write it on an application or a form.

He replied, and the couple sent more information, which he briefly scanned before paying for the dog right then and there, his finger abuzz while clicking Finalize Transaction.

———————

"You don't even have a *yard*," said Dan's best friend and former bandmate, Winston, in his usual distracted tone, "and your square footage is barely double digits."

Three years ago, Winston had accidentally impregnated Marta, then merely one of that species of desperate, tragic girl who often gravitated to their shows. Soon after, Winston ceased calling it an accident, quit playing music, cut way back on his drinking, married Marta and bought a house in Port Coquitlam, a suburb an hour out of the city. In a matter of a year, Marta had gone from a near-transparent chain-smoking waif to an extremely successful self-employed makeup artist and aesthetician—a success that baffled Dan, given that each time he saw her she managed to have rendered herself even more unattractive. They'd recently had another baby, and now Winston called only during his masochistic commute, his attention mainly on flaring brake lights and timely lane changes.

But Winston had a point. Dan's condo, a one-bedroom, was small.

"Tell that to all the other dog owners in my building," Dan said. "Plus there are parks, off-leash parks, and there's the seawall.

It's called public space, Winston. I don't need to own something to appreciate it."

Dan heard the first few seconds of several songs as his friend trolled for one that would best compliment his mood. Winston settled on a punk rock staple they'd often covered as their second encore—a song that once had shocked and inflamed them but now just sounded needy and indulgent, like a clamouring child. "And what's with this bloodhound? Never heard of them," Winston said. "Is this thing accredited?"

"Wolfhound," Dan said. "They're from Spain. They were used by the Republicans in the Civil War, but now they're making a major comeback," with a pre-emptive pride for his dog tightening in his cheeks.

"And how long do these things live?" Winston said.

From his research, Dan knew exactly how long, but he saw where Winston was going. Ever since his ultimate sacrifice, Winston had enjoyed nothing more than subjecting Dan to languid dissertations on all of life's inevitable and unromantic realities. Dan ignored the question.

"Because this isn't like yoga, Dan-o. You can't just quit after two sessions because there aren't any attractive women in your class."

"You know that wasn't why I quit. I'll never touch my toes, it's genetic. And plus the teacher was a flake."

"In a yoga class? Anyway, is this recognized Republican breed the kind you're going to have to walk? Like outside?"

"Of course."

"Well, I endorse anything that'll get you out of that Plato's cave you have going on over there. Maybe you'll even make it out this way for a taste of the good life."

The morning he was to pick up his dog, Dan spent an unusually long time in the mirror, meticulously shaving the horseshoe of stubble that grew, clinging there, around the back of his head. To him, the horseshoe didn't signify he was bald, but rather balding. It was evidence of a process that was to Dan much more humiliating than any barren result. At least shaving it put him in charge. It looked better anyway; his hair had not been anything much. He held his own gaze, wiping bits of shaving cream from the knuckles of his ears with a towel that smelled somewhere on the continuum between mould and fabric softener. Dan was not what he would call an attractive man, but this knowledge was also a kind of power. He felt he had a fair inventory of his assets and worked with that. He'd vowed never to be one of those— mostly European—men he'd seen at the public pool whose great hairy and gelatinous girth was slung with a scrap of spandex, their denial of reality being their primary offence. It was one of Dan's greatest desires to make it through his life without dis- gusting anyone.

Turning to check his profile, Dan smoothed his golf shirt over his stomach. It has to like me, he told himself. It has no choice. He pictured long invigorating walks in the woods, leash in hand.

He was stopped at a light on his way to the airport when a quantity of fluid was suddenly dashed across his windshield. A squeegee flicked from his right and began frothing the liquid. Dan hit the wipers, clacking them against the squeegee, and a brief struggle ensued that reminded Dan of duelling swordsmen. The squeegee recoiled and his wipers arced freely. His view cleared and there stood a street kid with a three-pronged green mohawk and dirty patches affixed to his rotting clothes bearing the names of punk rock bands Dan still remembered. The kid lifted his hands, the squeegee drooling suds on the hood, and Dan could hear his Québécois accent even with the windows rolled up. "Ah, what the hell, man, I'm trying to help." The light changed and Dan gassed as if in reply. Who knew what they put in that fluid—probably piss. It was something he would have thought was funny when he was a punk.

He arrived early. To kill time he parked in the econo lot and walked a good twenty minutes to the terminal through a grey, atomized rain. Inside, he stood beside a woman, mid-forties, black yoga pants and a few inches of hard-fought midriff. Not exactly a natural beauty, but she had obviously put in some effort, no doubt for the guy she was picking up. Cracking her gum, she let her gaze fall briefly on Dan. She smiled, so quick it seemed more of a grimace. He realized he was waiting for a loved one too— well, a potential loved one—and he felt a kind of kinship with this woman, and with all his fellow ride givers: brothers, friends, girlfriends, these people of the arrivals area.

Sandy was easy to spot among the passengers trickling through the automatic doors. She was tall, almost sideshow tall— easily over six feet—and wore the same flowery, ankle-length dress and hat she had worn in her picture on the website. The hat was a floppy, Cat-in-the-Hat style that had enjoyed a brief popularity in the nineties. It was a hat that women like Sandy referred to as funky.

Closing the distance, Dan noticed she wasn't carrying one of those dog-carrier baskets.

"Hi, Sandy," he said, offering his hand. "I'm Dan. Forget something?"

Sandy lit up and swept her body into his. Dan could feel her chin brush the top of his tender skull, and her body was warm and smelt of a wet dock drying in the sun.

She spoke in the singsong of someone who has spent a large portion of her life with dogs and children: "Our little guy is in special cargo, and you know what? He told me this morning that he can't wait to meet his new companion."

She guided Dan by the elbow toward special cargo, swirling the air with talk, commending him for his decision to share his life with a 'Lucian.

When they arrived at special cargo, an interval of loud buzzing issued from behind the doors. Sandy began rummaging for something in her leather-tasselled rucksack. She held a document to Dan's face, too close for him to read.

"What's this?"

"Standard contract: resale clause, guarantee of humane and ethical treatment, breeding restriction, standard stuff."

Dan began scanning what was an agreement between himself and Life Partner Kennels Ltd. that stated he agreed to care for the dog, refrain from breeding it or profiting from it in any way. If he failed to do this, he was to return the dog to the custody of Sandy and Ihor without refund.

An ear-muffed baggage handler burst through the doors and set some items on the rubberized floor: a guitar case, a snowboard, what looked like a djembe drum. No dog.

"You can do it on my back," Sandy said, turning to offer a wide, flower-patterned expanse.

Perhaps Winston was right and this dog idea had been ill-conceived. Purebred dogs were expensive, almost extinct ones even more so. Throw in Sandy's round-trip flight from Regina to deliver the dog, and Dan's savings had taken quite a hit.

He guessed the contract had been drawn up by Sandy herself—lawyers tended to steer clear of phrases like "Together embarking on a mutually majestic journey"—and it certainly wasn't legally binding. Nevertheless, it seemed to represent the kind of serious commitment Dan had always avoided.

Just then a baggage handler set down a medium-sized beige dog carrier next to a computer monitor box. "Is that him?" said Dan, hurrying over.

"Shhhhhhh!" Sandy exclaimed. "You'll wake the little guy."

She was right: inside was the chocolate Andalucian from the picture, curled up like a cooked shrimp, his chin resting picturesquely on his soft ivory paws.

"Look how calm he is," Dan whispered, hunkering down.

"Sedated," whispered Sandy. "Don't worry, it's herbal, should wear off in an hour or so, just something to tone down the trauma of air travel and relocation."

For a second Dan thought the dog might have suffocated in the cargo bay, but then it released a long, even sigh that played in the fur of his paws. He was exactly like the photo, only more real, and more beautiful. He was perfect.

Dan rose with the contract still in hand. "Turn around," he said to Sandy, and he braced his forearm against the warm sponginess of her back.

Dan set the carrier in the rear of the car, unsure if it needed to be strapped in somehow like a baby seat. He took extra care as he muscled his way through the midday traffic, all sorts of emotions ranging inside him, the most distinct being a sort of pleasurable impatience.

The carrier seemed larger on his living-room floor. He opened the gate and stroked the dog lightly on the head a few times, but it didn't stir. He hoped Sandy's herbal business hadn't vegetized it in some way that would necessitate spoon-feeding it mashed banana for the rest of its life. He realized in all of his anticipation, he'd neglected to buy food or a leash. He considered going to the organic dog deli he'd done the website for, maybe get some freebies, but figured he'd start off with some regular food to avoid setting the bar too high. In case the dog woke while he was gone, he left the carrier open so it wouldn't commence its new life in captivity.

When he got back, arms hugging a ten-kilo bag of kibble to his chest, he was about to call the dog when he realized he hadn't even considered naming it yet. No use in jumping the gun, he thought. He was sure a working knowledge of its personality would allow the selection of a more fitting name. Setting the bag on the floor, Dan clapped his hands and took a fair shot at a whistle.

The dog came into the hallway, alert and friendly, very much alive, claws skittering on the laminate hardwood, his tail wagging, jawing ecstatically at something hard.

"What have you got there?" Dan said, and it dutifully released a chunk of what looked like black plastic, pocked and gashed by its teeth. Dan scooped it up and turned the mangled artifact in his palm. In the end it was the rubber bit that read DVD/TV that allowed Dan to determine its origin.

The dog followed him into the living room, where he found long, raw claw marks in the Corbusier sofa he'd bought online at an orgasmically low price the previous spring.

"No!" was all he could think of to say as he investigated the condo for further damage. Multiple bite marks in the webbed rubber of the expensive computer chair that had cured him of chronic back pain; stuffing eviscerated from a cushion hand-sewn by an ex-girlfriend who'd moved to India. It was staggering that a dog could inflict so much damage in so short a time. Dan dumped himself on the ruined couch, already aware of his failure to take good advantage of the moment, the kind dog websites called a disciplinary opportunity. The dog approached him carefully, measuring its steps. "No!" Dan said again, maybe a little too loud, and he saw its ears flatten like a pair of little wings. The dog shuddered and flipped onto its back, emitting a pitiful whine and began pawing at the air with remorse. It was then Dan's eyes followed the curly fur of its belly down to the junction of its hind legs and saw there two rubbery masses, wobbling and lolling as the dog shook. Dan was sure they'd said he'd been fixed. Was it too late? The thought of ordering the castration of another living creature inspired a sensation of emptiness in his own nether region.

"This isn't what I wanted," Dan said out loud as he lifted his pelvis to retrieve the contract he'd wadded into his jeans pocket. He indulged himself in the brief consideration of what he knew to be schemes of a quitter, a coward. He pictured driving to a rolling field somewhere and throwing a stick as far as he could before dashing for the car. Or catching a flight to Saskatchewan to hand Sandy the leash personally and admit to her that he didn't, in fact, want to share his life with a 'Lucian.

The dog yelped playfully as if to suggest the ludicrousness of Dan's anger. Looking back, Dan liked to think it was compassion that compelled him to keep the dog, but to be honest, it was the thought of Winston's tone of voice when he heard Dan explain their incompatibility. No, it would have to stay, at least until he could think of a better way to ditch it.

The days that followed could be accurately called a nightmare. The dog barked at the ceiling fan and the television as if they were demonic intruders, which got Dan two separate written noise warnings slid under his door. It slurped greedily from the toilet—even when Dan hadn't flushed to conserve water. It hid hard, dark turds in increasingly imaginative places. Each morning Dan woke to the bed gently vibrating, the dog at his feet, trembling in anticipation of a command Dan knew he could never give. He wondered if the dog ever slept; he'd never seen it. During the days it roamed the condo with its secret purpose, searching, Dan imagined, for something to herd, longing to execute some genetic program bred deep into him by a thousand years of gentle shepherds, fluffy sheep and sunny meadows.

Even with its tireless seeking of Dan's attention—trailing him room to room, nudging open the bathroom door as he sat reading fitness magazines—any attempt Dan made to touch or stroke it sent the dog leaping back, barking sharply, its tail whipping like a weed whacker.

With all time Dan spent failing to prevent the dog from destroying his home, he was two weeks over schedule delivering a site for a fitness boot camp franchise and hadn't even begun the design phase. He took to locking the beast outside on the balcony, where there was nothing but wrought-iron patio furniture and his ancient neon snowboard. "Chew on that," Dan said, sliding closed the glass door.

———————

Dan didn't make it down to the exercise room as much as he'd have liked—he couldn't find the time—but maybe the dog was a good idea if only because fleeing it meant he'd work out more often. The place was usually deserted. Even with the five tread-mills, full free-weight setup, stairclimber, complimentary yoga balls, and ceiling-to-floor mirrors, residents of the condo pre-ferred to use the expensive health club down the street. Dan fig-ured they thought they weren't getting anything unless they paid for it. The exercise room was one of the amenities that sold Dan on this place. There was also a full-sized pool, a rooftop patio and a party area with a 65" plasma TV.

Buying the condo was the biggest decision Dan had ever made. When he put his deposit down, construction had only just begun. He would go peek through the square they'd cut in the ply-wood that surrounded the site, into what then was just a big hole bristling with rebar and lined by wire mesh. It was thrilling that someday this grey pit of sludge and concrete would support the shining tower of his home. And not only his home—the homes of hundreds of other young professionals, those bright, creative people who were also carving out a life for themselves in this part of the city, who'd also bought into a building and a lifestyle that would be like no other before it. Over the following months, he had watched the building rise under the ministrations of a massive crane and heard the workers on their smoke breaks complain about the foreman or their girlfriends, but never did they know they were building Dan's home.

It had been five years since he'd moved in, and during his lonelier moments Dan found himself weighing the life he'd envisioned in the condo against the life he was living now. He had to admit there were disparities. He hadn't really met anyone, save the occasional glimmer of polite greeting, the pittance of small talk with Paul who worked at Blast Radius, or Neeti who'd once said she worked in marketing somewhere. And as far as he could tell, nobody booked the party room. He thought at last of the dog barking itself into exhaustion on his balcony upstairs and pitied him. He too, Dan figured, had expected more.

2

A few months had passed. The winter rain had given way to a mercifully bright spring. Dan and Buddy—the name he realized he'd been calling the dog in his mind for the last few weeks but had yet to say out loud—had reached a series of necessary compromises.

Having wrung the novelty from every square inch of the condo, Buddy had taken to slumping lethargically in his spot of choice near the entertainment centre, behind the DVD rack. He no longer showed much interest in Dan, or anything, for that matter, which thankfully included the ceiling fan and television.

They'd spent New Year's alone, and when Dan got a touch too rowdy on his third cosmopolitan while play-fighting Buddy with his old leather motorcycle gloves on, the dog had nipped him on the forearm, drawing blood—two glossy blobs like ladybugs. Dan forgave him, and the next day picked up some bison pepperoni from the organic dog deli. "Don't get used to it," he said, as Buddy jawed the spicy tubes. But at least his digging and chewing had ceased, and Dan was back up to full productivity while Buddy lived only for the creak of the hall closet door and the Pavlovian jingle of his leash.

There were all kinds of people in the off-leash park that day. And all kinds of dogs: a few whippets, bred nearly into two dimensions; a jovial German shepherd with an endearingly bent ear and a long, pendulous tongue; two snobby-looking Scottish terriers, one black, one white. Dan passed by seven or eight squeegee kids sitting in a half-circle on the grass near the public washrooms and recognized the kid with the green mohawk who was scrubbing an approximation of a Nirvana song on an acoustic guitar. Their sign read: *Spare change for World Domonation? Merci.* Three of their unruly mutts wrestled and loped in the grass before them. When Buddy scented their dogs, he surged against his leash, breath rasping.

Dan tallied all the money he'd spent on Buddy so far, all those unanticipated expenses, vaccinations and special food. Why a street kid would go out and get a dog evaded Dan's understanding. If you had trouble feeding yourself, why incur an added burden? It seemed so impossibly selfish.

"Easy, boy," he said, tugging the dog over to a bench, where he sat and watched the wind bend the trees that stood around the park like chaperones.

Ihor and Sandy had replied to an email he'd sent over a month ago saying that 'Lucians were often more excitable in winter through early spring and that Buddy should calm as the months progressed. Dan took a deep slug of fresh air. Even though Buddy had turned out to be a handful, and Dan wasn't experiencing what you would call love for him quite yet, the dog sure was a great reason to venture outside.

Dan strained forward to grasp an adequate-sized stick. Since he hadn't yet allowed Buddy off his leash, a game of fetch would be a good way to keep him focused during his first taste of real freedom. Still holding the leash, Dan did a mock throw of the stick and the dog flinched but didn't run, somehow alerted instantly to the trick. Buddy sank low in jack-in-the-box readiness. He seemed to have entirely forgotten the homeless dogs, so Dan figured he'd give it a shot, unclipping the leash and hurling the stick as far as he could, which admittedly wasn't nearly as far as he expected.

Buddy exploded into motion. At first he flailed a little, careening on amateur legs, then settled into it, thrusting over the turf like a furry torpedo. He was already there to greet the stick as it hit the ground, but to Dan's surprise he sailed right past, leaving it to tumble in the leaves. Buddy picked up even more speed, then banked left and commenced pursuit of a large and lumbering black dog—a breed Dan couldn't identify—a good twenty metres ahead, itself chasing a pink tennis ball rolling in the grass toward the park's treed boundary. With great uncoiling strides, Buddy was gaining.

Dan traced the ball's trajectory back to a woman who gripped one of those ball-thrower wands, visoring her eyes with her hand. A brindle ponytail spouted through the hole in her cap, and her pants were the mint colour of hospital scrubs. She cupped her mouth and called something to her dog.

Buddy was now abreast with the black dog, and they bodied each other, like cars in a chase scene on a mountain highway. Buddy gave one final burst, lunging to snatch the ball from a tuft of weeds where it had come to rest, and took off. The black dog slowed to a defeated canter.

The woman hadn't yet identified Dan as the owner of the dog who was now doing victory laps around the park, a pink blur in his mouth. Dan considered walking away and just leaving him. He wasn't tagged, or even registered. This is what he wants, Dan thought, to go down running free.

Buddy came blazing past with a taunting grin and Dan took a half-hearted swipe at his collar, blurting, "Here boy!" Seeing this, the woman began a sporty trot in his direction. Dan's embarrassment was like an egg of heat cracked over his face. What kind of person has this little control of his dog?

As she approached, he saw her face sharpen, briefly appearing quite pretty, then it changed, as if someone had focused it too far and blurred her face into a kind of wrongness. Dan looked away. He felt like if he looked at the wrongness, he would be in some way complicit in it.

"Quite an energetic little bugger, isn't he?" the woman said, spectral in his peripheral vision.

"Yeah, sorry, he can be a bit of an asshole."

The wrongness split with laughter. "An asshole?"

At first Dan hadn't seen the humour in calling a dog a name normally reserved for people, but it felt good to make someone laugh, even if he could feel her gaze on his scalp. It was no doubt gleaming. Dan wished he'd worn a toque—it was cold enough today to get away with it.

"Do those thrower things work?" he said.

"Yeah, it gives you a little more time. You know, to think. They aren't nipping at your heels every second."

Dan felt less tense when she turned her attention toward the other dogs playing in the grass, watching them in the wistful way one does a campfire. Her own dog approached cheerily. Buddy was nowhere to be seen.

"I'm Ginnie," she said, placing a treat on her palm, offering it to her dog. "But more importantly, *this* is Josephine. Say hi, Jo." The black dog tipped herself to the ground and Ginnie rubbed her tummy vigorously.

"Hi Josephine," Dan said.

Ginnie had an easy way with Josephine, who Dan recognized now as a Kerry blue terrier. She asked her lots of questions, like "Who's that?" and "Where's your ball?" in a low, slack voice that used up lots of air. Dan watched her ruffle the fur around Jo's ears, explore the crevices of her neck, places the dog couldn't reach. She even let Jo lick her face, something Buddy had attempted but Dan had rebuffed. It was when Ginnie looked up, dog spittle shiny on her cheek, that he beheld the wrongness he'd momentarily forgotten: a thin line connecting the base of her nose to a slightly sneering upper lip, as if her nose had gone fishing for her mouth and was battling to reel it in. He was surprised it didn't affect her speech.

"Well, he looks like *he's* having a better time here than anyone," she said, referring to Buddy, who Dan spotted near the washrooms, still with the ball, playing cat and mouse with a frizzy Lhasa Apso. "What is he? Not a border collie . . . ?"

Dan cleared his throat and gave a description of Buddy's breed and history, careful not to make too much eye contact, lest she think he was looking at it. After his speech, he realized he possibly had overstated his own role in the heroic resurrection of the noble breed. But she seemed impressed.

"And what's this almost extinct Republican dog's name?" she said, with her dark eyebrow arched.

Dan briefly considered offering his own name, then thought better of it since that would mean he'd have to invent one for himself.

"It's Buddy," he said.

"He's gorgeous," she said, and Dan turned his eyes to the dogs.

Walking home with Buddy back on his leash, the closest to tired he'd ever been, Dan ran through his conversation with Ginnie in a barely audible whisper, as if he could deduce by re-enactment how insipid he might have appeared. His job never bored him more than when he was asked to describe it to others, so when she did, he'd let out a much too theatrical sigh before telling her, "Basically, I click, so that people will click where I've clicked." Which had made her laugh but now sounded flippant.

She was a nurse at St. Paul's, and while scooping out kibble, Dan pictured her at the hospital, working a double on dead-numb feet, attending to the belligerent, the deranged, the stoic sufferers of unholy affliction, the hypochondriacal, the high school volley-ball players of West Van with their twisted ankles. How could she choose a job so public? And how ironic it was that her job was to fix people, make them better, when she bore such an obvious deformity. Did people comment? Did children, awaking tonsil-less, ask her if she was an angel, and if so, then how could God let something like this happen to one of his angels?

I would curl up and die, Dan thought, as he and Buddy climbed into bed that night.

3

Weeks passed, and to Buddy's delight they'd found themselves at the dog park almost every day. Ginnie and Dan discovered they had compatible schedules, and Buddy and Jo were already great friends. Dan had noticed a big difference in Buddy's behaviour around the house, and they were making progress in his obedience training.

Dan was lounging on his tiny balcony when Winston called on his land line and spoke in the careful tone of a man coached by his wife: "So, we were thinking, why don't you and your new furry best friend come out and get a taste of that patch of splen-dour known as the well-kept suburban backyard?"

Buddy was lying over Dan's toes on the concrete, twitch-ing and whimpering his way through a dream. Dan was sure that Buddy dreamt about herding various animals, and that these dreams were much like the sex dreams of Dan's adolescence, rife with shadowy figures, unattainable goals. He pictured hundreds of sheep morphing into clouds, blown by a wind that originated from every direction. The dog twitched once more.

"I don't know. I think Buddy may have a hard time with a vehicle, behaviour-wise. I think the trauma of his relocation is still pretty unresolved."

Winston wasn't listening. "What's that, Mart . . . ?" The thud of Marta's voice could be heard through Winston's palm placed over the receiver. "And you could bring someone else if you like? How about that woman . . ." Dan could tell he was stalling for effect. " . . . uh, Ginnie? The one you mentioned the other day. I'm sure she'd like it out here."

Dan had been careful to mention her only in passing and was surprised Winston even remembered. Winston had often tried to set Dan up in the past, having worked his way into a low-level administrative position at the public library, where there was no shortage of women Dan's age. "It's like musical chairs," Winston had once said, "and they know you know the music stops when they hit forty." But Dan had never gone for it. People as desperate as he was weren't his thing. He was holding out, for what he didn't know. Then Winston mentioned his new baby, which Dan hadn't yet seen, and that made him feel like a neglectful friend, so he agreed.

———————

They met in the park the next day at the usual time. She said she'd go as long as she could bring Jo. "I get nervous in groups," she said, touching Dan lightly on the back. This touch was given in the way, he convinced himself later while shaving, that nurses must touch people all the time. Nurses were just used to having their hands on people, with all that spelunking into chest cavities and various orifices. Lower back, no big deal.

Ginnie pulled up in her compact car with a "Healthcare Before Olympics" bumper sticker and black dog hair blanketing every upholstered surface. They stopped and bought lamb shanks for the adults and some Italian sausages for the dogs. "It's Jo's favourite," she said, actually colouring slightly with embarrassment.

In the car Dan worried about having failed to prep his friend for Ginnie's harelip. Winston had once dumped a woman he'd dated for over a year, whom Dan had liked very much, because "her tits were like pool balls in socks and the fact she was a card-carrying idiot." Dan knew something like a harelip fell under the disability classification, those things that cannot be helped or commented upon. And as they exited the freeway, he reminded himself of this once more.

Marta met them at the front door, her face G-force tight with the hue of a professionally roasted turkey. "Wince is in back," she said, before hugging them rigidly, not batting a heavily mascaraed eye at Ginnie's lip. Dan figured she'd seen her share of disfigurement in the makeup-artist-slash-aesthetician business.

"Take the puppies around the side—we just had the carpets done," Marta said.

Winston greeted them in flip-flops, Hawaiian shirt fluttering open like two curtains drawn back for the big debut, a hairy belly that had grown since last time.

"So good to *finally* meet you," he said, as if Ginnie were the subject of frequent discussion. Dan looked puzzled then laughed to make sure Ginnie knew Winston was exaggerating.

They sat out in the yard on some plastic patio furniture.

"Quite a parcel of earth you've purchased here," Dan said.

"The city is no place for a kid to grow up. Too much stimulation. Too many distractions," Winston replied, ruffling his son's hair. It'd been ages since Dan had seen Jacob, their oldest, who was now three. He'd sprouted an odd tuft of black hair dead centre on the crown of his head, much darker than the wispy baby hair that surrounded it. It looked like he was growing out a bad dye job. Or into one.

"At least he's *got* hair," Dan said later, palming his own head and everyone had a chuckle.

Winston set a box of white wine on the table. "The good stuff," he said, then made a flourish of lighting the barbecue.

Dan noticed that Marta tensed when the dogs came anywhere near Jada, the new baby. Buddy sniffed then licked Marta's manicured hand and she batted him away.

"Tenacious," Marta said.

"You wouldn't believe it," Dan said.

Later, out on the grass, Jacob pulled Jo's tail and they both yelped, while Marta directed a barrage of questions at Ginnie, who handled them with grace.

"Well, some suggest the Kerry blue terrier is the result of a Portuguese water dog swimming ashore from a shipwreck and mating with the soft-coated wheaten," Ginnie told her.

"That is *so* romantic," Marta declared, glancing at Dan for some reason. "She's *such* a beautiful dog. Gorgeous."

"Well, she was destined for the show circuit, but her tail was too short. She's lucky they didn't put her out of her misery," Ginnie said.

"You know it's amazing the kind of things they can do now," said Marta, blind to the irony of Ginnie's comment. "You wouldn't believe it. I bet you could have the tail lengthened if you really wanted."

"Oh no, I'm happy with her just the way she is," Ginnie said.

To steer the conversation away from genetic defects, Dan said, "You know what they *do* have now is an organic dog deli. I did a website for them."

"Oh god. That's it. Too much," Winston said, as if this were the final piece in a puzzle he'd been slowly putting together. "You can't make that stuff up."

"And now they have these dog spas," Ginnie said. "I'm serious, you drop them off. They supposedly put them in hot tubs and give them pedicures—they call them paw-dicures. What I think is that they probably just stick them in a cage in the basement and then spray them with perfume and give them a Milk-Bone before you come get them. How would anyone know the difference? Isn't that ridiculous? I spoil Jo, but that's just excessive."

"Well, I think it's cute," said Marta. "Everyone these days needs to relax, why not dogs? And hey, if there's a market for it."

"Oh Christ, Marta, let's not use the *m* word at a time like this," Winston said with the ragged quality his voice got when he drank.

"I'm just saying."

"I think it's unforgivable we have all these people on the street and people are spending hundreds of dollars on organic dog delis and spas," Ginnie said. "It's insulting. And inhuman."

Marta seemed to interpret this as an insinuation and she shot up straighter in her chair. "Maybe if those people took better care of themselves—their looks, I mean—they wouldn't be in the position, you know, unfortunate as it is, that they're in."

"What, kids who are living on the street to get away from abusive homes just need to get nice haircuts?" Ginnie's voice had gone up what seemed like a whole octave.

"Well, I know what it takes to make a mohawk stay up, and that is eggs," Winston said, trying to lighten things up. "Am I right, Dan? And I have serious doubts about the poverty of a kid who is using eggs in that fashion rather than scrambling them with some toast, or feeding them to their dogs. Plus, more often than not these kids run away from good homes, am I right, Dan? That's what we did—it's part of growing up, they'll come around."

Ginnie was fuming, and it gave her a powerful, attractive quality. She turned to Dan with her jaw hanging and her eyebrows scrunched, and at that moment Dan realized he'd come to this house with a strong, smart woman who held real opinions, opinions about issues he'd never really considered, if only because he hadn't before had anyone to discuss them with. Willing to agree with anything as long as it united him with Ginnie against these people, he smiled and shook his head in the same way she had, knowing his head was by then sweaty and shiny, but for some reason not particularly bothered.

They had more wine and things cooled down. Someone handed Dan the baby and they all stared as if it looked different now it was being held by someone new. The conversation trailed off and Dan passed the baby to Ginnie, who received it with unselfconscious ease.

"Another drink?" Winston called, ducking inside before

Dan could answer, the box now weightless on the table. Same as always, if Dan was drinking, Winston could too.

Dan's mind wandered to the night Marta told Winston she was pregnant. He and Dan were living in a house with five other guys, some of whom were in the band. Winston came down to Dan's room in the basement, drunk. His hands were restless and he spoke very softly. In a disturbingly short period he went from asking Dan how he might convince Marta to have an abortion to what Dan thought they should name it.

Now, looking at this house and everything assembled here—barbecue, playhouse, lawn mower—Dan marvelled at how so much could spring from a decision at the time so seemingly insignificant. He watched Jacob chase Buddy around the yard like a miniature Frankenstein and knew it could really have gone either way.

"Winston. The baby is tired," Marta said later as if that meant the whole world. As if it wasn't actually she who was tired. Winston strained to his feet, pounded the remains of his wine, regarded them like a cop giving an I'm-just-doing-my-job-here speech and said, "It's been fun."

———

"Hey, my brother gave me an extra ball-thrower thing as a gift, you want it?" Ginnie said on the way home.

Keeping up with Winston had left Dan drunker than he'd planned, and he throbbed with the sort of sleepy freedom he'd forgotten larger quantities of alcohol could afford. Really, he preferred throwing to Buddy unassisted—it was a better workout—

Subaltus

but he didn't want to be alone quite yet. He agreed to stop by her place to pick it up.

It turned out Ginnie lived in a building called La Sirenza, built directly across the street from Dan's the year before and obscuring about 30 degrees of his once dazzling 180-degree view of English Bay. Before it was built, Dan had checked out the La Sirenza website and considered buying a unit as an investment, but in the end he put it off and missed the deadline.

Her building had a Mediterranean theme—his was industrial, New York gothic, which he much preferred. The entrance led them beneath some pretty believable faux arches and porticoes into a lobby that gurgled with a white, marble fountain in the form of a spouting swan.

"Wait here," she said when they arrived at her door, and she rushed inside. Dan felt the alcohol accost his centre of gravity and Buddy's breathing echoed in the empty hallway. He worried she was going to just bring the thrower and say goodbye.

"All ready," she said, opening the door out of breath, beckoning him inside.

Her condo was on the seventeenth floor—Dan's was on the fifteenth—and standing at the window, he saw that it faced his own. He counted up to his little darkened square in the grid of glass and steel.

The layout of her place was a mirror image of his own, giving it a creepy familiarity. This similarity failed to extend to her kitchen, however, which featured granite counters, white oak cupboards, built-in wine racks and mosaic tile. She must have spent a fortune in upgrades.

"This is Jo's," she said, opening a door to a room strewn

with bones, balls and a battery of chew toys. Photos of Jo and Ginnie were tacked in random-seeming clusters, low enough for the dog to see them. "There *is* a bed in there, but she usually just sleeps with me."

They shut the dogs in Jo's room to play and sat on her couch drinking wine, Ginnie drawing deeper slurps now that she wasn't driving.

"So what's with this band?" she said. "Sounds exciting."

It wasn't. Winston had played guitar and Dan played drums, and they only ever opened for other bands, leagues angrier and better than themselves. An alternative weekly had once called them imitative and redundant, and Dan couldn't find it in himself to disagree. It was a time that Winston had passed sleeping with debatably conscious girls while Dan got blackout drunk trying to figure out whether he was being appropriately punk by doing whatever the fuck he wanted at that exact moment.

He didn't miss it and he told her so.

Ginnie said her brother was into punk music. "I bet he's heard of you."

"Hope that he hasn't," Dan said, right before they were suddenly kissing, her mouth pressed to his, her tongue wet and roving. She exhaled heavily through her nose. He found his arms around her and she radiated a surprising heat. It occurred to Dan he hadn't once thought about her lip since he became sure neither Winston nor Marta were judging her. The lip felt slightly tighter than her lower one, though not much. The urgency in her breathing led Dan to wonder how long it had been since she'd kissed anyone. A while, he figured. Her hand brushed his stomach and it flexed. He could feel rolls hanging over his belt and he sucked it in further. He was light-headed and realized he'd been holding his breath.

She pulled away, a string of spit briefly trapezing between them. "What's wrong? You seem . . ."—she chose the word carefully—"uneasy."

"No," he said, needing to convince her he was enjoying himself, or was just starting to. "I'm good here," he said, chuckling.

They kissed again. It was different. It felt like a re-enactment. She was tense, and it made him tense. He could feel her monitoring him. She wasn't moving her hands. She somehow knew her lip had once repulsed him. He started focusing his kisses on her lip to prove to her it wasn't disgusting. He licked it and gave it playful nibbles, his tongue flicking over its ridge. He let out a sigh to show her how pleased and relaxed he was by all of this.

Just as he was really getting back into it again, she pulled away a second time, as if it was so she could take a drink of wine. Then she went to the bathroom. When she came back she said she was tired. She smiled at a joke he made at the door but didn't exactly laugh. She passed him the ball thrower on his way out and said she'd see them in the park. Buddy and Dan walked home across the street.

4

It was an upper-body day, and the weights were kindling dull smoulderings in his chest and arms. He grunted pathetically as he pushed, without embarrassment because there was no one there except for Buddy.

It'd rained for a week, and although dogs weren't allowed in the fitness room, he'd decided to chance it. Buddy had sniffed the gym with the thoroughness of a bomb detector while Dan cycled through his routine. Leaving Buddy alone in the condo, even briefly, seemed too cruel at a time like this—with the days being so dismally grey and the dank bales of clothes and towels he'd let accumulate in every room.

Buddy was depressed. He slept most of the day. He'd been ignoring the kibble Dan rattled into his bowl, mustering only little bites of people-food every so often. They'd made it to the park only once the preceding week and found most of it flooded with six inches of murky water. The squeegee punks were its only patrons, smoking and shivering beneath a tree. As Dan hurled a sopping tennis ball that Buddy begrudgingly retrieved, he remembered what Ginnie had said about those kids, how sad it was that they were abandoned, or wanted to be abandoned. Even in the park Buddy quickly grew bored. When they were leaving, Dan noticed the kid with the green mohawk, which was now hanging down, eggless perhaps, the tips of the once proud spikes dripping rainwater. Dan wanted to tell the punks he'd opened for a couple of the bands sewn to their jackets, but he thought against it when he remembered how much pleasure he, as a punk, would have taken in telling a guy like him to fuck off. "For world domination," he said, pouring a handful of change into their cup. They didn't notice him enough to ignore him.

Dan switched to the treadmill and watched an educational program about witchcraft as he ran. "In Salem, witches were often identified by the presence of their familiars, animals like cats or owls who would perform the evil bidding of their master," it said. "Many women were burned based on the evidence of a familiar alone." Dan looked over to Buddy, who was regarding, suspiciously, his own reflection in the full-length mirror. "We're getting pretty familiar, aren't we, Bud?" he said, realizing he'd lately started conversing with the dog in a voice that was not his own. Then Dan amused himself with the thought of Buddy running on the treadmill. He briefly considered trying it, setting him up there and punching the button, but he decided against it. You had to have a big brain to get used to things like full-length mirrors and running without moving.

He brought a water bottle to his lips, suctioned a mouthful, then let it release with a gasping sound. The sensation sent his mind stumbling upon his night with Ginnie, now two weeks past, a night whose meaning he'd not yet examined even though he'd found himself mildly annoyed she hadn't called. The kiss felt like a liability, a leak of information. He wished it hadn't happened. Or that it had kept happening. Or perhaps something else entirely. In the end, he decided it was selfish of them to jeopardize Buddy and Jo's relationship like that.

"There are no dogs down here," a reedy-voiced security guard said from the entranceway. Dan recognized him, a boy who usually spent whole graveyard shifts scouring skateboard magazines behind the concierge desk.

"There's a dog right there," Dan said, gesturing smugly, his voice croaky from exertion.

"Okay, sir, there are no dogs *allowed* down here, it's against strata regulations. You know, health issue." He glanced around as if the room were potentially infested by dogs.

With only thirty seconds left, Dan dismounted the treadmill, scrubbed a towel over his face, set it about his shoulders.

"This just isn't what I'd expected," he said.

"Something wrong with the equipment, sir?"

"Do you ever see anyone down here?"

He thought for a moment. "Umm . . . no, not really. You?"

"This place, it hasn't really worked out for me. I figured it'd be different."

"I understand that, sir, but the dog has to go," he said with his neck set and his slender hands folded over his crotch, gripping a walkie-talkie.

"Come on, Buddy," Dan said.

Dan's condo was much too hot. He checked the oven on the outside chance he'd accidentally turned it on, never once having actually used it. He cracked some windows, cursing the fact there was no thermostat, and noticed the rain had stopped. The sky was an elephant hide stretched over the whole city.

Then the phone rang. Dan whacked his shin on the glass top of his coffee table while he ran for it, crumpling him to the carpet. Buddy came to him. He didn't lick Dan's face, but Dan was happy to note a certain attitude of concern.

After a deep breath he set the phone to his ear.

"Where've you been?" Winston said. Dan could hear Jacob yelping nonsense in the background. He took the cordless out on the balcony where the air was refreshingly cool and sat, testing the swelling that was conglomerating on his shin.

Dan attempted to recollect what he'd been doing the past few weeks and came up with a mental summary as formless and without value as a handful of gravel. What had he been doing? Sleeping? Trying to cheer up Buddy, was all he could say with certainty. He told Winston he'd been working on something.

Winston then asked what happened with Ginnie that night and Dan told him the story, omitting the kiss.

"I liked her," Winston said. "She stood up to Marta."

"Well, she seems to be standing up to me as well, which is surprising because all I ever wanted to be was her friend, so there's nothing to stand up to."

Winston exhaled into the phone. It sounded like wind. "C'mon, you liked her, I could see it, you were unleashing facial expressions I haven't seen in years."

"I do really love her dog, Jo. I really miss her."

"Her dog? That's why people get dogs, isn't it? To meet other *people* with dogs? Am I not right? Sort of like joining a club?"

"No, I wanted a companion."

"Come on."

"Buddy and I understand each other. I don't know what I'd do without him. People say dogs are loyal, but they really are *actually* loyal."

"Speaking of loyal, I saw on the radio this thing about how if someone dies in their home and nobody drops by or smells the stench, and that person has animals—like so many lonely shut-in types do, may I add—then it only takes three days, *three days*, until the pet, doesn't matter what kind, cat or dog, whatever, will actually *eat* their owner's body to stay alive. How's that loyalty for you?"

The thought of Buddy feasting upon his corpse filled Dan

with a curious pride. Buddy would do what he had to do to survive. This stood as another example of what non-dog-owners could never understand.

"I just don't want to see you miss out on an ideal opportunity is all," Winston said.

"You know what the saddest part about this whole Ginnie situation is? Who the biggest losers are?" Dan said, excited like an oilman who'd struck it rich with a geyser of the unsaid. "Jo and Buddy, that's who. Those dogs love each other. You can tell. Buddy hasn't been himself all week. He's having trouble eating. And how cruel and immature is it for someone to deny these two innocent dogs their only pleasure."

"You're aware of my theories on female friends, Dan. Nonexistent. Oxymoronic. And I don't want to tell you who the moron is in this situation. Believe me, there are plenty others out there, and to be honest, she wasn't exactly Best in Breed at Westminster, if you know what I mean."

After they hung up, Dan realized his eyes had been tracing the geometry of Ginnie's building in the same way he'd doodled whenever on the phone as a kid. The drawings he'd found he'd done were always more interesting than anything he managed with conscious effort.

Sheets of light had punctured the clouds and were refracting in the facets of her condo. The structure seemed more in the way now than it ever had. Like it was a spaceship recently touched down and the crew, disguised as humans, were wreaking immeasurable havoc on the city. There should be insurance for something like this, Dan thought. There ought to be a guarantee on something as important as a view.

He saw movement in her window and realized this would look really bad. Him out there, it looked creepy. Great, he thought, now he couldn't even use his balcony.

That night, Dan and Buddy watched the special features on one of his DVDs, then Dan fixed himself a cosmopolitan and grilled some salmon.

"You know what the truth is?" he said to Buddy, because he seemed like he wanted to hear it. "The truth is there's probably— no, very probably—someone out there in the city, maybe someone even living in this building, my building, who's just like Ginnie in every way. She may even be a nurse for all I know, maybe she even has the same messy car and all the same opinions on things, only she doesn't . . . you know, without the, the affliction Ginnie has." Buddy's smacking of the blackened salmon skin seemed to be an agreement.

Dan hand fed him some of the filet and scraped the rest into the dog's bowl. Better to give it to someone who'd enjoy it, and he was having trouble tasting because of the booze. After a while Dan ran out of Cointreau and cranberry juice, so he started drinking the vodka straight, calling them vodkapolitans to Buddy as a joke. It grew dark and he turned on the lights. Reflected images of his home leapt into the windows and he could no longer see Ginnie's building or anyone else's, and both Buddy and Dan liked it that way.

They played for what must have been hours with one of Buddy's favourite toys, a rope connected to a rubber ball. Buddy's jaws were strong enough for Dan to pick him up and swing him like an Olympic hammer-throw. They were doing exactly this when Buddy unlatched and went flailing across the living room, his body glancing an end table and sandwiching a lamp against the wall, breaking its ceramic base in two.

Buddy lay there, his husky breathing laced with whines, and he flinched at Dan's touch. It seemed so sad to Dan that Buddy could never grasp the concept of intent. "I'm so sorry, Buddy," he repeated over and over as he ground his face into the carpet, level with the dog, whose breath was hot and meaty, his gums slick black. Dan found himself weeping. The dog squeezed out one final whimper and began licking Dan's hand, then his face.

In the same instant, Dan realized both that he'd been lonely and that he wasn't anymore, like a person waking up after routine surgery and being told in the same breath that they'd found a tumour and that it had been successfully removed.

Late that night, the vodka long gone, Dan flicked the lights vigorously, making a giant strobe light of his place, *like a fucking disco in here*, he said before he lost consciousness on the couch.

_____

She called early the next day.

"Dan," she said, "I'm sorry to ask you this."

"It's okay," Dan said, "just say it." His hangover was just getting going and he felt benevolent.

"My brother"—Ginnie's voice veered toward a sob but she recovered—"he isn't well, and I need to go to Toronto for a week to drive him to appointments. I need you to dog sit."

Dan told her he was sorry to hear that. "Have you known for a while?" he asked, with a selfish desire to be sure this was what had kept her from calling.

"I just found out. Look, Dan, I don't know who else to ask. You're so good with her. And Buddy is too. I would take her to a kennel, but you know how those places are."

"You could take her to a dog spa?" he said, wanting to stretch this moment out as long as possible, her needing something and him about to provide it.

She laughed, sniffed. "Yeah, not likely."

He met Ginnie and Jo in the lobby of his building. There was a flurry of phone numbers and intricate instructions for Jo's feeding and general care. Ginnie's hair was up but she'd left pieces to hang like spider legs at her temples. Ginnie was someone who still believed in dressing up to fly and he couldn't help but find this charming. Her voice was strong with tragedy and necessity.

"I think I might have made some kind of mistake . . . ," he said at the last possible minute, the beginning of a speech he hadn't known he'd been preparing.

She looked relieved. "Dan, I agree, it was a mistake, and I got weird the other night. Can we just be friends again and act like it never happened? Sort of block it out? I've thought about it and that's what I want. I just think it's really important for the dogs to stay friends."

"That's basically what I was thinking," he replied.

She kissed his cheek and they hugged and she got in a cab.

"Look who's here," Dan said, and Buddy leapt almost as high as the fridge.

He took the reunited friends to the park, ran them for hours and later grilled the last of the salmon, which was now officially Buddy's favourite. Buddy had more energy than Dan had seen in weeks, and as for himself, Dan found that another animal in the house simply doubled the amount of joy.

His life felt full, he thought that night in bed, populated. This business with Ginnie had convinced him once again of the irrationality of others. How awful it was that Buddy was the one who'd had to endure the worst of it. Dan decided then that he would get another dog, as a companion for Buddy. This way Buddy could never again have his best friend taken from him on a whim, and Dan could watch the dogs grow together. He knew another Andalucian would look a little obsessive, but he didn't care. The 'Lucian was the finest breed he'd ever known. He settled on emailing Sandy and Ihor the next day.

In the morning he woke to an odd, two-tone sound, like a faint police siren with inadequate power. He padded to his living room and discovered that the sound originated from a furry heap. It was Jo and Buddy. They were next to the couch, by his DVD rack, fucking. Buddy had mounted her, with something that resembled lipstick passing between them.

He wondered if he should stop them but did nothing. He watched. It wasn't a bestiality thing, nothing like that, he wasn't close to aroused, it was something else—a kind of vicarious admiration he'd seen on Winston's face that day in his backyard when he watched Jacob hit a ball with a green plastic bat. Buddy perked up and regarded Dan with a sort of smile, mostly on account of his mouth being just shaped that way, but Dan knew there was real joy there, the little guy probably felt like he was back in Spain, releasing some tension after a long day of vigilant herding. Dan wondered how he would explain things to Ginnie if Jo became pregnant. But even if Buddy wasn't fixed, he believed Jo almost definitely was, so he put it out of his mind. Dan watched as Buddy, in a workmanlike way, devoid of all the absurd facial expressions and ridiculous moanings of humans, pushed Jo around in a little circle.

"Enjoy it," Dan said, returning to his bedroom to let them alone, shutting the door as gently as he was able.

King Me

As he ate his lunch, Saul watched the stout Assassin feed Georgina—a stunted, moaning woman to whom God had accidentally issued a mollusk instead of a brain—guiding a plastic spoon of wobbling pudding into her mouth, with a little flick over her lower lip to catch what didn't make it in. The Assassin was a short, rotund Latino, and his presence rang Saul with alarm as he pulped the crusts of his tuna melt.

Saul had recognized the Assassin because he was a self-taught detective, which meant he knew what to look for. He'd seen men like this night after night on the news: inflamed guerrillas and private militiamen, nationless killers and hooded butchers, all either shooting into the air or wailing mournfully, draped across the body of a fallen brother. Saul shifted a table closer and his suspicions were strengthened by a deep scar that tunnelled the length of the Assassin's left cheek, the shape of a minnow, clean enough to be the work of a scalpel. A box-cutter duel in the steaming slums of Nicaragua, Saul suspected. Or perhaps he'd been a child soldier, his soul now turned mercenary and septic with hatred. All seemed equally possible.

He saw the man unlace Georgina's bib and lift it from her limp neck. Had he come for her? But Georgina couldn't even speak—not entirely true, she knew two words: one that sounded like *bah*, which meant "bad," "hungry," "bathroom" and "angry," and the other *roob*, which was used for every other linguistic purpose. Saul's thoughts were interrupted when suddenly she gurgled and whacked her plastic bowl from the table with a sharp pink elbow, slopping ivory pudding on the right tire of her wheelchair while she brayed with delight. The Assassin went scrambling for a mop, desperate not to publicize his incompetence on his first day.

Saul decided to launch an investigation. In the smoking room, he found Drew, who was relishing his 1:15 after-lunch smoke. At Riverview, all aspects of existence were subject to a schedule, an iron framework of meds, meals, sleep, bathing and activities over which the staff attempted to stretch the battered material of their ruined beings like the fabric of a tent. Staff controlled the smokes because patients like Drew would torch an entire carton in a day if given the chance. Not that he ever had.

"Who's the new staff? And what does he want with Georgina?" Saul said.

"You mean the Latino guy wire tap water wings?" Drew said, blurting the words as a prefabricated unit. Drew's mind had been shredded by wagonloads of methamphetamines and radio waves sent especially to him by his great-uncle's ham radio. At some point he'd correlated the entire inventory of his brain into a useless fizzling web. Saul didn't care to fraternize with Drew—

one got tired panning everything he said for nuggets of sense—
but he often divined things that others couldn't.

"Yes, the Latino guy."

Drew shrugged and exhaled a globe of smoke. "Not sure
footed the bill Cosby kids are all right now." Then he scoured his
face vigorously with his palm as if it were a blackboard and he
couldn't stand what was written there.

"He's new," said Kim later at the craft table, unfurling a battal-
ion of paper angels she'd spent the last five minutes cutting, working her jaw unconsciously in time with her pink safety scissors.

"I'm aware of his newness," Saul said, careful to control
the annoyance he found scurrying in his voice, a displeasure that
had in the past sent Kim wheeling into another of her depressive
cycles. "But *why* is he here?"

"Oh, I dunno, the same as the rest of them, I guess . . . to
help?" Kim set the scissors back in the craft box. "Here, I'll call
him over . . . Luis!"

"No that's—" Saul said, too late.

The Assassin hurried over from his organization of the
board-game cupboard, his hands stashed behind his back. Saul
panicked and looked to the reflective glass of the nurses' station
for anything weapon-like in the Assassin's grip.

"What's up, guys?" Luis said in the simultaneously droning
and cheerful way that Saul figured they must spend small fortunes
on training these people to employ, and then to Kim, "Oh, I like
your angels," and then to Saul, "Are you helping Kim with her
angels? That's nice of you."

"No," Saul said, reeling from the Assassin's attempted butchery
of his self-respect. "We are—no, pardon me, *were*—conversing."

Luis's good nature was unflagging. "Okay, well, looks like fish burgers tonight, and maybe I'll ask the duty nurse if we could watch some tube after dinner? You're a real TV buff, aren't you, Saul?"

Saul displayed the type of facial friendliness that was used as a currency on the ward, just to be rid of him. He watched Luis return to the board games and clumsily topple a whole stack to the floor. As Luis pressed his cheek to the tile in search of scattered game pieces, Saul realized his heart was galloping on the narrow plain of his chest. He'd been rattled by the Assassin's knowledge of his TV habits. How could he have known this? Had he been studying him? Gathering intelligence? For what purpose? It seemed so absurd. No one on the outside even knows I'm here, he thought. Well, his parents, and one other person, an unmentionable woman whom he'd long ago scoured from his memory. Then came the dull thud of Luis's head against the underside of the games table. The Assassin groaned, slowly, like he'd just heard crushing news. If someone really does want me dead, Saul thought, why send this amateur? A man so evidently a card-carrying fool? He's no more an assassin than any other of the psych nurses, Saul concluded, then passed the remains of the afternoon on a puzzle that depicted a windblown Spanish castle dangling gloriously over a turbulent sea.

The next day, just to be sure, Saul requested a meeting with Dr. Darko Kraepevic, his personal psychiatrist of the past thirty-six years. Kraepevic was a fine man and brilliant doctor whom Saul admired deeply. A hawkish Slovak with a sharp goatee and cloudlike puffs of white hair that encircled an expanse of flawless, gleaming scalp. A man who, as if to manually punctuate his sentences, liked to double-click the gold pen that, as he'd once confided to Saul, his daughter had bought him for his fiftieth birthday.

Saul shut the door.

"What's this issue, Saul? You seem troubled," Kraepevic said. The leather of his chair bleated and the doctor interlocked his fingers.

"It's this Luis. Who sent him? I mean, where is he from? What are his credentials?"

"You are well aware, Saul, that I'm not about to discuss the personal histories of new employees," Kraepevic said, no doubt quoting verbatim from a policy manual.

"Just curious, " Saul said. "I feel like I've seen him before." He slackened his face and feigned nonchalance.

"Impossible. Luis is new to us here at Riverview. Look, we don't want to have you getting overly interested in a staff member again, Saul. You've been doing so well since the Janet situation. All settled." Kraepevic was referring to a former psych nurse who'd made inappropriate advances toward Saul, and against whom Saul had lodged a formal complaint. Rather than face disgrace, she'd relocated to another province, after which Saul had spent a week in the Quiet Room collecting himself and mitigating the stress of the whole ordeal.

Kraepevic could see Saul's doubts still working away in his face.

"Without divulging specific information, let me assure you Luis has not been sent by anyone, and is qualified in every possible way for this position. He's taking Margo's shift while she's on mat

leave, and, like Margo, his job is to assist the psychosocial rehabilitation of you and the other patients here. Must I remind you,
Saul, there *are* other patients here?" he said, clicking his pen. "And
speaking of you, how are you doing? Because you seem a touch
pale. Sleeping? Any intrusive thoughts? How's the medication?"

Though Saul respected Kraepevic immensely, he sometimes
pictured him as a skittish islander with a bone-skewered septum,
scampering up a volcano in full ceremonial regalia with a small
payload of psychotropic medication the doctor and the other vil-
lagers had prepared in large steaming cauldrons, which Kraepevic
then shovelled into the great smoking orifice to sate the bloodlust
of an angry volcano god.

"All thoughts are intrusive, Darko," Saul said, rising from
his chair. Dr. Kraepevic, he realized, might have had more to do
with Luis's appearance than he'd suspected.

Attention: Martin Shenck
Minister of Mental Health
Province of British Columbia

Dear Sir,

Saul Columbo here and as you know and are aware Ive been
residing in the care of Riverview Hospital for most of my
long life because of my mental state being unfit determined
by my personal psychiatrist Dr. Darko Kraepevic. I do not
disagree with this please ignore any letters Ive made before

now that says anything else. May I state for the record in light of my dangerous past actions I feel happy and safe to live in the care of Riverview Hospital and please keep funding such activities as bingo, video rentals, pizza night, crafts, etc, thank you.

*But this is part two of my letter. I wish to tell and inform you that through my detective skills and from my own observations Ive detected an individual or a person who is almost definitely an <u>Assassin</u> sent here (it is not as of writing this letter to you sir clear by who) possibly and probably with the help of my personal psychiatrist Dr. Darko Kraepevic who has infiltrated my mind and my hospital of residence and who I suspect means as well as intends to cause me **harm** possibly of the grievous bodily type or also more in my mind which is as you know sir much more difficult to know is happening. Also he might be shocking me while I sleep.*

This is a situation I want you to investigate with EVERY POSSIBLE AGENT through the right channels of course. I ask you sir to have this be kept in strict confidence. There is no one else for me who I can trust.

Your Humbled Informant,

Saul Columbo, Compliant and Concerned Patient/Detective, Riverview Hospital, BC

Saul pitched a bolus of house laundry into the dryer, pressed Start, then filled the mop bucket and rolled it sloshing into the Dayroom to perform his next chore. Apart from TV and bingo, chores were his favourite pastime. They ignited in him a faint yet pleasurable feeling of competence that made his thoughts fall quiet as clouds. Chores also earned him the snatches of freedom called two-hour passes, which he spent walking the oak-strewn hospital grounds.

Sending the letter to Martin Shenck had put the Luis affair out of his hands and Saul had officially closed his investigation. Though Saul disliked going over Kraepevic's head, even if the doctor was in on it, once Martin Shenck intervened and Luis was exposed and all was returned to normal, Kraepevic would offer an apology, which Saul would generously accept.

After a few swipes under the couch that yielded a dusty domino and a bendy straw, Saul saw he'd neglected to add soap to the water. The laundry-room door had locked automatically and only staff could open it. He knuckle-rapped at the nurses' station window and mouthed *laundry room* to the duty nurse, Roberta, who sat with a cellphone clamped between cheek and shoulder. She put a hand over the phone and called out.

The Assassin emerged like a lion from the medication room. Saul hadn't seen him in days and was suddenly concerned he'd somehow intercepted the letter. Luis stepped into the hall, his freshly cut keys sparkly in his hands.

"I'll let you in, Saul, no problem," he said.

"I'd rather Roberta did," Saul said, knocking at the window again. Roberta didn't stir.

The Assassin's eyebrows vaulted. He shook his head and expelled a short burst through his nose. "Okay," he said and re-entered the nurses' station. While he spoke with Roberta, Saul noticed all the binders labelled with patient names and file numbers crammed together on a high shelf. His eyes landed on the binder bearing his own name and he saw that it was much thicker than the others. Saul took comfort in the knowledge that his file was mostly well-crafted cover stories he'd been feeding them for years. Even so, he detested the idea of Luis's unlimited access to any of it.

"Well, Saul, Roberta's busy at the moment," the Assassin said when he returned. "Looks like it's you and me."

Saul trailed the Assassin by a good four paces, listening to his brand-new nurse shoes grunt on the linoleum in the wide, echoic hallway. The sound brought to mind Georgina's repulsive habit of scratching her throat with the base of her tongue. Like a tree trunk come to life, Luis was at least a foot shorter than Saul, who was a gangly six-two, and moved with the wobbly power of an upright bear. Saul would have to use his reach advantage; the Assassin would crush him like a lamb if it ever came to grappling. Saul doused his fear with an image of Martin Shenck keying in a background check at that very moment, turning up all those poor souls Luis had tossed from the doors of unmarked helicopters.

The Assassin stopped at the door. There was more jingling as he sought the correct key. Saul feared he was stalling.

"There you go," he said, jamming the door open with his left foot.

"After you," Saul said.

"I've got to go get the medications ready," he said, unflinching.

There was no choice. Saul took a few steps. The Assassin did not move. Saul took a few more, shuffling his way through the doorway, his hands guarding his face, keeping perpendicular to the Assassin, just as he'd seen in the martial arts programs. But Saul did not want to fight; he'd always hated when the nurses had touched him in the past, forced him to do things, their unbreakable wills and their questions, their hundreds of latexed hands.

"Sore back?" Luis said as Saul passed safely into the room.

"I don't want trouble," Saul said.

"Yeah, I heard they cut aerobics. Too bad. Could have used it myself," he said, cupping his barrel of a belly.

"You don't get a face scar like that doing burpees," Saul said.

The Assassin chuckled, then grinned, his large white teeth like an open suitcase of money, as he traced the minnow with his thumbnail. "This? This is just something that happened to me when I was young. It's nothing." Then he let the door go and it hissed on its pneumatic hinge.

———————

Later, in the Dayroom, its floor luminous from the mopping job he'd done, Saul glanced up from a checkers game with Kim to watch the Assassin through the glass of the nurses' station. Roberta was teaching him to punch pills from blister packs into paper cups with initials markered on them. Luis worked, squinting like a watchmaker, wary of a mix-up, which in fact happened frequently and was no great cause for concern. Saul had once got Darryl's anti-seizure meds and his body went rigid for six hours until they stuck him with muscle relaxants and he'd melted into his bed.

"King me," Kim said.

Saul counted Kim as his only friend, a manic-depressive and a shrewd and brutal checkers tactician, especially so when she was depressed. Saul clacked one of her captured checkers atop the valiant soldier who'd survived a brave advance to the underworld of his deepest rank. Why this checker? Saul wondered absently. What's so special about it? He sat for a moment admiring its stacked, regal magnificence, even though it was about to be commanded by Kim to cut a swath of vengeful, bidirectional wrath through his already dwindling forces.

"Med time, folks," said a nurse named Parvinder as she cranked open the gate on the drive-through-style window where they dispensed pills four times a day. The patients assembled and Saul ended up with Drew ahead of him in line. Luis was behind the counter, and Saul felt his eyes narrow. He still couldn't grasp why Luis hadn't choked him to death in the laundry room.

"Here you go, Andrew," Luis said, sliding a cup across the counter.

"These pills have eyes of the tiger shark," Drew said. His cup brimmed with pills, a little buffet of shapes and colours. It took four swallows to get them all down and Luis had to refill his water twice. Saul pondered the pharmacological rodeo taking place in Drew's gut: Zyprexa, Carbamazepine, Clozapine, Seroquel, Effexor, all of which he himself had been given at one time or another, their names like alien cities, pregnant with syllables as unusual as the minds they were invented to reconfigure. Saul knew Drew was too far afield for a return journey, but as Drew tottered off for the smoke he received only after he took his pills, Saul pitied him for an instant. How horrible they couldn't fit it all into one capsule.

"You did a great job mopping, Saul. I'd eat off that floor, no kidding," the Assassin said, grinning as he pushed a cup of pills, one blue (what Kraepevic bluntly called an antipsychotic) and one orange (to inhibit the side effects of the other) toward him.

"Has the mail arrived yet?" Saul said, attempting to drain any eagerness from his voice. He should be hearing any day from Martin Shenck.

"No, sorry—I mean, yes. It came, but there was nothing for you—Oh, wait . . ." he said, reaching below the counter. He plunked one more large, urine-tinged pill into the cup. "I forgot to put this in, a multivitamin. Dr. Kraepevic ordered it, said you were looking a little pale."

Who knew what was fear and what was excitement in the sensation that gripped Saul at that moment. How silly it was to think the Assassin would risk hand-to-hand combat in the laundry room. This was no amateur; he was sophisticated, clandestine. Saul had often thought the perfect murder would be to poison someone slowly. A crime without a witness. Because watching the victim die was like attempting to see the hour hand move; people simply lacked that kind of attention span. This new yellow pill was no doubt laced with something vile and unnameable, and probably invisible to lab analysis. Even if Martin Shenck and his investigators arrived in time, they'd test the pill, find nothing and side with the Assassin and his extensive credentials spoken of so highly by Kraepevic in his office.

"Who signs your paycheque, Assassin?" Saul said, grasping the cup of pills in one hand, water in the other.

"Same as everyone else, Saul, the Ministry of Health," he said, crinkling the dark pelts of his eyebrows.

"And it's good money? I mean for what you do to people? It's worth it?"

"Hurry the fuck up," said a voice from somewhere in the line.

"I like this job," said the Assassin.

Saul tipped the dose of pills into his mouth, the new pill large and bitter on his tongue. He splashed them with water, swallowed.

The Assassin leaned toward him, his hefty forearms on the counter. "Saul, the doc said you were having some trouble adjusting to some of the newer staff, so I just wanted to let you know, if there's anything I can do to make things go easier for you—you know, adjustment-wise—just talk to me any time. Sound good?"

Saul nodded. He'd already manoeuvred the three pills under his tongue, a technique he'd mastered during that whole debacle with the sexually inappropriate nurse Janet, when he'd needed his mind unmuddled to successfully parry her advances.

"Okay, Saul?" Luis said again, his eyes wide with feigned empathy.

"Yup. Ochay," Saul said.

"Great," the Assassin said, visibly relieved.

Saul was relieved as well. Although fear was twisting his stomach like a balloon animal, it thrilled him to have detected such a diabolical plot. And at least he could spend the final days of his pitiful life clear-headed enough to muster some resistance, however futile it might be.

Saul took the empty water cup and plopped it into the other one that had held his pills, pushing the little stack of paper cups back to Luis.

"King me," he said, and walked casually to the washroom, where he spat the already melting and bitter slurry into the toilet.

———————

Other than twenty-four-hour news, Saul's favourite TV program was the detective show *Columbo*. This dishevelled, lazy-eyed dwarf, who acted the imbecile in order to lull criminals into a false sense of security only to spring his trap on them at precisely the most opportune moment, owned acres of Saul's heart. In today's episode was a blond woman whose father was murdered with a seven iron. This woman spoke words that Saul could not help but find personally relevant. "Sal, can't we just let the detective do his job?" And then, "Sal, we have to move on with our lives, my father wouldn't want us to act like this." Saul could tell that her words held something prophetic inside them, but to what purpose he couldn't decode.

It had been three weeks since he'd commenced medicating the sewer system and his brain was crackling with sharpness as the chemical fog burned off him. This morning, upon waking, he'd felt a sensation like a subtle tearing away behind his eyes, then sensed a spotlight flicking on, its beam falling somewhere at the base of his skull. Today he'd completed the Spanish castle puzzle, plowed through a crossword, and his normally forgotten childhood was returning to him in vivid, painful chunks.

"Do you think I need to move on?" he asked Tina as *Columbo*'s credits scrolled at an unreadable pace.

"Move on where?" she said.

Tina was a Voluntary, meaning she chose to be there. The story was, her parents brought her the day of her eighteenth birthday and made her promise to always sign the voluntary admission forms each year when they expired. People said they toured the continent relentlessly with one of the largest RVs allowable on the road.

Saul got up and flipped to the twenty-four-hour news station—no remote, because Georgina had dunked it in sugar-free Kool-Aid—to see what skirmishes men like the Assassin were concocting in the world's hot spots. Some hungry-looking boys had firebombed an armoured vehicle, incinerating a diplomat; vengeful machete-wielding militants had seized a town, killing all but those they wished to rape. As if the images weren't enough, words traversed the bottom of the screen like a freight train loaded with sadness. "What the people of this country need right now, Chris, is leadership," a reporter said, and Saul found that he couldn't agree more.

"But from where?" Saul said, possibly out loud.

"I hate news. Let's watch my movie," Tina said, the worn VHS tape clutched in her hands, still purple with lunch's dessert gelatin. The tape had been re-dubbed at least ten times, thus accumulating a permanent drizzle of static. Tina would pass every minute of her life viewing it if she could. To her, its joys were boundless. Staff would limit her viewings if she hoarded porridge in her room or cackled at something inappropriate, like the dropping of a plastic cup.

Saul sat watching Tina watch her movie while she picked obliviously between her legs with a long thumbnail. Back when there was funding, a volunteer group took Tina and some other patients—Saul was in the Quiet Room at the time—to ride on a miniature train that looped around a great treed park. The staff member who'd brought the video camera had no idea he was shooting a movie that would be viewed more times than *Jaws*, except by one person many times rather than by many people just once. In the movie, Tina rode up front of the train with the handsome conductor. The train pulled into the station to a recorded whistle sound, Tina clapping giddily as she hung from his arm, her sweatpants yanked up high near her armpits and a yellow sun visor pulled down uncomfortably over her hair like someone else had put it on her.

But this time something about the video was different: the sunlight had a greenish tinge and the train moved with a snarling lurch. Then Saul observed a man on the train, sitting alone, five cars back from Tina, in dark sunglasses and a hat like a reporter from the fifties. As Tina stepped from the train and the social worker said, "How was it, Tina?" and Tina said, "I've been riding the train, one . . . two . . . three . . . four . . . five! Five times!" counting the rides on her fingers for the camera, while real-time Tina counted on the same fingers as she leaned into the screen, the man dismounted the train and left the camera's view, moving with the very same waddling gait Saul had noted in Luis.

How had he failed to see this before? No wonder Luis was familiar—he'd been watching Saul for years, perhaps through this screen somehow, gathering information, biding his time, and now Saul possessed proof that even Martin Shenck couldn't deny.

The video concluded and Saul punched Rewind. This was how Columbo did it, his obsession with the case's even-most-insignificant details always paid off in the end.

"You like watching my movie too, don't you, Saul?" Tina said.

"Shhhh, I think he can see us now," Saul said, just as Jacob stalked into the room.

Jacob couldn't have been more than twenty, huge and meaty, ruddy like a farmboy. Saul felt himself squint from his cologne.

"Time's up," Jacob said. "I'm checking the weather channel," which was on 68 and the news was on 3, so Jacob started clicking the channel button with a frantic, masturbatory intensity. Every second Wednesday, Jacob's father picked him up and took him on an outing, which involved Jacob pressuring his father into a trip to the mall to buy CDs. He was one of the only family who came and visited any patient regularly.

Tina yelped. "We were, we were watching me! In my movie!"

"I'm sure the mall will be good, weather-wise," Saul said.

"Yo eat a fat dick, Saul."

"Jacob," Roberta said from the door, and Jacob stood, shrugging, ready to receive what passed for a reprimand on the ward. "Your father is here."

"Dope!" Jacob said, as a short, silver-haired man came in, a mesh cap wadded in his hands. His neck hung meekly, his shoulders hunched toward his large ears.

"Hello, Jacob," he said, timidly, and Saul realized he could see into the father's mind. Jacob was an explosive device that could be triggered by ill-chosen words. Saul's own parents were both elementary teachers, and for the first few years they'd come twice a month with second-hand paperback books, mostly spy thrillers and detective stories. Saul had a younger brother, Isaac, who his parents said had died logging up north. Over the years, their visits dwindled, and now all he got was a Christmas card with their three names, including his brother's, all signed in his mother's shaky hand.

"Hello, Doctor Jacob's Father," Tina said. Tina had been there so long—the only one longer than Saul—she addressed anyone from the outside as *Doctor*.

"Dad, here's what we're gonna do," Jacob said, rising to approach his father. "Since it's my birthday we can go get cappuccinos at the mall, then like sit and talk about feelings and shit, like how I'm doing mentally etcetera."

"Jacob, have you forgotten?" his father said sheepishly. "Your birthday isn't for four months."

"So?" Jacob said, lifting his monstrous white T-shirt to scratch at his back. His trousers were slung below his rear end, vibrantly printed boxer shorts pouting over his belt, skewing his body's proportions toward those of a toddler.

"Mr. Drubinski, I'm not sure you are aware," the nurse softly interjected. "We offer only decaffeinated coffee here on the ward, and I would say providing caffeine off the ward would be an unhealthy practice." She cupped her mouth, "Much more difficult to deal with when they get back."

"You stay out of this," Jacob sneered at her, and he placed a large hand on the shoulder of his father's coat. "Let's do this, Dad."

"Well," Mr. Drubinski fumbled, reinvesting his weight in his other leg, "I suppose we should do what the nurse says, Jake—"

"What the fuck, Dad?" his son bellowed. "What happened to my birthday being *mine*? Do you know all day I'm stuck in this bugged-out place with all these kooks?" he said, gesturing to Saul and Tina on the couch. Saul squinted and gave his best closed-mouthed smirk, just like Columbo. The nurse's hand drifted to the object dangling from her belt like a little plastic bat. Jacob saw this too. "So what are you going to do? Push your button? This place is so fucked! We have to go *now* if we're gonna get back in time for bingo!" Saul saw lithe waves of rage scribble across Jacob's face and told everyone to be quiet. But they did not react. Then he recognized that he hadn't said anything—he'd just thought it with an intensity that approached speech. At this he chuckled into his collar.

"Today probably isn't the best day, Jake," Mr. Drubinski said, examining his shoes. "Like you said, bingo is tonight—" and at this Jacob palmed the face of his father and drove it through the doorway, sending him limply screeching over the sheen of the hallway linoleum like a floor polisher.

"I want a real coffee," Jacob said, squeezing in between Saul and Tina, to the gentle clicking of the nurse working away at her button. Jacob's shoulder was balmy and Saul felt him breathing in quickly and out slowly. Within seconds, the Assassin appeared at the door. He was winded and seemed dazed, less menacing. Saul wondered if he'd seen it all happen through the television.

The Assassin asked Roberta if she was all right and she began briefing him on the situation. More staff came. They encircled the couch.

"Jacob, we're going to need you to go to the Quiet Room for a while so you can gather yourself," said a large male nurse from another ward whose name was Pierre.

"I'm calm. What's on TV, Tina? Let's put your movie back on," Jacob said, crossing his arms, plunging his hands in his armpits.

Pierre asked Tina and Saul to go to their rooms. Saul passed the Assassin on the way out. "Shouldn't you be riding a miniature train somewhere, you wretched bastard?" Saul said, and noted a quiver of recognition in Luis's cheek, deep beneath the scar. A tense second passed before the Assassin collected himself and thanked Saul for cooperating.

In the hallway, Jacob's father clutched the arm of a nurse, who led him to the elevator as sounds of a scuffle issued from the TV Room. Then into the hall came a large, white, wriggling caterpillar with Jacob's reddened face poking from one end. They dragged him like this toward the open Quiet Room door. The intercom said the TV Room was closed for the day. Saul would have to wait to get Tina's tape so he could mail it to Martin Shenck.

———————

The incident left the ward in unsteady stillness, and the patients retreated to their rooms to escape it. Saul could hear Jacob's bellowings all the way from the Quiet Room, the sound drawing strength from the dead air and landing furious in his head like crows shut in a closet. To drown it he pressed his face into his pillow and opened his eyes to a great void humming beneath him.

Some time later he glanced at his clock and saw that it was still two hours to dinner. He decided to use up his last pass for the week. He scrawled *Saul Columbo* in the sign-out book and rode the elevator down.

After his trial, when he was first admitted, Saul had attempted a handful of escapes—curiously, the doors to the outside were the only ones that weren't locked—but soon stopped trying, because the police picked him up each time within a few hours. "How did you find me?" he'd asked. They only shrugged. Their lack of enthusiasm was dispiriting. Upon his return, the staff made him apologize and agree what a mistake it'd been to leave. This seemed to Saul now the most hateful form of captivity.

The outside air was crisp. He walked an asphalt path away from the ward and entered a grove of bunioned spreading elms that lay between the buildings of Centre Lawn and West Lawn. A hundred grey birds watched knowingly from the branches. Saul could feel how each of his muscles fit together, like those Chinese temples built without nails. On the way, he halted at his favourite bench and beheld the river, a murky snake that wandered all the way to Vancouver and the ocean. Riverview Hospital sat on land that was, in Saul's youth, the middle of nowhere: a comfortable distance for a nuthouse. But from this bench Saul had watched the city break over the hospital, mazes of houses coiling up the river's banks all the way to the seam of the horizon. Years back, they'd closed both East Lawn and West Lawn and shipped those patients someplace else. Luckily, Saul was allowed to stay, because they'd concluded he posed a threat to the community. "What community exactly are you referring to?" he'd said to Dr. K. in his office when he told him the good news. "Well, Saul, the world," Kraepevic said, clicking. This was the period when they'd overhauled all the words: patients became clients, the Isolation Room became the Quiet Room, and the whole world became a community.

Saul continued on the path and met a few abandoned utility buildings. Kraepevic, in one of his impromptu dissertations, had once told him that when Riverview was founded it had included a farm, and the patients worked on the land as part of their rehabilitation. Some of these buildings were obviously part of the farm and others were for purposes he couldn't guess at. Now, word was that the hospital made a little money on the side allowing crews to shoot movies and TV shows in the closed wards where all those people were once held. Even some of the same programs Saul watched religiously in the TV Room.

He left the path and ventured around back of West Lawn, buffing his palm along its stone wall. The grey masonry of the hospital was castle-like. Why build a nuthouse of such sturdy material? Saul wondered. What siege was to be defended against?

Near the loading dock, Saul noticed a wooden door, one he'd never seen before, about five feet high and faded, so it blended in with the colour of the stone. Saul gripped the doorknob and the door squawked against his shoulder, swinging into a dark corridor. He had tried thousands of doors of the many buildings at Riverview and they'd all been locked. He couldn't help wonder why this door had opened for him now, on this day. He thought to fetch Kim to see if it would yield in the same way to her, then decided against it. He couldn't stand to endanger her.

He floated through a dingy hallway that terminated at a narrow concrete staircase reaching up. Could it be a trap? He held his breath to listen for the Assassin and heard only the distant sound of a TV, or perhaps a radio. He ascended five flights to the foot of a long institutional hallway, identical to his own ward except that the paint, the colour of a browning avocado, was flaking. He saw a bundle of thick cables on the floor and decided to let them lead him. He walked to where they ran under a door that was painted to look like wood, fitted with a brass knocker and the number 235 in brass numerals. The number felt compellingly lucky to him and he pushed open the door, also miraculously unlocked.

The room was furnished with a large-screen TV, expensive hi-fi stereo, leather couch, even art on the walls, all of it bathed by light from an arched window. He saw that the cables ran to movie lights at the edges of the room. The place was instantly familiar to him, maybe from the innumerable hours he'd spent in apartments like this on the TV shows he'd seen over the years, much like Luis had been familiar when Saul first watched him feed Georgina. This is a set, Saul said out loud.

As he inspected the place, the thoughts began to form. They began as an idea, an emulsion of insights laid over his vision. Then these thoughts birthed other thoughts, and those new thoughts came with sounds hidden in their pockets. They assembled in the city of his head like a murmuring crowd awaiting some great event. They conversed and argued, issued decrees from behind his ears. They were both everyone he had and hadn't ever known. They came together like starlings massing densely in a flock, if only for a second, and in this way they became impossible to ignore. So it was, there in the familiar comfort of the fake apartment, that Saul's voices instructed him to leave the hospital, move here and begin a new life.

Then he was in the bedroom, picturing his only jacket hung in the closet and his full colour spectrum of sweatsuits jammed into the drawers. In the kitchen he imagined the fridge laden with food, food he'd brought home on the bus from the grocery store. He saw his favourite blanket folded over the couch, where he would hole up and watch *Columbo* all day without people fighting and playing their depressing tapes whenever they pleased. In the bathroom he saw his toothbrush in a cup beside the sink.

Saul removed his clothes and donned the white terry-cloth bathrobe he found hanging behind the bathroom door. He felt fresh and sophisticated, regal almost, as he beheld the apartment's sweeping view of the river, a vista unmarred by bars or wire mesh.

Up this high, he could see so much more than he ever had from his bench.

The rustling of voices implored him then to sit on the blue lounge chair, and he did. He fell into the chair feeling free and competent, much like he did when he performed his chores, but the warmth of that sensation now twenty times greater. He immediately saw the hole in his plan: Kraepevic would never let him leave because he still believed Saul was unfit for the community. I'm not dangerous, Saul said, not anymore. At this notion something stood up inside him, a memory emerging in his mind like the sun from an eclipse: essential, beautiful and blinding to behold. A woman. He'd passed her twice each weekday that whole year he'd walked to and from work as a stockboy at Reno's grocery store. Fearful of the sound of his own voice, he'd never dared speak to her, but each time he passed he sensed her reaching out for him in methods beyond words. She described her moods with the clothes she wore. She drew him diagrams on the sidewalk with her flashing eyes. Strung in her hair he found codes that could only be unravelled with the other codes written on her lily-white skin. Each day this simultaneous beckoning and rebuffing tormented and inflamed him. Each night in the bath, he'd practise holding his breath and find her voice swimming in the dull water. He'd find it in the hissing spaces between radio stations as he lay sleepless. Even now, with his brain crackling and encyclopedic, he could not remember what she said in these messages. Braids of riddles and baroque details, challenges and dares, but the thrust of them was her desire to have her life derailed, disrupted. She was unhappy, her days were a brutal chore. She said she could never speak this out loud, had never told this to anyone.

Sitting there in his robe in his blue chair, he watched himself passing with her out front of a radio shop. He watched her draw breath as if before a dive, her eyes, green and bulbous as an owl's, set beneath a silk kerchief tied over hair glossy black as videotape. Beige leather gloves gripped tighter the handles of a vinyl handbag the hue of a poisonous frog. Then his hands were on her shoulders. An expression took root in her face, not fear, a determined concentration. She'd trusted him, even with the shop window now in glinting bits hanging around her like tiny stars and the heavy smell of new electronics wafting over them. He watched her delicate body strike a stereo cabinet and fall to the floor as scythes of glass dropped from the frame above and into Saul's outstretched forearms, shearing them to the bone, and he was gladdened for the openings and he drew into his mind her silvery voice: *thank you, thank you . . .*

In court, bandages swelling his shirtsleeves, Saul saw that she wasn't hurt and was relieved. Mostly, she hung her head, big tears tapping more codes on her skirt. When she was finally asked to speak, there before her parents and the jury, she was too afraid to face the truth of their secret communication. When Saul spoke to comfort her, to assure her she needn't be ashamed, the judge thundered in his direction. When Saul ignored him, he was whisked from the room and stuck with needles that filled his mouth with sand. After the trial was over, he'd asked his lawyer her name. The lawyer pursed his thick lips, thought for a moment, then told him it was Ada Plinth. He was eighteen years old. Saul had probably written her thousands of letters since, unaddressed, just her name in the centre of each envelope, all to no reply.

The memory now displayed to him so vibrantly, Saul was able to see he'd done nothing evil, or horrible, or unforgivable, nothing that could justify incarceration on the ward for the rest of his days. It had been Ada's wish they'd been caught; she had panicked, and he'd accepted the punishment to preserve her dignity. Saul now could see the bitter hollow of remorse he'd inhabited over the years and hated Kraepevic for having convinced him to call it his home. It then became clear to Saul that such a diabolical foe as Kraepevic wouldn't have made it his life's work to persecute and torture him if there wasn't something fundamentally important about Saul, something epic and dramatic, something innately good and worth destroying. He'd always suspected he was meant for great things and perhaps it was this very same fatedness that had drawn Ada Plinth to him, and had kept him from prison, and had protected him and guarded his sanity under Kraepevic and the Assassin's plot to poison his mind. And it was perhaps this same goodness that had led him here, to this new apartment. As he warmed to this idea, he felt the blue chair in which he sat throb beneath him like the cockpit of a powerful machine. But *was* he dangerous? He certainly wouldn't be if he lived here, free from poison pills and the cruelty of the other patients, with nobody scheduling him or scribbling about him in a binder.

It was settled. He'd never lived on his own but he'd learn. He'd keep the place clean, draw up a routine of chores for himself and, of course, he'd still return to Centre Lawn for bingo, the occasional hot meal or checkers match with Kim. Saul's mind soared like this for a while until it was grounded by his stomach—he hadn't been eating much since he'd spotted Luis mucking about in the cafeteria. His pass was probably up anyway, so he rehung the robe, got dressed and made sure the door didn't lock.

———————

The ward always smelled foreign after he'd been away, but this time it was startling: discount cigarettes, crayons, messed pants and bile curdling on the warm air. Bad as they were, the smells failed to bother him. He looked upon the whole ward as if from a high place, as though he were still in his white robe gazing out on the river. He saw Tina, Drew, Kim and all the other patients lining up for dinner and he pitied them. But he couldn't take them with him; the apartment was too small.

After dinner, a salubrious feast of noodly casserole, Saul approached the bingo table, a folding thing the staff set up each time. With Jacob still languishing in the Quiet Room, Saul knew his bingo victory was certain. Jacob always won. He never missed a number, due to a youthful concentration that hadn't yet been whittled down by meds and the lack of things to concentrate on. Saul vowed to put his jackpot toward supplies for his new place: food, candles and an alarm clock, because he'd need to wake early to perform chores when the staff wasn't there to rouse him anymore. Saul thumbed the stack of cards, trolling for vibrations. In bingo, the selection of a card was the only aspect you could control; the rest was just making sure you didn't mess up. He sensed the aura of a winner and fetched a paper cup of pennies. They didn't allow dabbers so the patients placed coins to mark the numbers called. A whole card was accidentally dumped at least once each game. Whoever dumped their card was usually dragged to the Quiet Room for a while to calm down.

The Dayroom was placid even with all the patients loaded in there. Saul marvelled at how much less insane they were on bingo night. There was a focus, a common purpose, or maybe it was just that everybody wanted to win. The lack of seating forced him next to Georgina, within range of the flailings of her elbows. Frieda, a tense, dead-eyed nurse, sat to the left of Georgina's wheelchair to place her pennies for her, sure to raise serious questions of fairness if she ever won, which she never did because she was terminally unlucky. All she'd ever seen was spoons shoved toward her and TV she'd never understand and someone dropping pennies on a card of nonsense in front of her. Saul read her mind for a moment and it made no more sense than the babblings of a child. He'd have room for her at his apartment, but he didn't know how to care for her, to change and feed her, and this saddened him.

Suddenly, the sphere of wire commenced churning the numbered balls. The Assassin was cranking the handle, grinning to the crowd like a Caesar. They locked eyes. Saul almost quit right there; he knew the Assassin would never let him win.

"Eye-thirty-seven. Eyeeee, thirteeeee, sevennnn . . ." he said, holding the first ball aloft, appraising it like a jewel.

Saul had I-37 and placed his first penny.

After that, Saul knew each number the Assassin was going to pick before he picked it. He and the Assassin were communicating telepathically. It was a covenant. Luis wanted Saul to win. And he did. He had the next three numbers after that—including the free space—and was first to get a line.

"Bingo," Saul said, and Luis checked his card.

"We *have* a winner!" he said, shaking Saul's hand with vigour. The first prize of the night was little bottles of shampoo and a new toothbrush.

"Keep it coming," Saul said, and cuffed Luis playfully on the shoulder. Luis winked and brandished his huge, beautiful teeth.

Saul was next to get two lines, then a plus sign, which earned him a hairbrush and some new black socks. The other patients grew suspicious.

"You win too much, Saul," Tina said from a few chairs over.

"The fix is in the house coat of arms," Drew said.

"About time," Saul said, returning to his seat with a foam goblet of decaf coffee for the final round. He was an athlete on a streak, an accidental millionaire, the king of one of those microscopic countries you can't find on a map but know are somewhere.

"Okay, ladies and germs, this one is called Blackout, and it's for the whopping cash prize of five bucks," Luis said, turning the handle, hamming it up like a showboat caller. His entire demeanour had changed. It seemed inconceivable to Saul that Luis was once the sort of man who'd pitch someone from a helicopter. Perhaps he'd fallen out with Dr. K., or maybe he really was a psych nurse.

Luis called every number on Saul's card except for I-25, which he remembered as two of the numbers on his apartment door, so he wasn't worried. Then Luis spoke some numbers Saul didn't have. Saul wasn't concerned; he only needed one. Saul began broadcasting *I-25* with his mind and could see blue brainwaves bending the air between them.

Luis called more bad numbers. Then more.

The grids of the other cards were filling with pennies.

Saul felt a blackness gathering in the room. "I-25!" he heard his voices threaten all at once.

"Would you sit down, Saul?" Kim said.

Luis regarded Saul and shrugged. There were only about six balls left. He pulled another and read it.

"Oingo bingo bango!" someone called from behind him. Saul thought it was his voices again until Drew came gamely jogging to the front like this was *The Price Is Right*. Then every face in the room ripened and turned from Drew to Saul like a field of pasty, deranged weather vanes, and it was fitting because, after all that had happened today, Saul felt he deserved the attention, he should be the contestant whose card Luis was now checking. Saul felt an itchy vibration in his chest and throat and found he was already in the act of describing luxuriously the day's events: the prophetic *Columbo* episode; Jacob's capture; the discovery of the apartment; his sobering realizations with respect to Ada Plinth and Kraepevic; and this new conclusion that Luis was not an Assassin at all but an ally, who was strangely not following through with what he promised. Then Saul saw his own fingers prying open the ball-tumbler. He just wanted to see if ball number I-25 was in there, while someone was repeating his name and a bunch of other words of minimal importance, until he heard amidst the din of voices the former Assassin say, "Drew didn't win, he only had three numbers, we have to keep playing."

Saul sat back down.

He watched Luis pull another ball. Saul didn't have to look to know it was I-25.

———

To: Marty S.
Czar of Mentals
The Province of Greeting Cards

From: Saul Plinth, Master of Columbo and Fine Dining

*Lots cooking way out here at Riverboat Hospital Marty the most specifically is this <u>Assassin</u> I detected has turned out to be a **bingo emancipator** a co-conspirator a <u>guardian angel</u> of some kind a real magnificent associate if you can locate my meaning. It's also come clear that my derangement may in truth be a PSYCHIC SHAM constructed with the help of Darko Kraepevic by yours truly to scare the bejesus out of himself for psychological reasons **unknown** (keep you posted on said reasons).*

*In fact I suspect my entire caged life so far has been something of one great Columbo episode of which we are only now reaching the electrifying conclusion. My bumbling veneer is SHED and I grow **more and more** powerful by the microsecond. Did I tell you already Martin? I found a little nook to call my own. Yes Martin big <u>changes</u> are on the way don't send authorities they arent needed. Before I go here are the charges I'm laying against you and your <u>stooge</u> Kraepevic:*

*In the care of the Riverboat <u>Gulag</u>, Saul Columbo-Plinth, The Desperate Grammophone, The Triumphant Detective, The **King** of Remnants has been the victim of:*

Glass assault, contempt of courtroom, note-scribbling, phantom-limb amputation, mail fraud, skimming of the books, mail terrorism, social security fraud, cyber-stalking, unreasonable bingo dabbery, medication management, puzzle piece apprehension, building code violations, copyright infringement, mind mapping, mind mastication, injury to wildlife, non-smoking, various war crimes, petty scheduling, land piracy, grave-robbing, tax fraud, price-gouging, hunting without a license and fratricide.

May I in closing tell you to fess up on your <u>own</u> GUILT surrender your position and do the only <u>honourable</u> thing by throwing yourself upon your silver sword.

With Fierce Sincereness,

King Saul Plinth-Columbo,
Eminent Fingerpainter, Majestic Vestibule

———————

A gorgeous wash of time had passed when Kraepevic called him into his office.

"Saul, there is an old story my abnormal-psych professor once told of a schizophrenic patient who was hooked up to a lie detector and asked by his psychiatrist if he was Napoleon. And to this, the patient replied, 'No,' and the detector said he was lying."

"So," King Saul said.

"What exactly do you mean by 'So'?"

"What if he was?"

"Lying?"

"No," King Saul said.

Kraepevic exhaled deeply and theatrically in the self-important manner of all doctors and lurched forward in his chair. "Saul, I just don't want to find the condensed *Art of War* written on your walls again."

King Saul neither feared nor loved the doctor. He pitied him. Kraepevic had dedicated his life to convincing the meek that they were to blame for their misery, that their brains lacked a chemistry they would never manufacture. The old Slavic fool had filled his own head with so much nonsense he was certainly too dull to grasp the majestic plan Saul and Luis had incubated in secret for the past few weeks.

"I never was dangerous, Darko," King Saul said, a regal timbre riding in his voice. "Not until now."

"Okay. May I ask why you are wearing that bathrobe and that pair of pyjama bottoms wrapped around your head?"

"You might want to consult the literature," King Saul said, gesturing to the red, blocky DSM-IV parked on the doctor's walnut-tinged shelf, a sort of Sears catalogue of ways the human being could malfunction. Saul vowed to burn it the day of the Electrifying Conclusion.

"Saul, I didn't want to do this, and I don't enjoy it, but I'm going to have to revoke your passes for the time being, as well as temporarily upping your dosages while you present yourself this way."

The doctor thought keeping Saul from his apartment and upping his dosages could stop it. But the apartment had only been a prop. He'd been back and found that the TV and stereo were fake, the taps didn't work and there was no electricity, but the remembrance of Ada had opened his eyes. He'd seen the selfishness of ignoring the plight of the other patients. The maligned, the ruined, the shot to shit, the perennially confused, the monstrous slack-jawed head-bangers, the unfit for community, the grotesque drooling legions with blown fuses in their eyes, they were his subjects. King Saul saw them for what they were: a people ripe with an untapped greatness. And if he, their Sovereign, didn't care for them, who would?

King Saul sculpted some sounds into words Kraepevic wanted to hear and exited the office, acting the role of the freshly strapped schoolboy. They would have to speed preparations. Outside he saw Kim sullenly navigating the hall. Saul had described the Electrifying Conclusion to her on Pizza Night earlier that week and she'd seemed, at first, a touch concerned before growing duly inspired when he assured her the staff would be unharmed. They would surrender or they would be humanely executed with med overdoses, and this had impressed her so much she'd gone to bed.

"Feel like checkers, Saul?" she said, glancing with apparent awe at his Intuitional Headwrap. He considered describing to her how the Wrap amplified his thinking, but doing so would force him to use upside-down words so he was silent. He'd so far avoided inflicting the infinite wattage of his brain on Kim and those sixty-four squares, fearing that a defeat as crushing as he'd administer could be ruinous to her already fragile mental constitution.

"I'm sure you'd be victorious, Kim," King Saul said, "but it is I alone who can provide the leadership that those broadcasters pine for nightly on their evening news."

"Okay, Saul," she said, carrying on, and Saul was fortified by her enthusiasm.

He found Luis in the bathroom across from the laundry, sprinkling a pink powder that smelled like bubble gum chewed by the fetid jaws of the devil himself.

"Got you on cleanup, have they?"

"Georgina had an accident," said Luis.

"Your talents are wasted here, friend."

"Oh, I don't mind," he said. "It's just smelly. Somebody has to do it. Hey, I'm done here. Why don't you come talk to me while I do lunchtime meds?"

Saul trailed him from the bathroom across the Dayroom to the med window. Luis ducked behind the counter and started popping pills from blister packs.

"So . . . what's the outfit?" he said.

Luis was many things—co-conspirator, guardian angel, emancipator, sidekick—but genius he was not. Saul overlooked his question so as not to cudgel him with his ignorance.

"Luis, I met with Kraepevic and he suspects something."

"Dr. Kraepevic is a great psychiatrist. I thought you liked him. He's really worried about you right now, and I think we all are. Your behaviour has been, well, bizarre lately. Here," he said, depositing a paper cup of pills on the counter, "this is your new dosage. And Saul, when I was cleaning the bathroom this morning, I found a pill behind the toilet, melted enough that I couldn't identify it. I'm not saying it was you, but I'm going to need to make sure you take these meds today. Okay?"

The poor fool's allegiances were so skewed that King Saul couldn't rebuke him. He could even forgive this lingering fealty to Kraepevic. The doctor had him on the same leash he'd used on Saul for the last thirty years, a barbed tether that had required every gram of his strength to break.

"There is no stopping it, Luis," Saul said, drawing the cup of meds to his lips. It held two of the same orange pills and a new capsule that was green and white, the markings of a deadly snake.

"Good," Luis said, exhaling. "This afternoon we're doing crafts. You could write some letters or put some more art on your head scarf if you wanted."

Saul scuttled the pills onto his tongue, sipped the water, and for the first time in what seemed like years, he swallowed. He opened his mouth as wide as it would go, twisting his tongue in a circle.

"All gone. Satisfied?"

"You bet, Saul. Thanks for making my job easy," Luis said.

As he returned to the Dayroom, Saul could feel the medication's tingle of dissolution in his throat, preparing for its short journey upriver to the palace of his mind. He would grow duller, meeker and less capable by the minute, and King Saul knew that if it was to begin, it must begin at this moment.

He went to the TV Room, where he found Tina basking in the gangrenous glow of her train movie, burrowed into the couch for all eternity if he failed to act. A videotape was actually much more difficult to snap in half with bare hands than one would think, and King Saul resisted the urge to put it over his knee because he'd pictured doing it in the air, over his head, his thumbs pressed at its centre—much more epic, statuesque—and he did this while expounding to Tina the new life offered her, after the Electrifying Conclusion had freed them all from bondage. There was a choked screech and she came at him with all of the glory and elegant fury of a wild beast. He twisted the glossy coils of tape around his forearms like a boxer readying himself for the fight of the century. Her small, hard fists bit into his shoulders and neck and her wailings were musical and ignorant of syntax. "Let it out," Saul sang, and he leaned into her, accepting her blows as one would a handmade gift, or Christ did his thorny crown.

King Saul then saw that she had driven him into the Dayroom. Someone was wrenching fists of hair from the back of his neck and kicking at his shins. He laughed, and tears stung his eyes, and King Saul knew instantly that these were her tears, that she'd given them to him. He called on his subjects to witness her transformation and be inspired by it. He'd managed to wind the videotape around his neck and face like a carbonized mummy and the hair-tearing ceased. Through his mask he could make out the approaching figures of nurses and a number of his subjects watching from the craft table, mouths agape. He heard Tina's name. Nurses had her by the arms and she kicked at them and roared. More nurses came. Saul saw Luis appear from the nurses' station, where, inside, he saw all their files up on the shelf, and he vowed silently to burn those too once it was over. Luis wrestled one of Tina's legs and they dragged her down the hall.

The miracle is underway, thought King Saul. I am only an usher to it now. By its own engine will it be brought forth. He tore the videotape from his face and climbed up on the craft table, where he kicked aside their artwork, crude portraits of their tortured dreams, their parents and their childhood homes, even a sheet that staff had beset with horse stickers and signed Georgina's name to. He saw that bits of glued paper and sparkles had affixed themselves to his slippers. From high he gazed down on his pitiful subjects. He saw Drew, Jacob, Kim, Tina, even some of the stunned nurses, all admiring him together, their faces pale and practically arranged like a keyboard. Words rose for them to hear, the boil of voices in his head now constituting his own true voice, the way colours together made only white, and he was unsure if they were telling him what to say or if they repeated what they read from his mouth. He informed his subjects that he was no longer just a self-taught detective, that he'd been crowned King in a ceremony of his own design. He vowed to rule kindly and justly. First, he would re-establish the farm—his subjects would cultivate tobacco, then in time other crops would be sown. Families would be forbidden any visitation. If they came they would be drowned in milk and buried at the bank of the river. There would be no more schedules. His subjects would be free to live as they pleased. Then as plainly as one peered into a bucket of water he saw into their futures. Kim would play checkers and keep her own darkness in her head. Drew would cease his meds and smoke without limitation, writing great nonsensical missives on the walls of every building and donning every manner of tinfoil helm. Jacob, free from his father, would grow into a kind and gentle man, maybe a farmer. Even Tina would come to understand what a great gift was given her with the destruction of her tape. Shortly after the Conclusion she would find a companion, not just a vision of a man long gone. King Saul then vowed to commence his reign by constructing for her a train that ran around the edges of the grounds, which she herself could pilot. And finally, Georgina. She would be venerated, an empress, and it would be thought of as a great privilege to change her linens, kiss her sores, and for her a great pool would be dug, and she would float for the rest of her life in the warm water therein and each day would be like the day before she was born, when she was still perfect.

Saul's eyes veered back into focus. Some of his subjects were dazed, their faces churning confusion, and he feared his words weren't as he'd intended, that they were bad models for the architecture contained in his head, or that the air itself was somehow sickening them. For a moment he felt like he had during his trial, like something important and irrecoverable was slipping from him. He could smell the fluorescent lights above and considered breaking them open and drawing their gas into his lungs and speaking the illumination contained within them. These thoughts were abruptly ended when in the crowd he saw her. King Saul knew that she'd heard what was transpiring here and had come to stand by his side. She'd come with his letters bundled in her bare arms and glass shards shimmering in her hair. A shuddering joy broke over him and he raised his arms and spread his palms like two wide eagles and called to her and she sent him a kiss tumbling into the air.

Then a booming voice was asking what he was doing. A clutching thing gripping his ankle. Things are happening wrong, he thought; there is no centre to them. King Saul called out to Luis, an entreaty, a royal plea for help, but not a soul could hear him. Saul saw only a gilded songbird flitting about the room, a rainbow in the air like gasoline splayed on water. He wondered if it was the pills. Then another voice spoke words about someone getting off a table. Luis was by his side. King Saul introduced him to his subjects as his second-in-command. This gentle bear Luis called him Buddy and gently wrapped him in his hairy arms.

Saul kissed the great scar that he'd once feared but now saw as a badge of boundless strength and perseverance. Then someone cut gravity in half. His feet were level with his head. King Saul heard someone who sounded exactly like himself ask Luis what was happening and Luis replied that everything would be all right all right all right and Saul was comforted by this exchange. He could see now that a whole group of them were carrying him aloft. Saul could hear the river licking the windows. He could hear cheering and the call of a trumpet in the close distance. They were taking him to the apartment in West Lawn to prepare for the Electrifying Conclusion and he felt himself loose a great bellow of triumph.

Saul watched the Dayroom recede from him and spoke tender words to Ada who he could see now had joined the ranks of those who bore him, her intricate hand in his own and the other pressed in the hollow of his knee. He regarded her twinkling face and told her that upon his return this kingdom would be more different than even they could ever imagine. The TV Room passed into his view and inside was Georgina slumped in her wheelchair amidst a gentle rain, dangling her small stunted head toward him, drizzling a shot-glass amount of drool into her lap. King Saul instructed his subjects to halt and grasped at the doorframe. She lifted her head, her stringy hair cast sopping across her gorgeous face, and fixed her deadened eyes to his. Georgina then uttered something so startling in its profundity, so divinely beautiful to King Saul's ears, that he feared it would light the rain on fire with its magnificence.

"Roob," she said.

The Quiet

Tonight he'd plucked an emerald green Benz S600 from the spiralling garage of the Queen Elizabeth Theatre. The sky hung with violet dregs of twilight, and a recent rain was held by tire ruts worn in the pavement like the prints of snakes. Finch piloted the Benz over the stately Lions Gate Bridge, up some switchbacking mountain roads to a turnout with a clear view of the city. He parked, mindful to leave the Benz running—it wouldn't start again without Stanislaw's laptop. He discovered a set of pristine golf clubs in the trunk and hit nearly thirty balls from the cliff out into the inlet. This took an hour: he held the tall clubs below the grips, took four swings at each, murmured boom with the miracle of each connection.

On his way down, he dropped the stick in neutral, retracted the sunroof, stood, and coasted with his head in the jet-engine wash of night air until his eyes went gummy and his lips recoiled like the muscled dogs Jerzy kept in their yard. Sitting down, he found the sedan's stillness and grace so deliciously amplified in the aftermath of the roar he executed a jerky three-point turn near a curve and climbed back up to do it again.

While Jerzy and his boys preferred the growling flutes of Japanese or Italian design—sleek as swelling waves and painted in lipstick sheens—Finch liked the quiet ones. Sedans mostly, executive models, the kind that diplomats were chauffeured around in, the kind with classical music in their television ads, cars so noiseless, so painstakingly designed to hush even the meticulous whirring of their own engines, they floated with the elegance of celestial things.

Finch took his first when he was twelve and emboldened by the sort of confidence that only youth can prop up. It was his brother, Jerzy, who'd retracted the slim jim and swung the door out like a valet. "You going from BMX straight to BMW, Ostrich," Jerzy said as Finch climbed into the leathery cockpit. Though he'd begged his brother mercilessly for the opportunity, Finch had never before operated an automobile—not counting arcade games you sat in. That first night, Finch ground the BMW's gears for ten whole minutes while the others bent at their waists laughing, until finally he hopscotched the car out from beneath the buzzing amber of the lot.

He'd driven hundreds since. Getting them was no problem. The expensive ones didn't even use keys anymore. They were too good for keys, as if keys somehow tainted a driver's hand. Stanislaw programmed laptops to open them. Twenty minutes near one was enough—digits and letters flipping on the screen with a shimmering speed.

Tonight, it was only twelve minutes before the locks of the emerald Benz thumped and the engine came alive.

"It's your brand, I'm right?" Jerzy said before Finch went for the car, a weighty hand on his shoulder. "But this time no tour."

Finch nodded.

"Where do you go with them?" Jerzy said.

"Nowhere."

"What? Speak up."

"Nowhere," Finch said, not much louder.

"What's this mouse-talking? Are you unhappy, mouse? Maybe you have a girl?"

Finch sunk his hands into his track-pant pockets.

Jerzy regarded him sideways, a grin turning on his lips. "It's no problem if you do. It would explain much."

"No girl," Finch whispered.

"Okay, no girl. Then you tell me, Robin, where do you go?"

Finch knew that once his brother got his teeth into something like this he would not relent. Growing up, Finch had seen him take hideous beatings from bigger kids, men even, because he wouldn't let something drop, once by a giant sauntering man who'd let a door swing closed on them at a movie theatre.

"I just like driving, that all right with you?" Finch said, sloughing the hand from his shoulder.

Jerzy laughed and cupped the back of Finch's neck to force an interval of eye contact. Like Finch, he was still a boy, really, but his eyes looked pleading and perennially tired like a pair of deflated blue balloons. Jerzy turned to spit through his teeth on the concrete floor. Finch saw Stanislaw shoot a panicked look to the stairwell.

"Well this time, my feisty driver-bird, no tour," Jerzy said. "We need to flip this one quick. There's people we need to pay."

He released Finch's neck. "At home in one hour. Not until every-thing is cool and clean."

Twelve a.m. by the dashboard clock and Finch was back in the city, giddy and ecstatic, his shoulders taut from swinging the clubs. He'd found four hundreds, crisp and brown like book-pressed leaves, folded into a golf scorecard in the console. Betting money, he figured. He'd seen greater sums piled on his kitchen table and never taken notice, but those bills had not been his own. All he could imagine buying was a ping-pong table they lacked room for, so he resolved to keep thinking.

He drove five under, captivated by the pavement's glisten and the innumerable signs—the Benz an exquisitely tailored coat he wore. He squirmed and adjusted the pillow he'd brought to boost him. Back when Jerzy took cars, his brother brought CDs—soaring orchestral samples over subsonic bass eruptions peppered by barking lyrics baroquely detailing the joys of wealth—that he let ring from opened windows with a strange pride. But it wasn't just rap. It was all music. It grated Finch, seemed to demand a response he could not give. As long as he could remember, he'd found contentment in the world's quiet places—pillow forts, clos-ets, churches he'd visited as a boy with his father in Łódź—but nothing compared to the sedans. And their stillness was movable: you could take it anywhere in the city you chose, especially when it was late, with the roads empty as fresh sheets of black paper.

After a couple more hours of aimless, blissful driving, Finch arrived home to see a few of Jerzy's boys on the porch, bottles of

Żywiec pendulous in their hands. The Benz insulated him from the thud of bass, but Finch could see it flexing the picture window of their house.

He should have killed the engine, but he needed to feel it. He half-yawned and removed his glasses to rub his eyes. He was beyond late. Jerzy would be more scathing with his boys looking on. It was doubtful Jerzy needed money. He'd always got paid, even in bad times. Four years previous, when Jerzy was fourteen and Finch was ten, their father, who worked security at the airport, was killed in a dispute out front of a nightclub. The hospital called and they spoke to Jerzy, who passed the cordless from one hand to the other like it'd just come out of the oven, clearing his throat mechanically. They had waited weeks for someone to come. When nobody did, they'd simply carried on. Jerzy had been a goofy, raucous boy, but this ended when he became their guardian. He built a bunk bed out of two weather-beaten doors they found in the basement and made Finch sleep above him in his room. He quit school, sold stereos, gram bags, bikes, shoes, fake pills, even umbrellas for a while—all of which he kept padlocked in Finch's old bedroom. This was before he ordered a fifty-two-piece lockout toolkit online and moved on to cars.

Then two years ago Finch was hassled on the way to school by some Hindu kids, and Jerzy and Andrzej went and beat them with leather skipping ropes. Later, people said the Hindus had gang-affiliated brothers and Jerzy got worried. He pulled Finch from school, stabled his crew at the house, and reinforced the doors with sheet metal. At home and bored, Finch pestered his brother to bring him along at nights, a privilege he finally achieved by suggesting he'd be safer with them than at home.

In the idling Benz, Finch considered inventing a story—he was followed, chased by cops—then let it go. Jerzy had a keen ear for fabrication. Yet in other ways his brother was a fool. It'd been two years, no Hindu gangsters, and his paranoia had not abated. Lately, Finch found little inclination to obey his brother, whose darkening demeanour increasingly reminded him of their father. Finch slept on the couch and locked himself in the bathroom to read encyclopedias. Now he saw Jerzy's warning for what it was: a desperate attempt to force his obedience—a bluff, really, because violence was his only remaining option, one he would never use, if only because their father had employed it with such zeal.

Perhaps it was the bills in his pocket, or the impending reprimand, or the idea of another night on the top bunk, a pillow wrapped about his ears, the bass dispelling any peace he'd gained tonight, that rendered him incapable of leaving the Benz. He dropped it into gear and eased quietly from the curb.

After a string of deliberately unconsidered turns, Finch found himself on a dark freeway, a greenish sea of city light churning on the clouds in his rearview. He wasn't tired any longer. He felt sharpened and jittery and electric, like he would after emerging from an arcade or drinking a two-litre of discount pop. He supposed he was driving east—west was ocean, south was America—but wasn't sure. The sedan had a GPS that he didn't activate for fear it could locate him. Just a short trip, he told himself, luxuriating in the joys of freeway driving: the way speed slowed the landscape, the geometric perfection of banking corners, the cinematic sweep of headlights, the thought of a million engineered parts spinning in unfathomable synchrony.

It was mostly trucks on the road, towns passing like fallen constellations. The night went blacker and Finch bent closer to the wheel. A light appeared in the dash. It looked like a robot pointing a gun to its head. He puzzled over this until a beeping sound came. Something was wrong with the car, and he felt a boy's sob gather in his chest. Then the same suicidal robot flashed by outside on a sign that read "GAS" and he swerved into the turnoff, nearly throwing the Benz in a ditch.

He came upon a station—an island cut in the blackness by a punishing white light—and pulled in. He'd never kept a car long enough to require fuelling. He studied a man fill his half-ton, then hoisted the heavy nozzle from the pump, unscrewed the cap, inserted the nozzle, and squeezed. Nothing happened.

"Need a hand?" a woman said with a wrecked voice.

"This doesn't work."

"You didn't select your grade," she said, approaching the pump to smack a button. She gripped the handle and digits spun. She didn't have a uniform. She wore a filthy puffy jacket and a mountaineering backpack with plastic bags strapped to it. She was middle-aged, about as old as his father had been.

"Oh, hey," she said, "you gotta kill the engine!"

Finch had never heard of this before. "I can't," he said.

Her forehead gathered into ridges. "You can't?"

"No."

She glanced around the station. Finch realized then that she was alone and didn't have a car.

"That's what they say, anyways," she said. "Doesn't bother me."

"What could happen?"

"Your car could explode!" she said in a voice like a pot bubbling over as she finished pumping. Finch knew that adults often said things they didn't mean, like how his father had always declared his love for his job at the airport, even though he used to be an engineer in Poland—not the kind that drove trains, but the kind that built them. He hoped what the woman had said was the same sort of thing.

Finch turned to the bright kiosk, the attendant already looking in their direction.

He extracted a brown bill from his track pants. "Can you pay?" he said, his ears turning hot.

"You bet," she said.

She went in, stood at the counter, and returned with his change.

"Here, keep this," he said, pushing back a twenty, which she took without thanks.

She paused for a moment. "Actually, I wouldn't hate a ride," she said.

The attendant was outside now, inspecting pumps and scribbling on a clipboard. Finch itched to escape the brilliant scrutiny of the lot. He was old enough to know there was no respectable reason for a woman to be stranded at a freeway gas station, but in her face he caught the same desperation, the same doe-like vacancy, he had seen in the girls Jerzy's boys brought over, or the glitzy women his father shepherded home from clubs, and in this he took a strange comfort. He popped the trunk and she tossed her bags in with the golf clubs.

"Where you going?" he said, merging onto the freeway.

"Just to Merritt," she said. "My kid—" then her breath cut off like a valve and she turned her face to the window.

Finch vowed off more questions and watched the gas needle's deliberate rise.

"This is a whole lot of vehicle you got here," she said, eyeing the pillow beneath him.

"My brother's," he said, checking his mirrors.

Then a quiet overtook them, and Jerzy loomed in Finch's mind. He was going to be furious, more so if he found out Finch had picked up a hitchhiker. Finch could see no boundary in his brother between anger and concern. Jerzy would either kick him out or further tighten his grip, neither of which seemed possible to endure. Finch just needed a little more time in the car, to think. He'd come up with a way to fix everything.

"You talk funny," she said as though he'd just spoken.

"I have an accent," he said, recalling for a second the blunt sweetness of his father's voice, when he did not raise it.

"I mean you whisper," she said, unwrapping a new pack of cigarettes, lighting one with a barbecue lighter pulled from her coat.

"I don't like noise."

"Makes sense, sweetie."

She reached for the radio and a bright breeze of enveloping sound—a hive of guitars, organs, and voices—leapt from speakers hidden on every side. Soon she began twisting in her seat, throwing her head in odd ellipses, unwashed hair draping into her eyes.

Finch tried not to let her see him looking. He'd never before driven with a passenger, never with a real destination either. He liked her there beside him, this dancing woman. He knew the car would have exploded by now if it was going to. It was the last sedan he would get, but they had three hundred dollars, a gas gauge that promised more than full, and he was taking her to Merritt, wherever that was.

As they shot through the dead-flat valley, with dawn lifting shadows from the weary shoulders of everything, the music reached out through the lightly tinted windows of the Benz, touched the signs and trucks and sulfurous lights and roadside buildings of no discernable purpose, enmeshed itself with this whipping landscape, enlivened it, and Finch was met by an unfamiliar and almost stupefying sense of beauty.

"I like this," he yelled into the fury.

"Sure you do," she yelled back. "It's a classic."

The Beggar's Garden

S am Prince lay awake, listening to a squad of raccoons loot his recycling. Since moving into the slumping structure behind his house—it backed onto the alley and was either a shed or a small garage, he'd never been sure—he'd taught himself to distinguish the noise of the raccoons licking his containers clean from the more orderly clanking of the men who came on trailered bikes to rummage his blue bins for anything they could return for deposit. There, in the interminable dark hours of recent weeks, Sam had come to the fearful knowledge that the alley doubled as a nocturnal highway where all valuable things were to be carted away.

The structure itself was a rickety assemblage of rotting boards with two barn-style doors that swung outward. Sam had never made good on the promise to both Anna and himself to undertake its renovation. It held their bikes, wicker garden chairs, rubberized bins of what remained of Cricket's childhood memorabilia, and an arsenal of tools he'd got when his father had passed—tools his father hadn't much used either. Black mould speckled the exposed rafters above, where a coiled badminton net, Cricket's crutches from four years ago, and Sam's old hockey equipment had found permanent lodging. The garage had always been the storehouse for the scraps of their life together, and Sam considered it fitting that it was here he'd sought refuge.

Earlier that night, he'd discovered some freeze-dried meals they'd purchased for a kayaking expedition in the Yukon that had never got booked. He boiled chicken à la king in a foil bag over a camping stove and spooned it from a dented tin plate. While he ate he listened to hockey on the radio. The stream of the announcer's play-by-play kept his mind from betraying him, as it did without fail during any manner of silence. His power supply was an orange extension cord running to the side of his house—a four-bedroom built in 1912 that he and Anna had gutted and renovated at great cost. It had become a place Sam could not tolerate. Mostly, he did not care for the linger of his family's scent, in the towels, the carpet, even his own clothes, which served only to feed the dark ruminations that dredged his mind without mercy. The house had always felt much too large, and now, after he'd locked all its doors and dropped his house key down the manhole out front, it was tomb-like, monolithic, laying a wide, grim shadow over his yard.

The ordeal had commenced benignly enough. Anna, a casting director who'd just wrapped a gruelling sci-fi film that had gone way over budget, had taken Cricket to her parents' in Calgary for spring break so they could ski at nearby Banff. Sam was to enjoy some "self-time," as Anna would say. The visit was first extended by a few days when there was a heavy snowfall, then by a week because Anna's father had experienced another heart arrhythmia. Sam filled most of this time by working late at the bank, spearheading a new fraud initiative involving digital finger-printing that he knew would never get the funding to clear the boardroom. It wasn't until she'd called to inform him of her plan to stay another two weeks that Sam knew something was amiss.

"I thought you had that Jeep thing this month?" he said.

"The dollar the way it is, they're shooting it in Detroit. Oh, that reminds me, can you call Cricket's school? I lost the number."

Sam said he would, then suggested he book a few days off and fly out for the weekend.

"Oh, don't bother, we're so busy here . . . ," she said, and when Sam insisted, her voice congealed. "Sam, this is hard to say, but I think I need you *there* right now."

Sam fell silent. He could hear some electronic debris on the line, a distant titter, and he wondered whose provider was responsible.

"I'm sorry," she said, "but we've just been so *isolated* in Van-couver. And I suppose I've been reconnecting with my family. I do have a family, remember?"

"The same oppressive one you were trying to escape by dragging us out here? Or have they been swapped out?"

There was a moment of quiet, during which Sam fought to corral his breathing.

"Sam, I've begun to suspect that either you or I is horribly unhappy," she said next, "and I'm afraid it may be both."

"I *was* happy," he said, feeling simultaneously witty and petty for the emphasis.

They'd been married eleven years, and Sam had long ago regretfully concluded they were a disagreeable species of person, fundamentally speaking, a reality he'd resigned himself to and was willing to endure. The years had cruelly revealed in Sam and Anna the very qualities they'd so zealously sought to conceal with copious amounts of false self-advertisement on those pivotal first dates: she, controlling and anxious; he, over-critical and distant. But Sam had always secretly believed that the death of their embellished fictional selves was inevitable and, ultimately, forgivable. They were things built to dazzle, then to be shed and to fall away like the fuel tanks of a space shuttle.

So it had mustered in him an acute sense of betrayal when she disturbed this functional truce to declare their unhappinesses. Yet even during the spiteful salvoes he made on her memory nightly, he couldn't dissuade himself from admiring her bravery.

"Sam," she said in a broken voice after a few hollow seconds, "it's simply that I . . . I've realized I've become someone that I think I may loathe."

"Can you put Cricket on?" Sam said, circling the kitchen island with brisk strides.

When Anna informed Sam that Cricket was out cross-country skiing with her cousins, Sam, more sternly than he'd have liked, took it upon himself to offer an itemized verbal summary of the errors she was right then committing in arriving at this decision. Though outwardly independent, she was at heart an impressionable woman, vulnerable to another's interpretation of her feelings, and Sam had always secretly feared it had been this ability of his to articulate how she felt, and what she needed to do to fix it, that had drawn her to him and kept her there. And for the bulk of that night, he lay in their bed reviewing his points, each of which was unquestionably true, then concluded that perhaps it was their overwhelming cumulative effect that had caused her to hang up with a delicate, jaw-like click.

————————

The raccoons must have moved on, because when Sam's clock radio went off it lifted him from a fitful sleep. It was a Monday. He rose with a lead weight in his body and stood at the small window that overlooked the garden. It already bore signs of her absence: weeds sprung amidst the vegetable beds; the rhododendron petals gone the nauseated hue of tobacco leaves; a defeated wither over everything. She'd always neglected to instruct Sam on the operation of the system of taps feeding the intricate vasculature of punctured hoses that wound about the yard. Despite the feminist outpost she dutifully occupied after the second bottle of wine at dinner parties, she was a woman who believed in household domains; she stalked the kitchen, laundry room, and garden like a wolverine and was determined to keep their secrets from him. Regardless, he'd begun to enjoy the garden's slow ruin and found himself compulsively checking forecasts on his phone.

He unplugged the clock radio from the extension cord, plugged in his shaver, and held the buzzing instrument to the wilds of his sleep-puffy face. He coughed down a few pieces of ragged multigrain bread, went out to his car, and pulled one of the dry-cleaner bags from the trunk. After moving out, he'd gone and bought five cheap suits, one for each day, the boxy polyester kind his father had worn. Relieved of the counterbalance of family, Sam's life had tipped wildly into the realm of his office. He was a director in the fraud department of a major bank, his main responsibility being to oversee and ever-update a byzantine formula through which each transaction was run, designed to detect any manner of banking irregularity. He'd heard from the old-timers that his job used to entail tracking down real flesh-and-blood con artists, cheque kiters, and crooked tellers. Now nothing near detective work was involved; if the formula flagged any statistically anomalous event, a follow-up was made by call-centre employees from a contractor in New Brunswick. Ones that didn't check out, the card was cancelled and the money replaced; ones that did, the card was reactivated. In either case the formula was adjusted accordingly.

Initially, his rise at the bank had been rapid, the position in fraud conceived by higher-ups as merely a way station on his ascent to more crucial departments like corporate finance or strategic initiatives. But Sam enjoyed fraud, the puzzle of it, the meticulous attention it required, this endless struggle to reduce loss, and politely refused the next two promotions they put before him.

That morning Sam sat through a gruelling project management round table on cheque security initiatives during which his head dipped twice. After the meeting he retreated to his office and redrafted a presentation he was to give at the national conference in Montreal the next month.

At lunch, he walked from the shadowy narrows of the financial district to an area consisting mostly of language schools and tiny eating establishments. Crossing Dunsmuir Street, he saw ahead of him on the sidewalk a young girl a few years older than Cricket, her face bright at the heart of a tempest of dark curls, walking hand in hand with her towering father. The sheer discrepancy of their heights was oddly delightful to Sam; the notion that two people could exist at such differing altitudes seemed immediately mystifying. Then an ambulance parked out front of a dollar pizza place whipped alive with lights and a piercing cluck of siren. Sam saw the girl recoil toward her father, setting her feet on top of each of his, nestling her back into the space between the solid timbers of his legs. They all watched the ambulance roar away, its on-board control somehow flipping lights green as it went. Sam was struck by the tenderness with which the man held the girl and the automatic way she'd sought him. They stood for some moments, the man whispering at her hair where her ear would be, until her face softened and they set off.

Sam went inside Top Choice Donair and ordered a falafel to the bracing sound of Arabic dance music, then stood on the sidewalk to eat. When he finished, he started back toward his office, balling the tinfoil wrapper tightly in his fist. He detoured into an alley, and after sidearming the foil into an open dumpster, he set both of his palms flat on the brick wall beside the bin like he was about to be searched and emitted a long, grinding sob.

The girl had brought back the way his daughter sought him in these situations of distress—not her mother, whom she consulted first in most other matters—the way she produced staccato blasts of sound and stood, arms outstretched, limp as a scarecrow, awaiting the vault into his arms.

"You all right, fella?" said an older bearded man, about ten feet to his right. Sam traced the man's arms down to his belt and realized he was urinating with surprising force. Sam removed his hands from the bricks and said nothing. It had always seemed overly intimate to conduct a conversation with a man relieving himself. The man zipped and left the alley. Sam noted he was still pulling choppy, hot breaths high into his chest.

Emerging from the alley, he was met by a cold drift of exhaustion and decided to walk home. He started east. He and Anna lived in Strathcona, the oldest residential neighbourhood in the city, besieged in recent years by the young, progressive, and wealthy, who sought to live within bike-commuting distance of downtown and could stomach the neighbourhood's close proximity to the riotous and hellish, but strangely contained, slum of the Downtown Eastside, through which was Sam's shortest route home.

They'd married after grad school, he with an MBA and she a law degree. She passed the bar and did four months at a corporate firm in Toronto before discovering her complete lack of interest in the legal profession. Her family was appalled by her decision to quit, and at one point her father hinted that he might want reimbursement for the schooling. The west coast had been Anna's idea of an escape. A few months after they'd arrived, an old friend offered her a position at a production company that specialized in American made-for-TV movies and commercials, and in a very short time that had led to her job as a casting director. At first, the city had been thrilling—as if their adventurousness, their willingness to scuttle the past, had been rewarded with their own earthly paradise, a temperate garden way out on the golden fringe of everything, far distant from the entanglements of her family and the yawning absence of his. Yet as years ticked by, something about the city nagged at Sam's prairie sensibilities. Its beauty now seemed to him almost obscene, as if to build a glimmering city of glass by the sea, at the foot of an Olympian rack of mountains, was to invite calamity. And over time this doomed neighbourhood he walked through had assumed a symbolic station in his mind, an unsightly eruption that the city somehow deserved and couldn't conceal. Much like his new backyard home, it was a tortured, unsettled dominion—a living monument to all unwanted things—and some part of Sam hoped it would be there forever.

He made his way past dismal blocks of vacant storefronts where sickened, twitchy people congregated like Antarctic penguins. He was offered drugs by palsied men who seemed nonplussed by his lack of response. He passed a vacant lot where two men stood over a large collection of VHS tapes laid out on a blanket, each holding the other by the hair, each pleading the other to let go.

After he'd walked awhile, the sun darted behind a ridge of cloud and the air fell cool. It was then he came upon a man sitting on the sidewalk with a yoghurt container before him. He was the man from the alley, in his fifties at least, lengthily bearded and swaddled in a ragtag assortment of dirty coats and vests; at his feet was a cardboard sign:

Spare Change? Drug/Alcohol Free, GOD BLESS.

Sam feared the man had attributed his silence to some prejudice he held, so he approached and plopped some larger coins in his cup.

"You startled me back there in the alley," he said.

"Not a problem," the man said affably but somewhat confusedly, and Sam wondered if he'd been specific enough for a man

who surely passed much of his time in alleys. He decided to spare
him any further confusion and made a step toward his home.

"I hope you didn't mind me saying that you look somewhat
rough around the edges," the beggar said. His voice reminded
Sam of metal put to whetstone.

"Sorry?" he said, turning back.

"I seen the look before."

"Look?"

"The one you got. Like a light gone in your face."

Sam grasped for a response to this.

"There's this story around here, kind of a myth I suppose,
about this fella who got hit by a police car and made himself a
whole bunch of money, like seventy-five grand, for his damages,
you know—broken femurs, skull, the whole shebang. He's on
welfare, never seen money like that in his life. So he steps out the
hospital and figures he'll have the biggest party anybody ever
seen. He gets himself a nice suit and goes and buys all the drugs he
can get his hands on and offers them to whomever and whoever
he sees on the street. People knew there's something screwy in his
head, because of the accident maybe, or some other reason, but
they didn't care. He drew to him every nature of mooch, hustler,
and wicked person there was, and of course this guy ends up broke
after just three days, just the clothes they gave him in the hospital is
all that's left. He said to somebody that he didn't care for this place
no more and he'd decided to go on vacation. The next morning he
walked on down to the docks and he hopped on the first container
boat he saw. Well now, this boat ain't bound for Maui, no sir, this
boat turns out to be a non-stop to Alaska. So here's this poor guy,
just the thin grey sweatsuit they gave him and those cheap velcro

shoes, no socks besides. So this guy sits there on the deck shivering and making a full-time job of freezing his ass off. Crew members walking past his little hidey hole, going inside the cabin and drinking coffee, listening to the radio and whatnot. But you know what? This guy? He don't say nothing to them. This fella was so determined not to ask nobody for help no more that he went all sleepy and just froze himself to death right there between them stacks of containers."

Sam sustained the interlude of silence that the story seemed to require. "He would have been arrested if he gave himself up. Am I right?" he said.

"I suppose. Wouldn't have been much of a charge, just trespassing maybe, would've caught a beating from the sailors is more likely. But the meaning here is two things: sometimes a gift ain't a gift, and sometimes people are just too iron-headed to go asking for help." The beggar waved a blackened hand over his change cup like a tiny magician's top hat. "Me? I'm not afflicted with that problem."

At this, Sam thanked the man, dug into his pocket, and dumped the rest of his change, a near handful, into the cup.

As he started away something occurred to him, and he turned back.

"Take some out," Sam said.

"What's that?"

"There are too many coins in there—it doesn't bother me, but people won't give because they'll think you don't need it. But don't take them all out, because people won't give to someone who no one else gives to—the same way people don't want to go to an empty restaurant."

The man bloomed a sly, craggy smile that looked to be carved out of margarine. "You think I don't know that?" he said, and scooped a handful of coins and began stuffing them deep in the pocket of his pungent coat.

Sam woke to the sound of a shopping cart buzzing up the alley, which was now lit by a yellow array of moth-shrouded streetlights. He ordered a pizza and met the deliveryman on the front steps of his darkened house. When Sam handed him a twenty, the deliveryman commenced his attempt to retrieve the change from the pocket of his punishingly tight jeans. Sam waited five long seconds and the man hadn't yet got a finger in.

"Keep it. You earned it," Sam said, and the deliveryman gave up, grinning.

Back in his drafty abode, Sam thought of the old panhandler. He had liked him, his lack of pretence. It seemed to follow logically that someone with nothing left would also have nothing left to hide. It delighted him to think that his advice had helped him, even if only modestly. He'd also liked the easy way he spoke. His co-workers rarely told stories so freely, or of that nature—concerning the tragic events that so often befell a human being—and the ones they did tell, Sam always found trivial and hard to relate to. Not that he could truthfully say he found anything personally relevant in the strange tale of a broken, stubborn man freezing to death on a ship; in fact he'd found the story puzzling. Most puzzling of all was how the panhandler came to know the story if the man had died. Yet it had moved him.

While he ate, Sam pictured the beggar wandering the road-side shoulders of Sam's old hometown. It was easy to imagine him there—easier than it was to see himself there any longer. There, fallen men like the beggar parked themselves in the tavern to tell woeful stories and drink away their disability cheques, while above the sun fenced with a few unfortunate dollops of cloud in the giant sky. Outright begging was not something that was done, not even on the reserves. Sam supposed that street begging required the anonymity of a big city; otherwise, in a small town like his, what another gave could only be thought of as borrowed. Those who could not work or for whom there was no work were regarded with a solemnity by men like his father, who'd hired countless dazed-looking men for menial jobs around their house.

Sam grew up with no siblings and his parents were now both long deceased, his mother when he was six, his father when he was twenty-one—this while he was out east at Queen's University. His father was an accountant who'd made his living filing returns for the various Indian bands outside their rural Manitoba town. He was a precise and generous man who detested error, most vehemently his own, and provided his services to the bands at deep discount. Few others would do the same, as he never failed to point out whenever, out of adolescent loneliness, the young Sam voiced his desire to move to Winnipeg.

"These people need me," he'd say. "They don't know their asses from tea kettles."

Sam had grown up privileged, at least in relation to his peers, mostly the sons of wheat farmers, mechanics, and RCMP highway patrolmen, and had never been subject to the small-town inertia that had cemented their fates. Sam had coasted through high school with the coy detachment of a partygoer making a brief appearance before leaving for a more interesting and better-attended function. His eventual enrolment in university had been a resolute fact that had roots in a time beyond his recall, a certainty as closed to discussion as the subject of his mother, who'd died from a botched medical procedure and about whom Sam had never heard his father manage more than a couple of sentences.

But at university Sam had his first glimpse of the iridescent sort of person only real wealth could mint. And Anna was the best of them. They'd met in a second-year microeconomics class. That same year, Sam's father was killed by a stroke and Sam stuffed Anna into the resulting void. They spent every minute they could together. At first Sam was disconcerted by how easily she described her untroubled ascendance through childhood and into the clever and joyful woman she'd become. As Sam came to know her, he decided that hardship, economic or otherwise, did not bestow character, that in fact the opposite was usually true.

Her parents and three sisters had greeted him with a cautious, incremental warming. Her mother was a self-described homemaker and her father was an engineer who'd made a king's fortune in the eighties by buying up drained Albertan oil wells and using a method he'd innovated to wring from them a few more thousand barrels of crude. They lived in a rustic log mansion at the heart of a rolling plot of ranchland and engaged in an intricate schedule of family vacations, retreats, and holidays to which Sam had always felt not entirely welcome. The thought of Anna winding herself and Cricket back into their lives made him ill.

Before descending again to an unsteady slumber, Sam recalled his car parked in a garage downtown, no doubt accruing a book of tickets. Though he and Anna were wealthy by most measures, a fear of poverty persisted deep in him—this being perhaps a legacy of his father—and at the bank he often felt guilty and fraudulent to be in receipt of such a generous salary. Despite their considerable savings, he couldn't shake the notion that he was just a few paycheques away from being stripped of all he held dear. That's what money's for, Sam assured himself about the tickets, now aware that tomorrow he'd have to wear the same suit, the one he hadn't felt the urge to remove before bed.

The next afternoon, Sam found the old panhandler in the same spot and held out to him a large slab of cardboard. The old man extended a grimy palm and took it.

"What in the hell is this?" he said.

Sam had spent that morning at his desk pondering the old panhandler's sign, the connotations of it, its brief, penitent request for alms, its assurance of sobriety, and its parting block-letter invocation of God's blessing. While unread messages simmered in his inbox and his phone rang until losing its charge, Sam had become convinced that the sign could be improved.

He rode the service elevator down to the loading dock at the rear of the bank tower and fished out a cardboard box from the recycling bin. He took a marker and inscribed it with his message, then lightly charred the edges of the sign like a pirate's map he'd once made for Cricket after burying her birthday present in a bed of kale in Anna's vegetable garden.

New to vancuver. Spare Chanje for food and medecine?
Thanks.

"This for me?" said the beggar. "It ain't even spelt right."

"You're right about that. But this one is more effective," Sam said.

"Oh," said the old man. "Why's that?"

Sam's reasons were many. *New to vancuver* suggested only a trip gone wrong, a more temporary impoverishment; the spelling errors hinted gently at mental dysfunction; and the *God Bless* of the old sign had seemed too obvious, in addition to the fact that Christians were now in the minority, statistically speaking. Overall, Sam had gone for a simple plea from a guy who'd just shown up in town, who'd fallen on hard times and was looking for an honest meal. He'd also added the cryptic *medecine* to imply a mysterious chronic illness and potentially expensive treatments. Cutting the *drug/alcohol free* part he'd wavered on, but in the end he'd figured it was best not to mention these matters explicitly. Most important, Sam had concluded, was that people believed their contribution would go toward something rehabilitory, not just serve as a reward for sheer laziness or be flushed down the thirsty drain of addiction.

"How much do you make, a day, would you say?" said Sam.

"Weekday or weekend?"

"There's a difference?"

"Oh, yes sirree there is, people are more generous in their leisure time, that's a known fact. A weekday? I'd say about fifteen. Weekend about twenty-five. That's sitting all day, mind you."

Sam made a note in his pocket account book and paused for some calculations in his head.

"I have a proposition for you," he said.

"Shoot."

"I want to be your manager."

The old man was quick to his feet and hoarsely yelling, "I ain't doing no fighting of nobody—"

"No, no!" said Sam. "Please, not like that! I mean more like a . . . well, a financial adviser."

"Ya don't say," he said, sitting slowly, wincing, like he was lowering himself into a hot tub.

Sam sat down on the sidewalk beside him and was bowled over by the unruly stench of animal and vinegar. He swallowed hard and made his proposition. Sam would offer the panhandler advice, at no charge, on how better to ply his trade, and the beggar would agree to follow his instructions, however odd they might seem.

The beggar looked miffed. "Why are you doing this if you don't get no cut? Ain't you got better things to do?"

For the first time that day, Sam's thoughts touched on his absent family, and recoiled from their memory with the sour bite of a tongue put to a nine-volt battery. "Not really," he said.

Then, as a show of good faith, Sam leafed five 20s from his wallet into the cup. "Consider this a signing bonus," he said.

The beggar regarded the bills with wide, blinking eyes, turning his lower lip inside out. "That'll work," he said.

They agreed the beggar would keep a twelve-dollar per diem, which Sam saw as ample, and the rest Sam would deposit in the bank and give to him whenever he requested it. They would start right away with the contents of the beggar's yoghurt cup.

When he returned to his desk, Sam opened a special high-interest savings account available only to bank employees, then walked to a branch across the street and slid the cup of filthy change to the teller, who greeted it with a tired shrug.

Weeks steamed past with all of Sam's waking hours occupied by this new partnership. He conducted an exploratory interview with the panhandler over gourmet burgers, two of which the beggar devoured in quick succession while Sam took scrupulous notes.

His name was Isaac. He slept under an abutment of the train bridge near the old sugar refinery. He was from Vancouver, and in 1964, at nineteen years of age, had left to work as a faller in logging camps in the north. After some years up there, he was working alone one rainy day on a big spruce that was all rotten inside. He'd already done the backcut and had only just started the undercut when the tree, with no good wood to hold it, cracked, twisted, and leapt from the stump, catching him just above his groin, snapping his pelvis, and pinning him to the emerald moss. He was found hours later by his crew boss, having screamed his voice to a whisper. They brought him down in a wooden float-plane and he spent almost a year at St. Paul's learning to make his legs work again. When he stepped out onto the street, he had no savings or family or inclination to find a job, so he just slept where he could and had done so ever since.

It pained Isaac to tell the story, and more than once tears had threatened in Sam's eyes. It was as if Isaac had entrusted him with a thing of great value, a sort of artifact that Sam felt honoured to possess.

Sam met Isaac each day after work, collected the change, paid him out, then went and deposited the money, tracking the growth of the account on a spreadsheet that could produce line graphs, though Isaac didn't seem to understand them when they were displayed on Sam's laptop.

Though he'd found the subject deeply uninteresting, Sam had sat through numerous marketing courses as part of his MBA. He soon realized that Isaac was essentially in the business of advertising; that his product was his story, the authenticity of it, the emotional power it brought to bear on those who heard it; and that this story was conveyed by his demeanour, his dress, his attitude. Isaac's job was simple, to win pity, and Sam knew he had to improve his product if Isaac was to be more generously and regularly compensated for his services.

"What are my services, exactly?" Isaac asked when Sam explained this.

"To tell the truth," Sam said, handing him a sweaty hotdog purchased from a nearby cart.

"That's what I always done."

"That's what I mean."

The first thing Sam had Isaac do was hide his shoes while he was working. A shoeless old beggar with beaten, dirty feet resting on the sidewalk was all the more pitiful for passersby to behold, and Sam saw big increases from this immediately, especially among older women. Next he coached him on the humble yet not overly articulate manner with which he should converse with patrons, and on the necessity of lowering his eyes, snatching only brief but friendly glances at the faces standing over him. Sam considered a more radical change in dress, more tatters and filth, to convey a greater need, but the acid burns he'd noted on his own designer jeans reminded him that real wear was difficult to imitate credibly. Finally, Sam considered doing away with the sign altogether and drafting a pamphlet that succinctly detailed the narrative of Isaac's sad life, which he could hand to customers. He suspected that no matter how poorly produced or pitifully worded, it would raise questions regarding how a beggar could pay printing costs. They'd just have to keep with the sign.

Sam soon observed that while they met, the flow of change dried up. Nobody wanted to donate to a beggar conversing with a well-to-do man. Perhaps Sam was a cop, or a drug dealer; either way, he only ratcheted up suspicion, so they agreed to meet a few blocks over in Oppenheimer Park, where drug dealers convened and a few old men threw a bent Frisbee around. What Isaac did with the money was the only aspect of the scheme in which Sam would not involve himself. He was clearly in need; the depth or texture of that need Sam had no business investigating. Occasionally, Sam smelled alcohol on his breath. But Isaac was discreet, and this Sam appreciated; it was better for business. He nipped from a jam jar he carried in the coat he wore in all weather and must have refilled it when Sam wasn't around. There were really no negative effects, aside from some mornings when for the odd fifteen-minute stretch his eyes seemed to function independently.

Best of all, their partnership proved to be a merciful distraction. The few times Sam had managed to speak to Cricket she'd been monosyllabic, and he detected in her tone the same limpness she'd shown on her eighth birthday when a girl gave her a pop-up book that she'd had memorized since she was three. His conversations with Anna were curt and perfunctory. A terrible mutual unfathomability had befallen them. Greetings and passing comments whipped up connotations in the other's mind that were far removed from their intended meaning. Now, when looking back at those months before Anna's departure, Sam couldn't say they had lacked signs of what was to come. Anna had commenced a campaign to rid them of clutter, donating furniture and clothes—theirs, Cricket's, anything that hadn't been worn in a year was her rule—to a church thrift store a few blocks over. This appeared now to Sam akin to the mute crew of a bombarded ship throwing their cargo overboard to buy a few minutes more before submergence.

———————

When a few weeks had passed with no measurable increases in Isaac's profit, Sam considered more drastic adjustments. Isaac had sat on the same spot for twenty-five years, thus violating the *begging must be only temporary* rule that Sam had established early on. After hours of searching, Sam found the perfect new place: "historic" Gastown, where hundreds of stunned cruise-ship passengers, mostly sturdy, khakied Scandinavian couples or wary American families all in the same leather-strapped baseball hat, washed ashore to lumber and gawk on the bricked sidewalks and hold aloft tiny cameras clasped between forefinger and thumb, aiming at landmarks such as the famous steam-driven clock. There'd be plenty of change in their pockets, left over from purchases of smoked salmon in mailable cedar boxes, authentic Coast Salish carvings, Cowichan sweaters, and four-litre canisters of maple syrup. The tourists were ideal—an ever-rotating and disposably incomed clientele who barely understood the Canadian system of currency—for Isaac to intercept and ply his trade.

The area already supported many beggars, who mostly encircled the bustling currency exchange kiosk. But this area was dark and crowded. Sam took two days off work to comb Gastown for a south-facing spot, as favourable lighting went a long way toward positive judgment of character. He found the perfect nook near a chain coffee shop, with a nice overhang to shelter Isaac from the rain.

"People been coming to me for twenty-some odd years," Isaac said wistfully when Sam informed him of the relocation. "I got a whole bunch of interest in this place, the sights're familiar to me, I could tell you who's gonna walk past just by looking at how the sun comes off that parking sign."

"I can understand that," Sam said, "but this is going to double our profits—that's a conservative estimate."

"I suppose it will," said Isaac.

And it did. The tourists were helpless against Isaac's dirty feet and murmurs of humble appreciation. To celebrate, Sam offered to take him on a road trip. It had been eight years since Isaac had left the neighbourhood, so Sam scheduled the next Monday off to drive him to a rainy beach where Isaac ate two ice cream cones and stuffed his pockets with the unremarkable grey shells that were scattered in the dark sand like bad coins.

"Looks like I gotta find a new patch to rest my head," Isaac said on the ride home. "The cops been coming round the train bridge and kicking over shelters."

"Why don't you rent a room?" said Sam. "You could afford it, we could do up a budget."

"Nope. That ain't me," Isaac said, doing his best to contain an indignance. "I'd rather sleep out in the air than shack up with the crackheads and rip-offs in one of those roached-up, firetrap hotels." To this Sam agreed and Isaac's anger waned. Isaac spent a quiet moment investigating the mechanism of his power window, stuttering it in place like a broken robot.

"I'll find something," Isaac said as they sailed over the Granville Bridge, high above the pleasure boats that bumped together in the False Creek marina. "I been very lucky in my life, for the most part, and I got a few good years left." Though Sam could not apply the same outlook to his own situation, the old beggar's almost pathological optimism, as misguided as it may have been, warmed his heart, like the astronaut dreams of children.

———————

That evening, when he returned home, he discovered a text message from Anna requesting he fly out to Calgary for Cricket's birthday. The message was worded with her usual legal precision melded with a kind of forced casualness, though underneath it Sam perceived a tingle of warmth, so he agreed and booked a ticket. The thought of his shed standing empty while Isaac wandered the city in search of a new cranny to crawl into did not sit right with him. He asked Isaac if he wanted to housesit while he was gone.

"They're really fixing this old neighbourhood up nice, aren't they?" Isaac said, as they approached Sam's house the following evening. "I used to live in a rooming house a few blocks over. This was years ago. Don't remember much of that, to tell the truth," he said. "Rice wine." These last words he uttered with a distal stare as if invoking the name of a demon.

Walking up to the house, Isaac emitted a long descending whistle that sounded like a bomb. Sam clicked opened the side gate and led him around back.

"This is most definitely kind of you to have me stay back here. No worry, I won't bug you or come by the house or nothing, because I respect a man's private moments and whatnot," Isaac said, setting his suitcase down on the cot beside the window.

"Actually, that's my bed," Sam said. "You sleep over there." He pointed to the bedroll set against the opposing wall.

Isaac's eyes darted to the square broken-out window that faced the rear of Sam's towering home. He displayed a puzzlement that arrived and dispersed almost immediately. "You're the adviser," he said, and rearranged his things.

For dinner, Isaac cut some stumps of wiener into a pot of baked beans that he warmed on the camp stove. It would be a long painful walk for the old guy to his usual begging position in Gastown, so Sam suggested he take a few days off, which he would reimburse of course. "I'm not sure I'm in need of too much free time to chew on," Isaac said. "It's always done me no good in the past. But maybe I'll go collecting some bottles."

While they ate, Isaac sucked brown sauce from the grey mottle of his beard, and it occurred to Sam that he hadn't touched his own shaver in weeks. He wasn't sure of the bank's dress code but could think of several bearded co-workers as proof he wasn't endangering himself. Granted, they were contained, manicured growths, clipped and neatly edged, not like the unruly mass of spindly blond that now abounded on his chin. The point was moot anyway, because Sam hadn't been at the office as long as he'd had it. There was just so much important work to do with Isaac.

"So it's your in-laws, then? My condolences," Isaac said swallowing. "Course I ain't never been married. But I managed to mix myself up with a few women—some good, some not close to good. But my overall experiences with family ain't what you'd call positive."

"You ever get in touch with your parents?"

"Well, my older brother, he's batshit crazy, locked up since he was just a young one. Did something terrible to a woman was what people said. After he was gone, my folks weren't the same. They didn't take much interest in me no more neither, afraid I'd go the same route. That's mostly why I went up north to cut trees."

After he'd packed, Sam did some dishes in a bucket while listening to zephyrs of air whistle through Isaac's nasal cavity. He'd bedded down, still in his coat, on his back with his head on his pack and his hands deep in his pockets. Sam knocked a tin plate against the galvanized watering can and Isaac's eyes opened, slick and yellowed in the moonlight.

"Can I put a question to you?" Isaac said.

"Shoot," said Sam.

"Why you sleeping out here exactly?"

"Because I can't stand being in my own house."

Isaac drew his hands from his pockets and threaded them behind his head. "I heard that," he said, and re-attained sleep with an instantaneousness astonishing to Sam.

Sam flew out the next morning—a parabolic jaunt over jagged spires of grey rock. Dennis, Anna's father, fetched him from the airport in an immaculate hybrid car. He talked quietly into his phone as they loaded his bags and continued to do so while they whisked over a dead-straight road through an endless procession of camel-tinged foothills. Sam nodded off, and woke to his father-in-law driving with an impenetrable air, two thumbs hooked at the bottom of the wheel. While Sam had slept, a carpet of white cloud had appeared, ridged and crumpled, like the roof of a mouth.

"You're growing a beard," Dennis said.

"It's growing," Sam said. "How much I have to do with it is debatable."

Dennis checked each of the car's three mirrors, even though they were alone on open highway. "Look, Sam, I don't hold it against you. Hell, I've always liked you, and God knows Gretchen and I have had our spats, but I've got to tell you that you have my daughter all twisted around."

"She's the one who's still on vacation."

"Son, I know you haven't had it easy. I lost my parents early on so I know the feeling, like there is no home left in the world, but you've got to give Anna a chance to think things through."

"Thanks, but I'm not really in the market for fatherly wisdom, Dennis. And I'd appreciate it if you didn't offer my wife any, either. She's already got enough wisdom of her own to deal with."

Dennis shook his head. "I just hope you are happy with yourself," he said as he clicked a tiny box hung from his sun visor that retracted a wrought-iron gate from the mouth of his two-mile gravel driveway. When they reached the house Sam informed

Dennis flatly that he was indeed quite happy with himself and levered open his door.

Anna jogged out to meet him in a jean dress he failed to recognize. She'd cut her hair—how exactly, Sam couldn't say, but it was angular and ill-suited to her easily flushed, curvy cheeks. These details dispelled any of the confidence he'd been able to scavenge during his flight; they spoke either of a dress rehearsal for a new life or of a regression to an old one.

"I like this," she said tugging on his beard, enough for him to wince.

"It's not a joke," Sam said.

"Didn't say it was. It's cute," she said, nearly giggling. Her apparent glee also unnerved him. She had a way of becoming giddy as she approached the summit of an anxiety. Though he'd visited the house before, she commenced a jolly tour.

At dinner, Cricket viewed him from beneath her party hat with a mixture of pity and skepticism, as if he were a thoroughbred limping to its trailer after a race. Earlier, she'd looked up from a book and called to him but then went rigid when he lifted her warm frame to his chest. While Sam ate, Anna's mother, Gretchen, moved about the kitchen and scooped various salads of grilled vegetables onto the plates of Anna's three sisters and their athletic husbands. Dennis leaned back in his chair at the head of the table with a self-satisfied look. Perhaps it was that he'd grown up in a house of silent, brooding suppers eaten with a book, or in one's own room, but Sam had always felt interrogated and judged by the expectations of festivity.

After dinner, they all sat in Dennis's basement home theatre for a viewing of Cricket's favourite animated movie. When it was over, Cricket tore into her presents with a feral tenacity. Dennis had given her a hand-tooled child-sized saddle that was wrapped in pink butcher paper tied with twine, and he insisted on strapping it to his back to go galloping her around the room, whinnying. Sam had been so consumed with getting Isaac settled that he'd neglected to buy his daughter a present, so he'd stopped at a cash machine in the airport and withdrawn one thousand dollars, which he stuffed into a deposit envelope procured from the same machine.

"Good work, Sam," Anna said, as Cricket fanned the bills with a somewhat horrified expression. "Thoughtful."

After the gift-giving, he and Anna slipped out for a walk on her father's ranchland. Sam kicked at dense tufts of bristly grass and nearly began a series of doomed, potentially spiteful sentences that he thought better of. They ascended a long rise of dusty ground that banked east in its climb up the ridge before halting at a post-and-rail cattle fence that ran for miles in each direction. Past the fence was a steep grade that fell into a splayed valley of verdant grass where a few hulks of cattle stood chewing, inert as mailboxes. The spring sun was weak, but Sam was winded and Anna had produced a dark spade shape on the upper back of her T-shirt. When they reached the fence she stepped ahead and put her back to it in the way Sam had seen her lean on numerous bars in college.

"I've enrolled Cricket at my old school—she'll be starting in September." This she said as if it were something they would both have to endure, like bombings, or a depression. This private school was, from what Sam had heard, a place where uniformed girls learned to beekeep and Nobel-laureate political science professors came to describe to the girls the workings of the Canadian parliament.

"She likes her school," Sam said.

"A school is a school last I checked."

"What about her old friends?"

"She's already made a few new ones at equestrian camp."

"She's been taking riding lessons? She's terrified of animals!"

"Dogs. She's scared of dogs. And you'd have known about this if you'd returned some of our calls," she said.

"I've been busy with something, I've been doing some advising."

"Well, a guy named Alphonse called from your office. He said you haven't been there in weeks. They were wondering if you were okay. Christ, Sam, if you are that busy *advising* someone else, you could just—"

"It's a business relationship, Anna. Nothing more. It's about the only thing I can handle right now. And neither of you is exactly eager to talk to me anyway."

She gasped and appeared to consider saying something biting, then released a long breath and turned to face the valley.

"I've made a decision," she said. "I can't live in Vancouver, but I might be able to live with you, on my terms."

Sam could hear her father's authority behind her words and it riled him. "On whose 'terms' do you think I've been living for the past five years? Vancouver was your idea. You're just too selfish to appreciate the sacrifices I have made."

"Why must the root of every problem exist entirely outside of you?" she said. "It seems a little suspicious, don't you think? Seeing how you're here too?"

This was the kind of misdirection from the real topic of discussion that Anna had honed in law school. "You just can't take criticism," Sam said.

"What you do is not criticism," she said. "It's vivisection."

Exhaustedly, she turned and started back down the hill. Sam followed some paces behind, his eyes cinching up from the low sun now dipping into the far-off hills.

Back at the house they had more cake and Dennis popped some champagne. Anna spent the rest of the evening in a determined sulk, and Sam suffered the chattering inquiries of her sisters with a brittle smile.

That night, he woke to blue spindles of light twisting on his ceiling, cast by the swimming pool that lay beyond the sliding door of his guest room. He rose and ascended the stairs to his daughter's room and stood by her canopied bed. He hooked a whip of hair behind her neat ear, recalling that the only effective way to soothe her as a baby was to clamp her to his chest and jiggle her with the vigorous, nearly imperceptible speed of a paint mixer. Forgetting his beard, he kissed her and she batted groggily at her cheek with a wrist.

Sam knew his marriage was in a condition way past hope. His terror he now reserved for the life in store for Cricket. If they separated, she would be unscrewed from him, every minute of every day not spent with her a counter-clockwise crank. She was a happy, adventuresome kid who would adapt, and as there were simply more of them here, she'd be helpless to the magnetism of Anna's familial cabal. Sam set himself down on the carpet at the foot of Cricket's bed, inhaling a dusty puff that rose from the thick, white pile. He considered for a moment relocating to Calgary—

he could implant himself on the periphery of their lives, perhaps retain possession of at least a pittance of their affections—and admitted this to be his only recourse if Anna decided to stay.

Sam left early the next morning and checked into a motel beside the airport. He spent almost a week there, stacking greasy room-service plates outside his door and taking shrivelling hour-long showers where, in the dizzying steam and torrential fury of the motel's Herculean water pressure, he held tight to the grippy stainless-steel bar affixed there for the disabled. Emerging pink and flagellated, Sam would crawl into the tightly made bed in search of refuge from the polar climate visited upon the room by an inadjustable air conditioner. He'd kick the sheets out from the corners and behold channels that advertised pay-for-view movies in short, entertaining nuggets, all he could stand to watch.

On the plane, Sam offered himself the sad consolation that he hadn't told Anna about Isaac. He could only imagine her lawyerly unpacking of the ethics of what he was doing. He was using him. He was enacting a dubiously selfish plot in order to convince himself, and her and Cricket and everyone else, that he was actually a good person—a point that Sam couldn't say wasn't entirely true.

———

When Sam returned home and opened the gate into his wife's garden, he couldn't believe what was there. Hoses were spritzing a fine mist skyward, sending shimmering sails of rainbow light to unfurl across the yard. Each of the beds was meticulously weeded, the earth black and freshly turned with ruby worms straining for air. New tomato plants were carefully staked in beds that had previously been empty. A few lavender bushes had exploded in a purple froth and there was a walkway that Sam didn't remember, made of flat polished stones that meandered from the peeling side door of the shed all the way to the rear of the house. Even the grass bore a lush, perky resilience.

"Wow," Sam said.

"I think you might have a nitrogen problem," said Isaac, appearing behind him in a dirty undershirt and cut-off trousers. "Too little, I mean, and too much potash. I got you a compost going over there. But if you want, you could piss on the beds. It might help. That's what I been doing."

Isaac pointed a trowel over Sam's shoulder. "That there parsley's gone to seed, don't blame me, nothing I could do, you should eat it up soon as you can. Oh, and you wanna wrap that elm in foil this year or the army worms will strip it clean come winter."

That evening, they pulled two wicker garden chairs from the rafters of the shed and sat out in the sweet night breeze drinking lemonade that Isaac had squeezed fresh.

"You been gone a while. Which I guess could mean it went good or bad depending," Isaac said.

"Not the best," Sam said, taking a long slug of lemonade.

"She'll come around."

"No," Sam said. "Not if she's smart she won't."

They sat for a bit, watching tiny grey birds flit and dogfight amid Isaac's handiwork. After a while, Isaac went and relieved himself into the kale bed at the side of the house.

"I think I might have got the taste for sleeping indoors again," he said, sitting back down. "And my hips feel a hell of a lot more spry not parked on the pavement all day."

"You know, I don't mind having you around, really," said Sam. "You could stay a while, keep up the garden, just until you find something else."

Isaac drew a slow breath. "Sam, what's my balance running?" he asked.

Sam crinkled his nose, then extracted his pocket notebook and descended the column of his neat script with a finger. "With this month's interest, it looks like twenty-two hundred and some change."

"I been thinking I may go out to that crazy institution and try to drum up my brother. I never found nothing but trouble in this city besides, and with that much cash in my hand it might help if I had someone else to take care of. I never done so well fending on my own."

Sam drove to a twenty-four-hour teller. He had to call some tech guys at the bank to lift his thousand-dollar withdrawal limit so he could empty Isaac's account. Before he left, Sam slipped a thousand from his own account into the wad.

"Sometimes I didn't even believe you'd actually give it to me," Isaac said when Sam returned, clacking the edges of the bills on the garden table like a deck of cards.

That night, Sam woke to a figure standing over his bed holding a garden spade.

"Someone's trying to get in," Isaac said.

Sam stopped his breath and strained his ears. He heard only Isaac's wheezy inhalations. "In here?" Sam said, sleepily. "Why?"

He rose to follow Isaac to the door, who slid the bolt lock back and nudged it open with the tip of the spade.

Outside they discovered a group of raccoons rummaging a torn-open orange bag of yard clippings. They'd surprised them, and the largest one reared and bared its teeth but made no sound. Sam stood with the cool air licking him between the buttons of his pyjamas.

Isaac drew the shovel over his shoulder like an axe. "Say the word," he said.

Sam raised his fist in a halting gesture he'd seen in Vietnam movies and took a step toward the hackled raccoon. Tiny stones bit into his naked heels. When Cricket was four she didn't speak to him for nearly three weeks after he refused to let her try to pet some raccoons they saw in Stanley Park. It was common knowledge that raccoons were dangerous things, especially vicious when cornered or defending their young. In minutes they could cut a man to ribbons with their sharp furtive claws. But looking down into the face of this particular beast, Sam wasn't so sure. It seemed to him more like a gentle, nomadic creature. A lonely thing. Something that would rather live at night off table scraps and garbage than face the roaring bustle and endless conflict of the day. And this was its little family, he supposed, judging by the way the smaller ones skulked at its haunches. Really, it looked more weary than anything as it completed its appraisal of them and settled back on all fours. Then it swung its white snout toward the garage of Sam's neighbour, mustering a final glance over its shoulder, holding Sam and Isaac in the hollows of its eyes before ushering its family beneath a camper van.

"Whew," Isaac said when they were back in bed, and Sam heard the slosh of his jam jar.

In the morning Sam woke and Isaac was gone, just a gamey smell on the bedroll that he'd folded up and tied neatly with a shoe-string. Sam sat out in the garden awhile. A few frigates of white cloud inched west toward the ocean. Fragrant wafts tore through the lanes between the houses and rustled the leaves of his garden with a pleasing hush that reminded Sam of rough hands passing over soft skin. After some time, he stood and clicked open the side gate and walked around to the front of his house. He climbed the three steps, took a little jump, and drove his brown loafer into the centre of his front door.

Acknowledgements

Thanks to:

Linda Svendsen, Rhea Tregebov, Maureen Medved, Jen Farrell, Conan Tobias, Bryce Firman, Arnie Bell, Jackie Bowers, Leslie Remund, Sheryda Warrener, Claire Tacon, Michael John Wheeler, Sheila Wilkes, Dennis LeDoux, Lee Henderson, Iris Tupholme, Jennifer Lambert, Stephanie Fysh, and my agent, Anne McDermid, for their invaluable contributions;

Alex Schultz for his incisive editorial ministrations;

Benji Wagner, Dylan Doubt, and Rick McCrank for their friend-ship;

my brother, Jason Christie, for his expertise and encouragement, and my father, David Christie, for his love, support, and the unlimited use of his library;

my dearest, Cedar and August.